Dis§ Murder and Community Spirit in Little Mallow

Patsy Collins

Chapter 1

Monday 30th March

"Control just came through with a sudden death," the duty sergeant, said.

The shift briefing in Gosport police station had only just finished, so Crystal wasn't immediately certain who was being addressed. She glanced around to see if anyone else had responded before getting her hopes up.

"Yes, Student Officer Clere, I'm talking to you," sergeant Imani Freedman confirmed.

Realising how inappropriate her excitement was, Crystal attempted a neutral expression. Although what some still called a probationer, attending a sudden death was something she'd already done. The first time was shocking, tragic, and very clearly the result of a road traffic incident. As the skipper was assigning Crystal this task, it probably wasn't another RTI.

"Sudden and suspicious," sergeant Freedman confirmed.

Yes! This was exactly the kind of thing Crystal joined the police for. "Great! Thanks, Skip."

PC Trevor Harris, Crystal's training mentor, returned from checking the computer. "What's great?" he asked.

"The skipper has a suspicious death for us."

"I thought it would be right up your street." The sergeant's eye twitched, almost as though she'd winked at Crystal.

Trevor repeated Crystal's, 'Great! Thanks, Skip,' but in a much flatter tone of voice.

Crystal could partially understand his lack of enthusiasm. Suspicious, in terms of a death, meant without any immediately obvious explanation. Usually it stopped being in that category after an initial investigation, or medical examination, but there were exceptions.

"What do we know?" Trevor asked.

"He's definitely dead," the sergeant said.

"That's something I suppose."

"Where are we going?" This, just possibly, could be a murder case. Not yet being in CID didn't stop Crystal wanting to be involved.

Sergeant Freedman gave the address. "The paramedic isn't convinced it's a natural death. He's still on scene. You're to take a look and, if necessary…"

"We know the routine, Skip. Come on, lass," Trevor said.

As they headed out of the station Trevor suggested Crystal drive. "Save you keeping on at me to put my foot down!" He said it with a smile.

"Thanks." She wouldn't really have nagged him to hurry, but would have felt like it. Trevor had no urgency about him. Often that was the right approach, but she was eager to get to the potential crime scene.

Trevor would be hoping one look would somehow prove the deceased had slipped away peacefully in his sleep and they could write up a report which was the official version of 'nothing to see here' over a leisurely mug of tea. He was far from lazy but, after nearly thirty years in the job, he didn't ever complain a task was too easy.

Trevor gave a chuckle when they arrived. "More my street than yours!"

He was right. Although she rented a modern flat in Gosport, Crystal currently lived in Little Mallow with her great aunt Agnes in an ancient house with a big garden, while the old lady recovered from a hip replacement. The house they'd been sent to was nothing like either, being late Victorian and in a row of terraces, just like the road where Trevor lived.

She'd visited Trevor's home several times as she'd been the one to help out when he'd suffered a sprained ankle and broken collarbone in the line of duty. He recovered quickly. No surprise there as Crystal took him Aunt Agnes's special chicken soup and that cured almost anything. About his embarrassment that the injuries were sustained falling out of a tree while failing to rescue a child's kite there was nothing to be done, except resist adding to the 'you'll soon be flying high' and 'you're treemendously missed' type comments on the get well card signed by all his colleagues.

"There seem to be a lot of houses like this round here," Crystal remarked.

"Yep, there are loads in Gosport and Pompey. Probably lots of other places too. Back then, most building firms used to buy the plans instead of employing architects."

Crystal had already teased him that week about knowing so much history because he'd lived through it, so chose instead to take advantage of his local knowledge. "Trevs, why is Portsmouth called Pompey?"

"I'm not sure there is a reason, lass. It's just what everyone says."

The last bit was true – Crystal had found herself using the nearest city's nickname herself. There had to be a reason for it but solving that mini mystery would have to wait.

The paramedic was waiting, with his motorbike, outside the home of the dead man.

Trevor made a small hand gesture, indicating he was happy for Crystal to take the lead.

She introduced herself and Trevor and asked the paramedic his name. "What can you tell us, Pete?"

"The deceased is a Mr Colin Argent, according to the neighbour, and lived here alone. Mrs Owen's not aware of him having any medical problems and says he seemed well when they spoke yesterday morning. 1 haven't touched him, other than to check he really is dead. He's just in there." Pete the paramedic jerked his thumb towards one of the front windows, then led the way into the house.

As they stepped inside, something reminded Crystal of her great aunt Agnes 'feeding' home made Christmas cake with whisky to help it keep. What an odd thing to think of in March, particularly under the circumstances.

Crystal noted the array of coats, shoes and other clothing in the hallway. Most looked of good quality but were old and drab. The exception was a baseball cap so new it was still encased in cellophane. The embroidery of a vivid red dragon contrasted with the deep green material. It wasn't something she'd expect to be on sale locally. Maybe Mr Argent was Welsh, or someone he knew had recently been to Wales.

The curtains of the room they went into were shut. The room was lit by a single, shaded electric lamp on a small table. Mr Argent was sitting on his sofa, fully dressed with a blanket wrapped around him and his eyes closed. Crystal guessed he was about seventy. Other than a strangely pink look to his skin it appeared he'd sat up late the previous evening, fallen asleep and never woken.

On his lap, close to his right hand, was a prettily shaped glass. The way it sparkled in the lamplight suggested it was made from crystal. She deduced it was for whisky, based on a strong smell of the drink and an almost full bottle of the stuff on the cluttered side table. That smell was what had made her think of Christmas cake. The position of the man's hand suggested he'd dropped the glass after death, or possibly fallen asleep holding it. Either way, it seemed unlikely he'd known anything was wrong.

"Any ideas as to the cause?" Trevor asked the paramedic.

"We won't know for sure until the autopsy, but he doesn't look the way I'd expect if he'd died from any of the common causes of sudden death. I'm none too sure it's natural."

Neither was Crystal. Mr Argent was too young for age to be the most likely cause of his death. The table on which the whisky bottle stood held no medication of any kind, not even cough sweets or a pack of tissues. Their absence didn't prove good health, but was suggestive.

Crystal glanced at Trevor, who again gestured for her to carry on. "Who called you out?" she asked.

"Lady next door." Pete pointed in the appropriate direction. "But it was a delivery guy found him. He knocked with a package and got no answer. Said that was unusual. Mr Argent always took in his own parcels, plus those of neighbours who were out, so the driver looked through the window and saw him. His banging and shouting raised the neighbour who noticed the deceased hadn't put his bin out. She called 999 and took the driver's contact details." The paramedic handed them a sheet of notepaper.

"The curtains are drawn, the lamp is on, and it looks like he was having a nightcap. Does what you've noticed fit with him dying last night?" Crystal asked.

"That's most likely."

"What you going to do now, lass?" Trevor asked quietly. Right from the start he'd had her try to work out what to do, not told her and left her unsure whether she'd have remembered correct procedure herself.

"Let the skipper know."

He nodded. "Go on then."

Crystal radioed through the bare facts which would begin the investigation. She was, for the moment at least, involved in what had the potential to be her first murder case.

While Crystal finished speaking and was given orders to keep the scene secure, the paramedic received an emergency call. Trevor told him to, "Go to the person you can help, and leave us with the man you can do nothing more for."

Crystal wanted to take an initial statement from the neighbour and search the house for clues, but knew they must wait for sergeant Freedman.

"The curtains are closed but don't quite meet," Crystal pointed out. "Mr Argent could have looked out some time after shutting them. Perhaps a visitor called and he checked who it was before letting them in?"

"That's possible, but if he was the sort of person who didn't close his curtains properly when looking out during the evening, he was the sort of person who might not always close them properly to start with."

"I suppose."

"I'm not saying you're wrong, lass. You're right to notice things and ask questions – just don't go jumping to conclusions about this being a murder because you want to solve one."

"I'm not. At least I'm trying not to."

"I know. And anyway I was wrong about you wanting to solve a murder."

No he wasn't.

"You want to solve hundreds, thousands, be the best detective ever."

Ah. "Is it that obvious?"

"You work with someone for a while and you get to know things about them."

"True. You like beer and women with bright blue eyes, Skip is a Scrabble addict, and Sergeant Dylan is very fond of carbs."

"I like you too, despite those chocolatey eyeballs of yours." He chuckled. "Maybe they're the reason Dil Dylan likes you?"

"He doesn't, does he? I mean not particularly?"

Trevor made a face which she knew meant 'don't be daft' but whether he thought she was daft for assuming that to be the case, or for not having realised earlier, was less certain.

"We'd best do as we were told and secure the scene. I'll stand out front and make sure nobody comes in who shouldn't. You make sure nobody comes in the back way."

"OK." A glance through the window showed the tiny back garden had no gate, so getting out there wasn't urgent. An intruder could have climbed over from the neighbouring gardens or alleyway behind, but no innocent person was going to stroll in, destroying evidence as they did so. It might be better if she didn't go outside in case there were footprints or signs of a forced entry which she accidentally obliterated. That thought led to another. There had been no damage to the front door, and the paramedic hadn't mentioned breaking in. "Trevor," she called. "Could you check you really can see him from outside?"

"Yes, boss!"

She knew he was teasing her. Had he been doing the same about Dil Dylan? Possibly, but if the sergeant really did have a particular interest in her it would be a good idea to formulate a plan to, very tactfully, discourage him. Now wasn't the time.

Taking another look around the living room, it struck Crystal that although the whisky and glass went together, they didn't match the rest of the room. The carpet was worn, the furnishings well used, and although the place was clean, nothing else sparkled. She pulled out her phone and did an internet search for the whisky. It was nearly £30 a bottle. You could buy ordinary whisky for less than half that, but this was single malt and everyone deserves a treat.

Crystal couldn't help thinking whisky would hide the taste of all but the most bitter poison. She half laughed at herself for jumping to the conclusion of murder despite a complete lack of evidence. But then there was no evidence of a natural death either – no indication of an accident or illness. And no obvious trauma so, if he had been killed, poisoning was a definite possibility.

If Mr Argent had died from something he'd drunk, he almost certainly didn't take it accidentally. The lid was on the whisky bottle and the seal was there too. Crystal was certain he'd opened it for the first time that evening, and done so in his lounge. The house was tidy with no rubbish to be seen, so if he'd opened it previously, the foil seal would be in the bin.

There was no sign of a container for anything he might have added, accidentally or otherwise, to his drink. Crystal lay on the floor and looked under the sofa. She learned two things – Mr Argent didn't regularly move his furniture to vacuum underneath and there wasn't anything there but dust.

On the side table were three ballpoint pens with company logos on, the kind of thing often given out as a free gift to prospective customers. There was a plastic tray, with a fork resting in it. The remains of something yellow smeared both. Another mismatch – he ate microwave meals straight from the carton, and drank posh whisky from a crystal glass.

Below everything else on the table was a stack of magazines and papers. From the bits Crystal could see they were women's magazines, not the kind of thing she'd expect a single man to buy. Mr Argent was a puzzle. Through the debris she could see something hand-written on a sheet of paper. A suicide note?

Crystal noticed movement outside. It was Trevor giving her a thumbs up to indicate the delivery driver could have seen the body just as he claimed. Crystal headed for the back of the house.

The middle room was gloomy. The equivalent in Trevor's home was too, but he'd brightened it up with pale yellow walls and cheerful paintings. In this house it held piles of used boxes and packaging materials. Maybe Mr Argent ran some kind of business buying and selling online, although there was no sign of a computer.

A key was in the lock of the back door. Nothing indicated a forced entry. The kitchen was scruffy, but not dirty. Upside down on the draining board was a glass tumbler. Perfectly adequate for drinking whisky, but definitely not crystal.

Someone arrived and spoke to Trevor, then Crystal heard them approach the kitchen.

"Hello, Student Officer Clere?" a voice called. It was deep, not that of Sergeant Freeman.

"Yes that's…" Oh. Wow. She mentally reminded herself she was a professional woman of twenty-nine, not a twelve-year-old schoolgirl with a crush and mustered a suitable tone of voice. "Hello again, sir," she said to Detective Inspector Shortfellow.

"I happened to be in the area and heard your radio call, so thought I'd take a look myself."

She couldn't blame him as she was taking a good look herself. Of course she'd noticed his physical appearance when they first met, but it never hurt an officer to remind themselves of the facts. The DI wasn't short, not anywhere close. The same applied to the adjectives pale and unattractive. He had an irresistibly wicked grin, which sparkled in his grey eyes.

Crystal's hopes of working on the case couldn't have got much higher, but they tried.

Chapter 2

Monday 30th March

A car pulled up alongside Arnold as he headed towards Palmerston Avenue in Little Mallow. "Hello, Mr Stewart," a schoolboy said through the open back window. "Are you delivering magazines for Mrs Patterson?"

"That's right." It was true he was delivering the community newsletter, Little Mallow's Little Mag, on what was theoretically Agnes Patterson's round. With young Adam it seemed best to give the least complicated answer.

"Can I help? Please."

His mother mouthed 'sorry' as she did whenever Adam attempted to help people with whatever they were doing, bombarded people with questions or, as was most usual, both at the same time.

"It's stopped raining and I don't have any homework."

"In that case I'll be glad of your assistance and will walk you home afterwards." As Adam cheered and leapt from the car, Arnold told Lorna Milligan, "We'll be an hour at most and I have my mobile with me if you need to be in contact."

She seemed to be trying not to laugh as she started the car and checked it was safe to pull away. Albert hoped that didn't mean the boy's questions would be difficult. They weren't usually, but Arnold recalled the confusion he'd got into when Adam asked why gravestones often, but not always, stated the person had died.

"How old are you, Mr Stewart?"

"Thirty-six."

"I'm eight. That means I'm… twenty-eight years younger. Mum is twenty-eight."

"Oh."

"When's your birthday?"

"It was last week." Arnold took one of the folded newsletters from his bag.

As Adam took it, dashed up the path and stuffed it into the letter box, Arnold began to understand how Agnes Patterson managed her round. When he'd taken over as editor and realised one of the distributers was eighty-nine he'd assumed he'd have to find someone else. In fact he'd had to arrange cover for her only twice in three years. She rarely did it all herself, but nearly always managed to persuade someone to help. Most recently that was her great niece, Crystal, who was staying with her.

"Do you know why I like helping with deliveries?" Adam asked.

Arnold admitted he didn't.

"So I have 'sperients when I'm old enough for a paper round. Granny said that would be a good idea."

"She should know." Mary Milligan ran Little Mallow's combined post office, newsagents and village store. Although Arnold could see that getting to know his way around local streets might be helpful for a prospective paper boy, Arnold suspected it was also a way to get him out from under his grandmother's feet. Adam was so interested in everything all the time that he was exhausting company. Arnold didn't mind – in small doses.

"Is that what you want to do when you grow up?" Arnold asked. He was sure the boy had a more ambitious job in mind.

"I wanted to be an astronaut, but I read they don't come home for months and months. Is that true?"

For the first time ever, Arnold contemplated the life of an astronaut. "I think it is. They must have to do a lot of training and they'd need to go to a special place for that, and when they're in space they have to stay there for the whole mission."

"That's what I thought. I'd miss Mum and Dad."

"There are lots of different jobs," Arnold pointed out. "You might like to find out about as many as possible before deciding."

"That's a good idea. Is doing the Little Mag your job?"

"I am the editor, but it's not precisely my job." He worked voluntarily on the free community newsletter. It wasn't part of his job as verger of St Symeon's, as the publication had no official connection with the church.

"Do you like it?" Adam asked.

"Very much." The previous verger had started up Little Mallow's Little Mag and Arnold had promised to try to continue running it himself. After learning the basics of what to do, he'd realised it would take only a few hours per month and would give him a certain amount of status in the village. He was fortunate to have inherited enough regular advertisers and contributors to keep it ticking over, even if he did no more than type up physical submissions and proofread, collate, and format, the copy emailed to him.

"I like the puzzles best. The ones with the photos and you have to work out what it is or what someone is doing. Which is your favourite?"

"I like those too. It's fun making them up."

"If I can make one up would you put it in?"

Arnold would like the magazine to cater more for younger members of the community, but he'd never considered encouraging children to contribute work. It seemed an excellent idea. "Yes I would. Or if you'd like to write a story or anything."

Adam nodded, then shot off to deliver another magazine. "Do you like delivering?" he asked on his return.

"Yes, because it's good for me to get some exercise."

"Is that because you're getting fat?" Adam asked.

Arnold knew the boy hadn't meant to be rude. Somehow that made it worse. He'd hoped nobody had noticed his expanding waistline, clearly he was deluding himself. The same was probably true about the one part of him which was getting thinner – his hair.

Arnold came home to find a thick padded envelope, addressed to him, waiting in the lobby. He brewed tea, then lifted the tape and carefully unfolded the packaging. The padded envelope contained fifteen ten pound notes and a peculiar letter.

Dear Arnold Stewart,

I desire to make a booking for the new hall for the eventide of 3rd June, for a surprise social gathering. The event itself is to occupy the time from 8 until 11 and I would like an additional hour preceding and afterwards to allow caterers to set up and for removal of trash.

I request you supply 50 chairs, or as near to that number as possible, arranged with an adequate quantity of diminutive tables in informal groups. In addition, a lesser amount of larger tables on which to place a buffet and drinks sufficient for 70 people.

In order to preserve the roguish surprise element of this event, I must remain entirely anonymous. To that end, I enclose payment in cash. I trust it is more than sufficient. The surplus is to be used to expedite preparations of a habitable hall.

To confirm this booking, please place a missive in the next issue of Little Mag saying precisely, 'The new hall has received its first booking! The first of many we hope!!'

Regards,

Mystery Party Planner

The comment about expediting preparations would be because Little Mallow didn't have a hall yet. There was only a derelict area for which they had planning permission to erect something suitable for organisations such as the Brownies and photography club to meet.

Arnold had tracked down two enormous second-hand Portakabin type structures. These, he'd been assured, could relatively easily be connected and converted into a suitable structure. The parish fund could just about afford to buy them, and Arnold had obtained promises of help for all stages of the work, but to his frustration nothing had happened yet. The problem was that Reverend Jerry Grande had decided he and Arnold shouldn't make all the decisions themselves, but involve the local community. Well-meaning volunteers had declared themselves 'the committee' and since then no decisions had ever been made. It wasn't that they disagreed, just that nobody would commit to anything. It was exasperating.

Arnold felt it would be wrong to get cross about the unofficial committee's procrastination and then be guilty of the same thing himself, so he took a deep breath and switched on his phone.

"Hello, Arnold," Jerry said after a short space of time.

"Booking, cash. Strange, but good incentive?"

"You've had a booking, paid for in cash, for the new hall?" Jerry confirmed.

Arnold gave a relieved sigh. People said that sometimes he was slightly abrupt on the phone, making it difficult to understand him. He'd tried hard to improve and, as Jerry obviously understood, clearly succeeded. Knowing that gave him the confidence to respond in detail.

"Yes. For third of June. Could be ready... if."

"The committee, yes. I'm in the Crown and Anchor, and I owe you a pint. Would you like to come and discuss it?"

"Yes." Arnold had no doubt that would be easier. And there would be beer. As with chips from someone else's plate, calories in beer didn't count if the vicar ordered it.

His employer and a pint of best bitter weren't all that awaited Arnold in the pub. Martin Blackman, the landlord, had moved from behind the bar to join the vicar. In front of him was an opened package which, other than the name and address, matched the one Arnold had with him.

Arnold took the letter from his, opened it and placed it between Martin and Jerry. He indicated Martin's package. "May I?"

"Help yourself."

Martin's package contained more money than Arnold's. That was explained by the fact the letter, using very similar phrasing, was an order for buffet food and wine, rather than room hire. Martin was to confirm the order via a precise Facebook post on the pub's page. 'We've got another outside catering job! Lots of sarnies and plenty of wine!!'

"There's a thousand quid with it," Martin said, when they'd all finished reading. "Whoever sent this seems weird, but they're not totally stupid. It's about the right amount for a basic party package, I could do with the extra business, and can do it that day – if the hall is open by then, and you get an alcohol licence."

"Mine has one hundred and fifty pounds," Arnold said. "That is quite a lot more than we were considering charging for room hire. As suggested, a bit of spare cash might help move things along."

"I'm sensing a but from both of you," Jerry said.

"It's just that the whole thing is so odd."

"Martin's right, and there's the committee," Arnold said.

"We need a quorum."

"It's not Sunday, vicar. No cause for Latin," Martin said.

As Arnold was wondering whether Martin really didn't follow, or was kidding, he noticed Ellie Jenkins at the bar. When she turned in his direction he beckoned her over. As the schoolteacher was a sensible young woman and, like the three of them, on the committee for the new hall, they would have their quorum – four people who could make a decision on behalf of all the rest.

Chapter 3

Monday 30th March

Sergeant Imani Freedman arrived almost immediately after the DI, and was clearly surprised to see him.

"Due to several ongoing cases, if Mr Argent's death is a case for CID I'll be handling it myself initially," DI Shortfellow told her.

After Trevor and Crystal told the DI and their sergeant everything they'd learned, Trevor said, "Skip, unless something has cropped up since we were sent here, we could probably stay on if a couple of uniforms would be any use to CID."

Even though it would most likely be the kind of routine house-to-house enquiries Crystal had assisted with after burglaries and road traffic incidents, she could have kissed him for making that suggestion.

"That would be appreciated," Shortfellow said.

She could have kissed him too. In fact, it was difficult not to.

Sergeant Freedman shrugged. "OK then," she said, and left them to it.

"Boss, can I show you what the delivery guy would have been able to see?" Trevor asked the DI.

Crystal noticed the informal term of address – the two men must know each other better than she'd realised. She was slightly miffed at Trevor's use of 'I' not 'we' especially as it had been her idea he made that check. She wouldn't tag along though. The tiny gravel courtyard in front of the house wasn't big enough for a crowd, and her temptation to be in a confined space with the DI wasn't exactly professional.

A sudden bark of laughter, presumably from DI Shortfellow, irritated Crystal. She understood that detachment from, or humour in, unpleasant circumstances were ways to ensure police officers could remain effective in their jobs while protecting their mental health, but the happy sound indicated she was being left out of something. She hated that.

Both men were forgiven when the DI returned alone and said, "Trevor is starting house-to-house enquiries, but he tells me it would benefit your career development to assist me more directly."

"Yes, sir."

"And that it would make his life easier if I were to allow that."

She'd been right, Trevor knew the DI well enough not to have to call him sir – and to make suggestions about how he deployed the uniformed officers assisting him. They hadn't exchanged any of the remarks she'd have expected if they were friends though. What *had* Trevor said to him? Whatever it was, playing along might allow her more involvement in the case than would usually be expected. She kept it safe with another, "Yes, sir."

"In that case, I'd like you to check the house for any medication which might give an explanation for Mr Argent's death, and to keep an eye out for anything unusual."

"Yes, sir!" If Crystal found something, she could potentially solve this thing immediately. A natural death wouldn't be as interesting as murder, but getting the right result quickly would still be good.

"But don't contaminate the scene!"

"Absolutely not." She explained she'd not stepped outside the back door, in order to preserve possible evidence.

The bathroom was cleanish, but not sparkling. It smelled floral. The towels were threadbare and it was unclear what colour they'd been originally. A bar of rose coloured and perfumed soap rested in a plastic dish on the sink. On the corner of the bath was a bottle of high-end, violet scented oil. It seemed an odd choice and judging by the fact it was almost full and dusty, wasn't often used. A gift, she guessed. Or maybe it was something a late wife or former partner used and he kept it from sentiment?

Nothing else was visible, so Crystal gloved up and opened the bathroom cupboard using her pen. She photographed the contents on her phone before using the pen to carefully move items aside so she was sure she'd seen everything. The contents, what there was of them, were inexpensive looking. A multi-pack of soap from which the one on the sink had almost certainly come, plastic toothbrush, disposable razors and can of shaving foam. There was no trace of medication beyond indigestion tablets. The small roll of those was almost intact and faded, so didn't indicate a long term and serious stomach issue. A tube of toothpaste was perhaps the most revealing find. Unlike the other toiletries it was branded, not supermarket own label. It would apparently relieve sensitivity, gum irritation and bad breath. She guessed he'd either had a painful condition, or was keen to avoid dentistry bills and therefore invested more on toothpaste than other forms of self-care.

One of the two bedrooms had the same floral scent as the bathroom. The bed had a dingy mattress and pillows, but no sheets or quilt. The bedside table held a single lamp. There was a stack of quilted toilet paper, eleven more tubes of the same kind of toothpaste as she'd already seen, and more multi-packs of the same kind of soap. Crystal thought it most likely he'd bought them all when on special offer – they didn't seem old enough to indicate COVID related panic buying.

In what must have been Mr Argent's own room, the bed was made. His clothes weren't new, but were ironed and neatly folded. The upstairs rooms matched downstairs in that almost everything looked old, cheap and was reasonably clean. An exception was a glossy clock radio by his bed. That seemed new. Crystal concluded Mr Argent bought the necessities of life as economically as possible, allowing himself just a few extravagancies. He didn't like waste – that was proved by the fact he'd kept the fragrant bath oil, and that he'd retained so much packaging material.

Her initial guess, that the piles of that she'd seen downstairs were to be reused in connection with a business was seeming less likely. He might have been the kind of person who'd use his home for work in order to avoid paying for alternative premises but, other than the toiletries, there was no stock of anything to send out. Nothing obvious he could be selling on for a profit. Maybe he was involved in some kind of scam. That might explain why someone wanted him dead.

Crystal went downstairs and reported the bare facts of her findings.

"Good. Keep looking," the DI said.

Crystal made a more thorough inspection of the packaging materials. All the visible address labels were for the property she was searching. The topmost boxes had been neatly opened, then closed again. None of the boxes, even those at the bottom, were collapsed or folded. It was frustrating not to be able to touch anything, but she knew better than to do so without permission.

Trevor came back from questioning the nearest neighbours. "The lady who called this in is out. There's a note on her door saying she's taking someone for a hospital appointment and will be back soon. General opinion is Argent was a nice, quiet man who kept to himself and never caused anyone any problems. He got on better with dogs than people apparently."

"But didn't own one?" The DI voiced Crystal's thoughts.

"Used to. Apparently when it died he was devastated and hardly left the house for a time, then he started volunteering at a rescue place and helped neighbours out sometimes. Letting the dog out for a run if they had to work late or walking them when people couldn't, that kind of thing."

Maybe the saved cardboard boxes could make temporary dog beds, but Crystal hadn't seen any leads, poop bags or even dog hairs. Although Mr Argent was tidy he hadn't been meticulous – there would surely be some sign if he'd run an unofficial boarding kennel.

"Other than delivery drivers and a relative, he didn't have any visitors," Trevor continued. "The woman opposite mentioned him not being married nor ever likely to be, which seemed a waste to her. No men friends either."

"So, he was polite to her, but not interested in the way she'd have liked him to be?"

"I reckon you're right there, boss."

"Sir, all the boxes and packages are addressed to Colin Argent, as far as I can tell without touching anything," Crystal reported. "They all appear to have been opened, but in some cases at least I don't think the contents have been removed."

"And you have a theory?" Shortfellow asked.

"There must be a reason for him to get sent so much stuff, sir. According to his neighbour the delivery person who realised something was wrong said it was unusual for him not to open up and accept deliveries – meaning he must have called frequently enough to remember."

"Good point."

Crystal continued with her partial theory. "Maybe he acts as a sort of PO box for people who don't want these items coming to their homes. Not that there's anything which seems to warrant that, and it looks as though everything was sent by whichever company produced it. And him not getting many visitors goes against the delivery point idea. It's a puzzle, and a frustrating one as otherwise I'm getting a clear picture of the dead man."

"Oh?" The DI's tone sounded vaguely encouraging.

Crystal explained that Colin Argent seemed frugal, but to have sufficient money not only for necessities but to buy them in quantity if that saved money in the long run, or otherwise seemed like a good idea.

"Why would buying a lifetime's supply of toothpaste seem like a good idea?" the DI asked.

"Favourite brand going out of production? Accidentally over ordered and didn't like to admit his mistake? Tokens on the packs he could save up for comedy teeth?" She'd noticed some kind of offer printed on the outer packaging.

DI Shortfellow emitted another short burst of laughter. "Carry on then." He indicated the kitchen.

Crystal discovered the cupboards in there were mostly quite sparsely stocked. Mr Argent had a large collection of assorted mugs – the kind made for promotional purposes and often given away to customers of the businesses whose details were printed on them. None of his crockery looked anything like a dog bowl and there wasn't any animal food or treats.

There was a whole shelf of the same brand of soup. They were neatly arranged with their labels all facing out. Lots of different flavours and, assuming each row contained the kind indicated by the one at the front, there was the same quantity of each. People usually had preferences – maybe he had a poor sense of taste? But in that case, why not go for own label, and wouldn't a cheap blended whisky appeal as much as the more expensive single malt he'd been drinking when he died?

Crystal heard more people arrive and speak to DI Shortfellow. Whether it was scenes of crime officers, generally known as SOCO, or more CID detectives she wasn't sure. Whoever it was went into the room with the dead man and nobody told Crystal to stop her search. As the last order she'd been given was to continue, and that fitted with her own wishes, that's what she did.

She eased open the fridge. There wasn't much in there. Milk, mushrooms and eggs. All looked as though they'd come from the nearest convenience store. There were also three jars of pâté. They looked expensive and oddly familiar. Crystal almost laughed aloud as she remembered Aunt Agnes asking why anyone would pay good money for squished up liver when they could have a nice bit of cheddar on their toast.

Crystal called, "I've worked it out!" as she headed to join Trevor and the DI.

"Steady, lass," cautioned Trevor.

The CID officers looked even less impressed.

"Sorry, I didn't mean the death, just the odd things around the house. Probably all those boxes too."

"Go on," Shortfellow said.

"He did competitions. That pâté was a prize in a magazine competition recently and I spotted some women's magazines by the sofa. I'm sure he won at least some of the other apparently out of place items, and others might have been bought because there was a chance of a prize with each purchase."

"That's possible," Shortfellow conceded.

"Makes sense," another officer agreed.

"When you're able to look at the magazines on the table there, you'll probably know for sure if I'm right," Crystal said.

"We'll let you know," DI Shortfellow said. "There's a bit of a crowd outside. If you and Trevor could see if any of them have anything useful to say, that would be appreciated."

"Happy to, sir," Crystal said, meaning it. Most likely they'd learn nothing, but by taking care of that task they were freeing up CID to do what they were trained for, and therefore she was aiding the case.

As expected, the crowd had questions, not answers. Trevor said Mr Argent had died peacefully the previous night and the police were carrying out routine enquires.

There were comments along the lines of, "There's a lot of you just to check if an old chap is really dead, aren't there?" and, "Don't you have any crimes to deal with?"

Trevor, asking for the names and contact details of anyone who had known the deceased, or had any information, dispersed quite a few onlookers. Crystal giving a couple of cars, which had been inconsiderately parked, a close inspection shifted some more.

They were left with a few people willing to give their names and say Colin Argent had been a considerate neighbour who, other than when it came to dogs, kept to himself. One said Mr Argent had a cousin, a girl she thought was called Lucy, who visited sometimes. "I think she must be his closest relative, as he's not mentioned anyone else and nobody else came near him, poor soul." She waved at a woman outside the house next door to Mr Argent's. "That's Winnie Owen back. She knew him best, I think."

"I'd like to interview her," Crystal told Trevor.

"Can you do that?" He knew the answer of course, but wanted Crystal to work it out herself.

She sighed. "I guess not. It's CID's case now."

Trevor said nothing. If she'd given a completely correct answer he'd have given a quick nod, or even a 'well done' to indicate the fact. Silence meant 'give it more thought'.

"It was CID's case when you spoke to the other neighbours and we were asked to find out if local people know anything useful. Yes! This is a routine enquiry. I can do it. But CID are right here... The information about the cousin could be a useful lead they need to follow up on quickly and interviewing Mrs Owen will probably wait for a few minutes. We should update the DI first and then inform him the neighbour is back and we're going to speak to her."

Trevor nodded.

So did the DI after hearing the update and their intention. "Before you do... " He gestured to a ring-binder with 'results' written in block letters on the front. "Confirmation you were right about your competition theory. He kept letters confirming wins. The last one is dated just over a week ago – it thanks him for entering a competition for whisky, a decanter and set of crystal glasses, and states that he was a runner-up. His prize is a crystal glass in a presentation pack, to be delivered by courier within five working days."

"The one he was drinking from when he died," Crystal stated.

"Almost certainly. By the way, SOCO think that as well as whisky, they can smell almonds."

"Oh! I thought of Christmas cake when I first came in. I assumed it was because of the whisky Aunty uses in hers, but it could have been the marzipan too. That smells of almonds... and so does cyanide."

Chapter 4

Monday 30th March

Colin Argent's neighbour observed their uniforms with her bright blue eyes. "He's dead then?" She looked to be about Trevor's age and as though she cared about her appearance.

"Yes, Mrs Owen. I'm sorry to say he is." Crystal introduced herself and Trevor. "Could we come in and ask you a few questions?"

"Would you like tea? I was just going to make myself one."

Before the more official questions, Crystal asked, "Do you live alone, Mrs Owen?" That was just in case Trevor was interested to learn she'd been a widow for three years. He was complimentary about her home and very appreciative of the refreshments they were provided with, but that was no indication. He was always polite and did his best to create a positive impression with any members of the public they encountered.

As Crystal made notes, Mrs Owen confirmed what the paramedic had told them. "The delivery chap was knocking and calling out like he was trying to wake Colin. Mr Argent, you know? I went out to say if he weren't about I'd take the parcel. He's done the same for me, often enough."

"And then what happened?"

"He said he was in because he could see him through a gap in the curtains."

"The delivery driver could see Mr Argent?" Crystal asked, checking she'd understood correctly.

"That's it, but he didn't come to the door and his hearing is fine, so we was worried and then I saw he hadn't put his bin out, so I called 999. The ambulance man got here on his motorbike very quickly and I let him into the house with my key."

"You didn't go in yourself prior to that?"

"If he'd been on the floor or something I would have, in case he needed help, but I was pretty sure there was nothing I could do and I had to pick up a friend and take her for a hospital appointment. Perhaps I should have… Is that why you're here?"

"No, no. It's routine for us to investigate any sudden death," Crystal said as though this wasn't her first potential murder. "You staying wouldn't have made a difference. He died some time before the paramedic arrived."

"Went in his sleep then. That's the best way, isn't it?"

"How well did you know Mr Argent?" Trevor asked, neatly saving Crystal from having to reply.

"At least fifteen years we've been neighbours, but I don't know him well if you know what I mean. Not sure anyone did. I never saw him show any real emotion until that old dog of his died. Scruffy little terrier it was. Didn't even have a name, he just called it Pup, but I reckon he loved it. After, he was even quieter than before."

"He was a loner?" Crystal asked.

"I wouldn't say that exactly. When it came to people with dogs he was proper friendly. He'd always fuss it and sometimes he offered to let them out to do their business if they'd be on their own all day. But with anyone he'd chat a bit when people saw him coming and going, or down the shop. The usual stuff. Or he might ask questions or ask us to save labels and things like that for all those competitions he did. And sometimes he'd come round to give us things he'd won. Me more than others I suppose. He didn't have a car and I gave him lifts sometimes."

"And you held his key?"

"That's right. And he had mine, for emergencies, you know? I've never had to use it before, but he used mine to feed my Binky a couple of times. He wasn't one for cats, but Binky isn't the kind to come up to people much."

"Did he hold the keys for people whose dogs he let out."

"Must have done."

"What about when his dog was alive? Did anyone have a key to come and let it out or feed it?"

"I don't recall him ever going away, but he might have made arrangements with someone just in case, I suppose."

"He didn't have visitors?" Crystal asked.

"Only his cousin as far as I know. She popped in for tea sometimes, after she finished work, I think. I thought she seemed quite nice really."

"When did she visit last, do you know?"

"Couldn't say, but I doubt it was more than a month. She didn't have a regular day, but I think she came about that often."

"Do you know her name, or that of any other relations?"

"I think there's only Lucy. Oh dear, she'll have to be told. I'd rather not do that."

"Don't worry, we can let her know."

"I'll get you her number."

By the time they'd finished their tea, Crystal had typed up the witness statement on her phone app, had it approved by Trevor and electronically signed by Mrs Owen.

"I don't think she's a murderer," Crystal remarked once they'd left.

"With eyes like that? No chance!"

"The knowledge that attractive, blue-eyed women are entirely innocent will save me loads of time once I'm a detective."

Trevor chuckled. "Oh no, lass. They might not go around murdering their next-door neighbours, but I can tell you from experience they're not always innocent."

"Trevor!"

Crystal updated DI Shortfellow, confirming they had a signed statement from Mrs Owen, plus the name and phone number of the person who had probably been Mr Argent's next of kin.

"Would you like us to do the notification, sir?" Crystal asked hopefully, but in the expectation of disappointment. If Mr Argent really had been murdered, his only relation and only visitor had to be considered a potential suspect.

"Not on this occasion, thank you."

Crystal opened her mouth to plead her case and shut it again without saying a word. If Lucy Carter had something to hide, her initial reaction to being officially told of her cousin's death might be illuminating. It was entirely possible someone as inexperienced as Crystal might say the wrong thing at the wrong time and therefore not get the best out of the witness.

"Thank you both for your assistance," DI Shortfellow said. "CID will be handling it from here, but as you're obviously interested, I'll do my best to keep you informed and perhaps some routine enquiries will come your way."

Crystal was amused. It wasn't a complete novelty for someone who was theoretically addressing both her and Trevor to actually be speaking to just one of them, but this was the first time the older, male officer was getting the dismissive treatment.

It was Trevor who responded with, "If there are any, I'm sure Sergeant Freedman will make that happen."

"Good. Thank you, Trevor. Officer Clere, you have good instincts. You'll be an asset to CID and I look forward to working with you in future."

"Thank you, sir."

Something about the inspector's and Trevor's attitude to each other seemed a bit odd to Crystal. They weren't antagonistic, but there must be some kind of history between them. Not for the first time, she felt there was something about Trevor she didn't know.

And what about the handsome inspector? He'd indulged her, no doubt blindingly obvious, wish to play detective and been very encouraging. Did he fancy her, or was she kidding herself? More importantly, did he really think she showed potential as a detective, or was he kidding her?

Once they were in the car, Crystal and Trevor headed towards the first of their routine tasks for the day. They were to speak to people who lived close to Stanley Park to gather information about anti-social behaviour, work out if any offences were being committed and, depending on the answer to that, either point out that young people having fun wasn't a crime, or assure the well-heeled residents that something would be done to keep them and their property safe.

"Thanks, Trevor," she said.

"You're welcome, lass. To which of the many kind things I've done for you are you referring?"

"Asking DI Shortfellow to let me help him, rather than make routine enquiries."

"Thought it would save you the embarrassment of pleading."

"Was I that obvious?"

"No, lass. If it weren't for my keen observational skills honed after thirty years in the force, I'd never have spotted you drooling."

"No! I wasn't?"

He laughed. "You weren't. It was your interest in a potential case, not a potential boyfriend which was clear. I'm not ruling out the other though."

"I'll admit he's quite attractive. You know him, don't you?"

"We've met before."

"And you're not exactly friends, yet you persuaded him to let me investigate a bit. That must have taken some doing."

"Not really. He's met you."

"Yes, he knows I'll be joining CID in a few months and it makes sense he'd prefer officers with some experience... But from what he said you'd... I don't know, not applied pressure exactly... And you don't call him sir."

"It's no big deal. Old timer like me can get away with a bit of cheek, besides he owed me a favour."

"Oh? What did you do?"

"Made a tit of myself and in the process messed up a major case he and his team had been working on for months."

"Oh." His delivery was so neutral it took a moment for his words to sink in. "Eh?"

"The long version is full of drama, excitement and opportunities for belly laughs at my expense. It requires total concentration from my audience and a couple of pints for me."

"We'll have to do that sometime. Would it be ruined by giving me the short version now?"

"Probably improve it to be honest."

"Come on then, spill."

"Late one night I saw what I thought was a hostage situation. Couple of youths tied to chairs, surrounded by armed thugs, in an industrial unit near St Ann's Hill. Then one was shot in the head."

"Oh god!"

"In the long version I'll give you the atmosphere and tell you about those little details I'd picked up on which alerted me to the fact something just wasn't right before I'd got anywhere near, and which made me so certain of my facts when I called it in. I'm an experienced and reliable officer, so my every word was considered credible and it was treated as a major incident. An armed response unit and ambulances raced to the scene and the chopper was on standby."

"And what was it really?"

"Students making a film."

Crystal did her best not to giggle. "Oh dear! OK, I get the drama, excitement and opportunity to laugh at your expense. But how did it mess up CID's operation and why did that result in him owing you a favour?"

"They were about to move in on a nearby unit, where a major drugs thing was going down. Months of work, including undercover officers, had gone into it. All the blue flashing lights in the area, just as key players started to arrive, put a stop to it."

"I bet."

"It was a right cluster. We'd been informed about the undercover stuff, but the deal they were about to bust didn't have a confirmed date and location until very shortly before it happened and they forgot to tell us."

"And DI Shortfellow was the person who should have passed that information on?"

"He certainly should have made sure it was done and… let's just say that if, when he's your boss you feel you're getting criticised for something which isn't your fault, or he's publicly saying something which should be aired in private, he hasn't learned his lesson as well as I hope and believe he has."

That last bit explained why Crystal hadn't heard of the incident. Whether or not a mistake had been someone's fault, if there was the potential for humour they'd be reminded of it quite frequently. It sounded as though the DI's reaction hadn't been funny.

In Stanley Park they found a group of kids who looked like they should still be in school. Coincidentally, within throwing distance, there were a number of beer cans, half still unopened.

"Those were already there," one of the youths assured the police officers, before they'd asked. "They're nothing to do with us."

"Any idea who they belong to?" Crystal asked.

"Nope." There was a lot of shrugs, head shaking and mystified expressions.

"We just know we definitely didn't buy them."

"We can't, we're all under eighteen," another added.

"We'll pick it up and put it in the bin," the most chatty one offered. "No need for you to worry."

Crystal and Trevor decided to help with that task, emptying every drop of lager as they did, and explaining the risks, legal and physical, faced by underage drinking. "Pass that on to your mates if any of them are silly enough to try it," Trevor said.

"They're silly enough for anything," the chatty one said. To Crystal, it felt almost as though he were apologising.

"Do you think we did the right thing, lass?" Trevor asked as they walked away.

"I think so. Pretty sure we gave them a fright. The fact the beer was the cheapest you can get and they had at most two cans each tells me they bought rather than stole it. The issue is with the shop who sold it to them. I'm not the only one who recognised the carrier bag, am I?"

"No, lass, you're not."

They visited the resident who'd made the complaint about the youths, saying they'd confiscated their drinks and given them a warning.

"Hopefully that will do the trick," the lady said.

"We'll keep an eye out whenever we're in the area," Trevor promised. Afterwards they made a formal report of their suspicions about the shop selling alcohol illegally, in hopes the owner would end up with more than an informal warning.

They still had enough of their shift left to stroll through Gosport High Street. The chief, rightly in their opinion, felt it was important for police officers to be seen 'on the beat' as much as possible. It reassured law-abiding people and there was anecdotal evidence of it reducing petty crime and anti-social behaviour.

"Oh dear, another shop closed down," Crystal remarked. "There seems to be another each time I come."

"I suppose that's not so often now you're staying in Little Mallow?"

"No, although to be honest I didn't shop here all that often before – which I suppose makes me part of the problem."

"Have you decided whether to stay on with your aunty, or move back to your flat?"

"Don't rush me – even the landlord has given me two more days to decide."

"Is it a difficult decision, lass?"

"I only ever intended to stay in Little Mallow until Aunty Agnes had recovered well enough from her hip operation to cope on her own. I thought we'd both be glad for me to leave after a couple of months max, but I was wrong. She's doing brilliantly – at her age she needs help with some things, but she's fine day to day. She says she's got used to my company and would be very happy for me to stay on if it suited me, but also made it easy for me to say if I'd rather not."

"So, it's totally up to you?"

"Yep. If I didn't stay I'd still call in regularly to see if there was anything she wanted or needed, so I don't even have guilt to worry about."

"It might help to make a list of the pros and cons."

"Can I try them on you? That will help me see if they make sense."

"After all I've done for you, I'm just the back of an envelope, am I?"

"A birthday card one, not a bill."

"Flatterer. Go on then."

"For is easy. Aunty would like it, and the rest of the family would be happier knowing she wasn't on her own. It would be cheaper. Even if she lets me pay towards the bills, which she currently refuses to allow."

"That's awkward, I suppose. Any other cons to staying with your aunty?"

"I couldn't invite a bloke back, at least not for more than tea and cake."

"Pretty sure DI Shortfellow has his own place."

"Trevor! But yes, dating a string of lads who still live with Mummy is something I can live without. I suppose the biggest reason to stay in my flat is Jason."

"The photographer who lives next door and hasn't had the bottle to ask you out yet?"

"Yes, him. But it's not lack of bottle I don't think. We're friends and he might not want to spoil that."

Trevor cleared his throat in a manner she was familiar with as meaning she was acting like chump.

"I haven't done anything to let him know I might be interested in anything more than borrowing milk when I've run out," she admitted. Trevor was right, she wasn't helping herself.

"You don't have to have front doors which open off the same landing to be friends with someone, you know."

"That's true. And maybe telling him I'm moving would make him realise he'd miss me, if he would."

Chapter 5

Monday 30th March

As always, when Ellie Jenkins walked up to the bar in the Crown and Anchor she subtly scanned the room to see if there was anyone she knew. Only once she'd ordered and received her gin and tonic did Ellie look round in a more obvious manner. Teaching small children had given her a remarkable ability to quickly recognise people and note whereabouts they were in the room and therefore seem to notice the right people first. Generally, when it came to those drinking in Little Mallow's only pub, people she knew were also people she was happy to join for a chat, but occasionally there were exceptions.

Getting her own drink before joining anyone avoided the dangers associated with having one bought for her. Some people believed the price they paid for her drink entitled them to a lot more than a polite thank you. It could be anything from an admission their child was an infant genius and the promise of unstinting efforts on her part to make that true, to a wonderful opportunity to make some man breakfast in bed the following morning. Of course, she was never offered a drink by a parent she was anxious to have a quiet word with, and rarely by a non-parent whose head she wouldn't mind seeing on the pillow next to hers.

On this occasion, the first person Ellie noticed was Arnold the verger. As he was quite a big man and actually gesturing for her to join him and his companions, it would have been impossible not to see him. He was with the

41

vicar and the pub landlord. Although it was quite likely they wanted something from her, she knew a polite refusal would be readily accepted with no hard feelings. That meant she was quite interested to learn what she might be able to help with.

"Miss Jenkins," Arnold said. "Now there are four of the new hall committee present, I propose an extraordinary meeting."

"Can you do that? Don't we have to notify the others?"

"It's not in the rules, as there are no rules, at least not yet. The committee appointed itself, so I don't see why we shouldn't appoint ourselves the executive committee and have a meeting just for the four of us."

Ellie blinked in surprise at the verger's display of decisiveness. Then grinned as that was exactly what the committee most needed. "One where something actually gets decided, you mean?"

"Exactly." Arnold was backed up by encouraging nods from the other two.

"Count me in."

Arnold's wish to hold a meeting which wouldn't just be further procrastination was explained when they showed Ellie the anonymous and unorthodox booking requests.

"Do you have any idea who or what could be behind this, Ellie?" Martin Blackman asked.

"None, sorry. It's very odd…"

"It is," Arnold agreed. "But I don't think knowing who wants to make a booking is as urgent as actually having a hall in which events can be held. I propose that we accept, and confirm as requested, call for volunteers to clear the site, arrange for delivery of the buildings, book a plumber and electrician, and apply for an alcohol license as soon as possible."

"I second the motion," Martin said.

"Arnold, you astound me."

Reverend Jerry Grande had voiced Ellie's thoughts. "Is that a yes?" she asked.

"It is."

"Then the motion is carried unanimously," Ellie declared.

They clinked glasses, took a celebratory sip of their respective drinks and began to speculate about who was planning this surprise party and why. That seemed like a pointless exercise to Ellie. Whoever it was had taken trouble, and a bit of a gamble, to ensure they remained anonymous. Even if one of the four guessed correctly it was unlikely they'd know that until the event. By then all would become clear anyway, so they may as well wait. Besides, if they did work it out they might spoil the surprise for the person in whose honour the party was being held.

Ellie's attention wandered towards a woman of about her own age who'd just entered the pub. She recognised her as the relation of Agnes Patterson, who was staying with the old lady while she recovered from her hip replacement surgery.

As people rarely went to the pub for solitude, Ellie decided to see if the newcomer would welcome a chat and went over. "Hi, it's Cynthia isn't it? If you're not waiting for someone, do you mind if I join you?"

"So long as you don't call me Cynthia." Although Cynthia was written on Crystal's birth certificate that name was only used by official form fillers, cold callers, and occasionally Aunty Agnes.

"Oh, sorry. I thought … "

"It is my name, but I don't like it. Even worse is when people shorten it. Can you imagine what it does to a girl's reputation if she acts like she's been summonsed every time anyone mentions sin?"

"I see what you mean." Ellie placed her drink on the table and slid onto a chair. Then, because she thought it would even things up said, "Officially I'm Danielle, but there were two boys called Daniel in my class when I first started school and apparently I had a bit of a meltdown over it, so now I'm Ellie."

"Crystal. I didn't choose that either, but my surname's Clere so it was an obvious nickname."

"I get called Miss Jenkins a lot. I'm an infant teacher, at St Symeon's. There are worse things I could be called, I suppose."

"I felt the same and decided to embrace the nickname. I like to think it suits me – the whole thing that is. I'm a pretty straightforward person, what you see is what you get kind of thing."

"That's good," Ellie said. She liked the little she knew about Crystal and hoped they'd be friends.

"I hope I'm clear thinking. I'm in the police and will be a detective in a few months."

"Oh, wow. That must be interesting."

"It really is. Today was... a good example. Of course there's plenty of paperwork and dull routine, but you get that with any job."

"Tell me about it!"

"I've not yet been in three years, so a lot of it is still a novelty."

"And you're being promoted to detective already? You must be good."

"It's not promotion, more a specialisation. I joined to be a detective, but we all have classroom learning and work experience in uniform to get a grounding in the basics. During that time I have to do a bit of everything for my SOLAP – that's the student officer learning and assessment portfolio. I am good though, at least that's what a CID inspector told me... when I helped out in the early stages of a case."

"Wow!"

"That's what I thought the first time I saw him, and today when he came striding onto the crime scene, all tall dark moody good looks. Think a younger Aidan Turner with serious hair."

Ellie had the feeling Crystal wanted to talk about whatever had happened at work that day, but had decided against it. Perhaps she couldn't say anything because the investigation was still ongoing. Ellie understood about confidentiality as it was important in her job, but it must be frustrating to have to keep exciting events to yourself. Perhaps that wasn't the only frustration? "Is he single and are relationships between different ranks allowed?"

"From what my tutor said, I think he's single."

"Tutor?"

"The officer I usually work with."

"Cool. So, once you're fully trained and qualified, can you and the inspector…?"

"People do get together in the police, the same as in any other job and it must sometimes happen between different ranks, but he'll be my boss when I join CID and a lot more senior, so getting involved isn't an option."

"Shame."

Crystal shrugged. "It's actually a pretty sensible rule."

"Oh?"

"It could be awkward working alongside someone who was sleeping with the boss. And if you're them, will you get resented for getting all the good jobs, or be given the rubbish ones so it doesn't seem like favouritism? And what about if you split up?"

"You're right. I was thinking more of my job than yours, but even there it could be awkward at times. Getting started must be tricky too – a move by the boss might be difficult to refuse."

"Or worse. Imagine turning them down and they hadn't meant it like that? I'm rubbish at telling if a man is interested or just being friendly – and at letting him know whether or not I am without being embarrassingly obvious."

"Same here." To Ellie it felt as though she and Crystal had been friends for years, rather than having just met.

"Come off it. You're so pretty and have a great figure, you must have got far too much interest not to know the signs."

Ellie thought Crystal was way overstating her attractiveness, but she was right that sometimes Ellie got far too much interest from men. "That's sort of the problem. Loads of men are interested in a blonde with boobs, but how do I tell if they're interested in this particular example, or if anyone with broadly similar looks would do?"

Crystal nodded and looked thoughtful. "Talk to them? You've clearly got the knack of making friends."

"But then I've got your problem of not being able to tell if he's just a friend or it could be more, and no clue if all my subtle hints that more is an option are not being picked up because friends is what he wants, or if I'm just being too subtle."

Crystal laughed. "What's yours called? Mine is Jason. He's my neighbour in Gosport."

"Mine's Mike, the vicar's nephew. He visits a lot and we've been friends since we were kids."

"What a pair we are," Crystal said in mock despair.

"Maybe we can help each other somehow? Shall we have another drink and try brainstorming brilliant ideas?" Ellie suggested.

"An excellent plan."

When they were again settled with drinks, Ellie asked Crystal when she was moving back to Gosport. "Not that I'm trying to get rid of you!"

"It's a good question. I've got to decide pretty quickly whether that's going to happen or not." She explained the entire situation.

"I don't see how Jason comes into it at all," Ellie said. "If he's really a friend, that doesn't need to end because you move a few miles up the road."

"You're right. I don't know why I'm making such a big deal about this. If nothing romantic has happened between us while I've lived next door it probably never will."

"Maybe telling Jason you're moving will make him realise he'll miss you?"

"Possibly. In fact it's the only thing likely to make any difference now." She sipped her drink. "Thanks, you've helped me make up my mind."

"You're staying in Little Mallow a bit longer?" Ellie didn't want to push Crystal into anything, but it would be lovely to have a friend of her own age living so close.

"Yep. It really is the sensible thing to do. I'll insist Aunty takes enough to cover my share of the bills, but I'll still save money, and it'll be a quicker drive to CID once I'm working there."

"And Jason?"

"He gets one last chance!"

Together they drafted a note, telling Jason of Crystal's decision to move out, her sorrow about no longer being his neighbour, and her hope they wouldn't lose touch. Crystal included a reminder of her phone number, her email, the handles of the social media accounts she now rarely used because of her job, and Great Aunt Agnes's address.

"It's not at all subtle, but if it doesn't work I probably won't ever see him again, so it doesn't matter," Crystal said.

"That's the spirit!"

"What about your Mike? Are we going to give him a chance to come good?"

"What do you have in mind? Remember, it won't be so easy for me to avoid him if it doesn't work. I'll still be living here and he'll keep coming to see his uncle."

"He does that a lot, does he?"

"Yeah. They've always been close and Mike likes to get involved with village life. I think he'd quite like to live here, but his job is up country and buying somewhere isn't easy – I suppose you know about that?"

"Aunty Agnes told me there's a weird covenant meaning you can't buy property here unless you already live here."

"That's right, yes. It was good for me as although I'd moved away it was for Uni and teacher training, so considered temporary. When my cottage became available I was able to buy it – I'd never have afforded it if it had gone on the open market."

"Which one is yours?"

"Just over the road." She pointed in the appropriate direction.

"Oh! It's lovely."

"I am lucky."

"Unlike this strange copper who's moved into the village and latched on to you because she doesn't know anyone."

"Crystal! I don't…"

"So you feel really sorry for her and want to invite her round for a meal or something, to introduce her to people and will Mike come too?"

"Ah! Even better, I'll say you're a detective and you've been asking strange questions. That'll probably have him begging for an introduction."

"Likes a mystery, does he?"

"He's always joking that Little Mallow is a front for something. I don't know if he'd be amused or horrified that the police thought so too, but he'd definitely want to find out more."

"OK, I'm game. What are my great aunt, the verger, and that grumpy chap who grows the vegetables up to? Drug smuggling? Counterfeiting? Plotting to overthrow the monarchy?"

"Money laundering."

"You sound very certain."

"Just before you arrived I was in a meeting about what to do with hundreds of pounds worth of used notes!"

"If that's true, you're going to sound very convincing when you tell Mike I was asking questions, because I'm going to start right now."

Crystal really did seem quite interested in the unusual booking. Not enough that Ellie expected a SWAT team, whatever that was, to descend on Little Mallow, but definitely enough to think mentioning it to Mike would result in another visit from him fairly soon.

Chapter 6

Friday 3rd April

Crystal called in at her old flat to check if there was post for her, and definitely not in the hope of seeing Jason. It was nearly a week since she'd left the note explaining she was no longer a neighbour and supplying numerous ways he could stay in touch. He hadn't attempted any of them. Clearly, he wasn't interested.

She keyed in the entry code which hadn't changed in all the time she'd lived there, and checked her mailbox. Nothing but junk and a free paper. If she'd still been living there she'd have flicked through before binning it, so that's what she did. Crystal wasn't prolonging her time in the lobby in case one particular resident happened to go in or out. It just seemed wasteful to throw the paper out unread.

There was a short piece about the unexpected death of 'quiet and unassuming' Mr Argent who was a 'retired man who loved dogs and was well-liked by his neighbours'. The photo of the deceased wasn't recent or of good quality. It was almost certainly cut from a group shot. Perhaps to fill space, there was also a photo of Lucy Carter. As the brightly smiling image didn't go with the caption of 'his only relative is shocked and saddened by this tragedy' Crystal doubted the woman had supplied it herself. As the entire article was heavy on cliches and very light on facts of any kind, it seemed likely she'd not spoken to the press, for which Crystal didn't blame her. Hopefully she'd been more forthcoming with CID.

Monday 6th April

Crystal and Trevor had caught up on paperwork and were preparing to go off shift when Sergeant Freedman informed them of a message from DI Shortfellow.

"The autopsy on Mr Argent confirmed he'd been poisoned. The DI thought you'd like to know you were right and you're to feel free to contact him if either of you needs any further information."

"Of course we do!" Crystal declared.

"You do, lass. I'm happy knowing we've done our bit and CID are dealing with it."

"I can't just leave it at that."

"I'm sure DI Shortfellow realises that." Sergeant Freedman's words lacked her usual upbeat tone.

"So, you think it would be OK for me to call him?"

"I'd say that was pretty clear."

"Crystal clear," Trevor added.

Crystal phoned the DI. Conveniently he happened to be in the area and was just going for a coffee. "If you'd care to join me, I'll answer as many questions as I can in the time it takes me to drink it."

She guessed the skipper had said Crystal was going off duty soon when the DI left the message, which is how he knew she was likely to be free. Trevor apparently wasn't, so she went alone.

"Poisoned with what, sir?" Crystal asked after they'd exchanged greetings.

"Cyanide. It would have acted quickly anyway, but the acid in the whisky sped things up. He most likely went into a coma almost immediately and probably suffered as little as his appearance suggested."

Crystal was pleased about that. It made her feel less guilty for her pleasure about being involved in the case. "Cyanide can't be easy to get hold of?"

"A licence is required to buy it."

"That'll help us narrow down the suspects."

"Yes, that gives CID a useful line of enquiry. Officer Clere... Cynthia."

"Please don't call me Cynthia."

"I apologise."

"It's Crystal. I'm only Cynthia to people who don't like me or when I'm in trouble, so obviously I don't want you calling me that."

He smiled. "Crystal... Your help when Mr Argent's body was discovered is much appreciated and I have no doubt you'll be an asset to CID when the time comes."

"But I'm not there yet and this isn't my case?"

"I'm afraid not. That doesn't mean you can't know what happens. Given your initial involvement and chosen career path I'll be happy to update you when time allows. And there may be routine enquiries which we'll ask uniform to assist with and which will hopefully come your way."

He'd already said that when she was on duty. Did he mean the updates would happen when they weren't? "Thank you, sir."

"I imagine your sergeant and tutor will allow you to carry out such tasks when your other duties permit."

"Yes. Trevor's a good man, sir." In case speaking up for him implied criticism of Sergeant Freedman she continued, "The skipper's great too. They all are. I was expecting a bit of... um reaction to me being young and female, but there's been none of that."

"I'm pleased to hear it, although saddened that we've not yet reached the point when a person doesn't think they're lucky not to experience discrimination just for being themselves."

"Things are getting better, sir, but there will always be idiots – just as there will always be criminals. And detectives. Is there anything else you can tell me, sir?"

"There was cyanide in Mr Argent's glass of whisky, but not the bottle," DI Shortfellow explained. "What do you deduce from that?"

She thought for a moment. "I didn't see anything which could have contained the cyanide when we first arrived. Was anything found after his body was moved?"

"No. Not in that room, elsewhere in the house, or even in the bin he'd failed to put out."

"So, someone other than him put the cyanide in his glass and took the container away. Presumably not long before Mr Argent drank the whisky. As it would have been quite late at night, and the neighbours seem to notice what goes on, it's most likely to be someone who has a legitimate reason to call, or appears to. The timing rules out tradesmen... " Crystal tried to think of ways someone could have put poison into Mr Argent's glass without arousing his suspicion. There was no evidence he'd had a caller on the night of his death and judging by the remains of his meal it didn't seem he'd been expecting anyone. As the whisky in the bottle was uncontaminated, the poison hadn't been added to that in advance.

"His cousin seems the most likely person to have been let in. There was a glass on the draining board – maybe they both had a drink and... But that's one of the first things you'd have checked."

"She did visit him that day, and it was she who supplied the whisky. That was in the morning. Not long after six that evening she met friends for a drink. They made a night of it, staying at a nightclub in Chichester until they were chucked out."

As she'd thought, Lucy Carter was such an obvious suspect they'd already considered and eliminated her. "Did you find out if any of the neighbours, other than Mrs Owen, had a key to Mr Argent's home?" The DI had asked her opinion, and she couldn't form one without facts, could she?

"None have admitted to it, nor thought it particularly likely anyone else had one. The lock is the same one which was there before he moved in, and several neighbours have moved in that time, so it's a possibility someone somewhere has a copy."

If someone had used the key to gain entry and kill Mr Argent they'd hardly admit to having been given one. Again that would be clear to CID and the lie by omission would do nothing to protect the guilty party should a motive, or any incriminating evidence, come to light.

"Could it have been a bizarre accident and the company sent out the glass with cyanide in?"

"Good thinking, but no. They don't use cyanide in the manufacturing process. Something else which might interest you is that although they did run a competition, they didn't send single glasses as runner up prizes."

"But he had a letter in his results file, saying one would be sent by courier... The killer must have been someone who knew about Mr Argent's habit of entering competitions, faked that letter and somehow used the delivery of the glass he didn't really win, to their advantage."

"That's certainly possible, but giving someone a gift in a complicated manner isn't proof of murder."

"Not proof exactly, but..." He was right. The killer might have known about the letter and used the arrival of what they, and Mr Argent, thought was a genuine prize to slip poison into his drink. It might even have been pure coincidence the murder occurred on the same evening the glass was delivered. Unlikely, but possible.

"The way they sent the glass wasn't just complicated, sir, it was secretive and they've not come forward. And yeah, I know that's not proof of murder either, but whoever sent it must be a suspect surely?"

"They are most definitely a person of interest."

"OK then." Crystal was still convinced the sender of the glass and killer were the same person, but if she were wrong it would still help the investigation to rule them out. And the best way to do that was to learn their identity and reason for acting as they did. "Whoever sent that letter and the glass must have known he entered competitions. Maybe not which ones, but it does seem they really wanted him to believe he'd won it."

"I tend to agree."

"Mrs Owen knew, as she said he sometimes gave her prizes, so it's entirely likely other neighbours did too – if he didn't tell them, she might have. There was a post office counter in the local shop. As the victim had most likely bought his magazines and sent his entries there the staff probably knew of his hobby. The delivery driver called frequently, so he might know too."

The DI nodded.

"Do we know when and how the glass arrived? If a neighbour called with a package and said it came to them by mistake and they're wondering what he won, Mr Argent might show them and then, because he got the whisky that day, decided to use it straight away. The killer could easily ask to take a closer look."

"Very good. We're looking into that angle."

Encouraged by his praise, Crystal asked, "Who stood to benefit?"

"Mr Argent's cousin Lucy Carter was, as we suspected, his closest relative. Closest in blood and geography, but not a close relationship. She was the main beneficiary of his will and showed no surprise at that."

"Main beneficiary?"

"Technically the only one. Mr Argent had completed a form to leave a legacy to the dog rescue shelter where he volunteered, but hadn't got it witnessed so it wasn't valid."

"If Lucy knew she was going to inherit, her cousin might have told her he was changing his will…"

"And decided to kill him before it became valid?"

Crystal nodded to show that's what she was thinking.

"She did know – and has promised the charity they'll still get the ten thousand pounds."

"Oh."

"Don't worry. Having theories is only a problem as long as you don't let them blind you to the evidence and other possibilities."

"It's not that. Lucy Carter seemed such an obvious suspect I didn't hesitate to mentally consider her a heartless, greedy murderer. I feel bad about that."

The DI nodded. "She displayed distress on learning he was poisoned via the whisky she'd bought him."

That made Crystal feel worse. It must be horrible to feel you'd played a part in someone's death. Then it occurred to her that DI Shortfellow had said 'displayed distress' not that she actually was upset. "Was it Colin Argent's birthday?"

"No."

"Then it's odd she'd bring him pricey whisky if they weren't close."

"She said he spent a lot of time 'comping' as he called it and was quite successful. He'd often given her his prizes, so when she heard he'd won a glass but nothing to put in it, she decided to treat him."

"You sound as though you don't believe her."

"On the face of it, buying him a bottle of whisky was thoughtful, and going for a malt instead of a less expensive blended whisky was generous."

"But?" Crystal prompted.

"It was on offer, so the cheapest single malt she could easily have bought and she'd just discovered he planned to alter his will to her disadvantage. Maybe the whisky was a calculated gesture to keep him sweet so she'd still get the lion's share of whatever he had to leave."

"That's a bit cynical."

"Nature of the job," Shortfellow said.

"I meant her going for the one on offer. That makes it 100% an investment and not a gift at all."

He laughed – a loud, abrupt sound, but not unpleasant. "Was it a long or short term investment? That's the question."

It was, and not one Crystal, who'd never seen or spoken to the woman, had a hope of answering. That was frustrating but… "Sir, thank you for sharing all this information, I really appreciate seeing how the case is developing."

"Noted."

Afterwards Crystal called in at her old flat again, to check for post. There was just one letter for 'the occupier' which she no longer was. Outside it had started to rain. Hoping the April shower would quickly pass she used her phone to look up the company who'd made the whisky glass sent to Mr Argent, but not by them. A photo of the competition winner holding her prizes was displayed under 'latest news', together with the fact she lived in Doncaster. Crystal spent a few minutes finding the woman on social media and checking whether she had any contact with anyone called Argent. Nothing.

Crystal scrolled through and discovered a single glass packaged as Mr Argent's had been was available for less than ten pounds including postage and packing. That wouldn't have added much to Lucy Carter's investment and, if an order could be traced to her, it would be a strong indication she'd been attempting to gain in the short term, not wait for her cousin to succumb to natural causes. CID would have checked up on that, surely?

The website showed images of glasses being made and decanters engraved. The workshop appeared to be small and open plan. It was hard to imagine an employee stealing a glass without being seen and far-fetched to imagine them trying to do so with murder in mind.

As Crystal, unofficially and ineffectively worked on the case in the lobby of the flats where she'd previously lived, residents came and went. Most she recognised, but not all. A few exchanged greetings but none seemed surprised to see her. That was good and bad. She'd made enough of an impression that seeing a police officer in uniform didn't alarm anyone or make them curious – Crystal was just a neighbour coming home from, or about to leave for, work. Despite her having lived in Little Mallow since late February, they didn't appear to have noticed her absence. Or maybe they had but thought, as she had when she first went to stay with Aunty Agnes, that it was temporary and she'd be back. Yes, when Karen from her floor spotted Crystal carrying suitcases, she'd said she'd return within a few weeks. Jason thought the same. They'd probably told anyone else who was interested. Or the landlord had. Once people got an idea in their head, it tended not to change without good reason.

Like her and Jason. They'd been friends from the start and it had taken her months to realise there was, or at least could be, more to it in her case. Then on Valentine's she'd received flowers she was almost positive were from him. If she took his lack of response about her change of address into account, things had gone backwards.

Jason wasn't one of the people who entered or left the flat while Crystal sat there pondering and in any case she hadn't been waiting for him, so she went home to Agnes's cottage in Little Mallow, where she was greeted by a wonderful aroma.

"Are you baking, Aunty?" she called as she headed for the kitchen.

"There's a couple of rhubarb crumbles in the oven. One for our tea and one for the freezer."

"Nice. I love rhubarb but rarely have any – it's so expensive." As she spoke, Crystal noticed a bundle of the glistening red stems on the worktop. "You know someone who grows it?"

"Old Bert Grahame has rows of it on his allotment. He sent young Adam up with as much as he could carry."

Crystal smiled. 'Old Bert' was at least twenty years younger than Agnes. 'Young Adam' was right and Crystal didn't doubt the accuracy of 'as much as he could carry' as Adam was often given tasks designed to tire him out.

In theory he was a great kid. In reality he was too – for very short periods. He was cheerful, polite, intelligent, and always wanted to help. He'd attempt to help anyone with anything and could be genuinely useful, but he preferred trying new things and currently had the ambition to be a police detective.

"Adam isn't still here?"

"I was tempted to get him to trim and chop some of the rhubarb for me, but wasn't sure if his mum would approve."

Crystal, seeing the size of the knife in question and knowing Agnes kept them all razor sharp thought she'd made the right decision.

"Luckily the kitchen waste bin was full, so I got him to take the contents to Bert for his compost heap."

"To thank him for the rhubarb?"

"Bert won't mind. He likes the boy and always has jobs for him to do."

"I can chop the rest of the rhubarb, if you'd like."

"Thanks, love. It takes it out of my wrists. While you're at it, think about what I can do with it. If I put it in the freezer like it is, it'll just stay there."

"Flapjack?"

"Don't think that'd work. It's so wet I'd end up with porridge."

"I had some gorgeous rhubarb flapjack not long ago. It was quite squidgy, but in a good way."

"That phone of yours have recipes?"

It didn't take Crystal long to find some. A few minutes were needed to narrow it down to one which Agnes thought sounded promising and only required ingredients she already had. A large batch had been cooked and was cooling when Arnold arrived.

"Your timing is as good as ever, verger," Agnes said. "Got something new for you to try today."

"I'll put the kettle on," Crystal said.

"Thank you both. That's very kind and… um… I'm hoping you might be persuaded to do something else for me."

"Anything we can, verger," Agnes said.

Crystal hardly had time to realise her great aunt was speaking for them both when she discovered it was her Arnold wanted a favour from.

"It was very kind of you to help out delivering the Little Mag," he said.

"Not at all. It helps make me feel like I belong here."

That reply seemed to give him confidence. "I was wondering if I could persuade you to share a little of your professional knowledge in the Little Mag? A local policeman, Trevor Harris, kindly wrote a piece for us but that was over a year ago and the focus was on home security. I was hoping for something more personal – and modern. Not getting caught out by internet scams, safe use of electronic payment methods, that sort of thing?"

"I could do that." There was plenty of advice online she could rewrite and it wouldn't hurt her professionally to say she'd taken a proactive step towards local crime prevention. "Did you say Trevor Harris?"

"He's a friend of Reverend Grande. They often share a pint in the Crown and Anchor although come to think of it, I've not seen him lately. Do you work with him? Is he OK?"

"I do, yes and he's fine. We have been very busy lately." That last bit was true. No more so than usual, but Trevor might feel the need to excuse his absence.

Thursday 9th April

Crystal offered Trevor a piece of the rhubarb flapjack she'd had a hand in making. She'd taken a boxful to share with everyone at the shift briefing. Aware sergeant Dil Dylan would be present, she'd only put out one piece per person and kept the rest back for her and her tutor.

"You didn't tell me you had a mate in Little Mallow, Trevs."

"You've met Jerry Grande then?"

"Not really. The verger asked me to write something for the community newsletter and mentioned you'd contributed in the past."

"I see."

"He said he'd not seen you lately."

"He probably will now you know I'll be in the village to meet my old friend, not spy on my colleague."

"No! Tell me you've not stayed away on my account."

Trevor grinned. "You still can't tell when I'm teasing you, lass?"

"I'm beginning to suspect it's when your lips move." That wasn't quite fair, but his laugh showed she was forgiven.

Chapter 7

Thursday 16th and Friday 17th April

Crystal was tempted to go by Lucy Carter's home for a nose. She could easily make an excuse to do so while on duty, but it really would be an excuse, and she couldn't risk it seeming the police were targeting or hassling her. If Lucy was guilty it could harm the case. No reason Crystal couldn't take a walk in her own time though – and Lucy lived near enough to Little Mallow for Crystal to deliver some surplus Little Mags. The small pile left in the Crown and Anchor under a note saying 'free – help yourself' hadn't reduced in the last week, so she wasn't likely to be depriving interested readers.

Crystal delivered to Lucy's side of the street one day, and the other side on the following day at a different time, to increase her chances of catching Lucy Carter coming or going. It was second time lucky. Lucy walked briskly right past Crystal, who didn't risk speaking to her, or even looking back. Instead she delivered the remainder of the leaflets asking herself what she'd hoped to achieve. She'd learned nothing of Lucy's personality and not much more than the photo in the paper had revealed. Lucy was a little older, shorter and heavier than Crystal. Her mid-length hair was glossy brown, probably her natural colour. She wasn't noticeably made-up. Crystal had caught a slight whiff of something floral, which could have been perfume, Lucy's shampoo or even fabric conditioner. Her clothes were similar to Crystal's and the kind of thing most youngish women in the area wore. She seemed a perfectly normal person in her mid-thirties, who had somewhere to be.

Monday 20th April

Crystal didn't attend Mr Argent's inquest. If she'd not previously had to give evidence in court she might have been asked to do so to help complete her SOLAP. If she'd been off duty she might have gone out of interest, but she was working so that wasn't an option. Fortunately it was standard procedure for all officers to be officially notified of the outcome of all court cases arising from any incident they became involved in. The result was murder by person or persons unknown. That wasn't a surprise – if CID had enough evidence for the suspect to be named, that person would already have been arrested.

DI Shortfellow called, offering to update Crystal. He again suggested meeting for coffee when she went off duty. Him remembering her shift pattern didn't mean anything. The pattern was standard and it was no surprise an effective detective had a good memory.

"My turn to get them, sir," she said when he asked what she'd like. This wasn't a date.

"So, what's new?" Crystal asked.

Although DI Shortfellow told her of the detailed routine investigations they'd been making into Mr Argent's background, that of his cousin Lucy, and his neighbours, the answer boiled down to nothing much. That surprised Crystal. She understood that a lot of detective work was slow and painstaking, more about elimination than breakthroughs but, as the DI had offered an update, she'd assumed there had been clear developments in the case.

Instead she drank half her coffee as she learned that Mr Argent had worked as a street cleaner for the council, got on OK with colleagues but not stayed in touch, that there hadn't been any disputes with his cousin or neighbours, that Mr Argent had no close friends or any enemies. Everyone seemed to quite like him, but even those people whose dogs he'd helped with, and other volunteers at the shelter, were really just casual acquaintances. Dogs and competitions were his real interests. He subscribed to magazines about both and made regular contributions to the Dog's Trust. The standing order he'd set up had been increased to £100 a month at the start of the year. All necessary research, and fascinating to Crystal, but not what she'd been expecting from the DI's phone call.

"I imagine you've been thinking of the case a great deal," the DI said.

She had of course. "The glass Mr Argent was sent must be important somehow. If it was simply a nice gesture then the giver would just have bought it for him, as Lucy did with the whisky. Someone took the trouble to make him think he'd won it. Maybe if he'd never won anything, someone close could do that to make him happy, but he'd already got a lot of prizes, and it doesn't seem as though he had friends who'd do that kind of thing. And even if they did, it would be a huge coincidence if it arrived around the same time as his killer turned up with cyanide, looking for something to put it in."

"I agree. That's strengthened by the fact we've been unable to trace any courier or postal delivery company taking the glass to Mr Argent. There's no sign of the outer packaging which would not only have made that easy, but shown where it was sent from and in theory who by."

"That makes it more likely someone brought it by hand. He wasn't one to throw packaging away and in any case didn't have time. The killer must have taken it away with them. Did the cousin say whether he already had the glass when she brought him the whisky?"

"She says he didn't mention it but, as she wasn't able to stay long, it's possible. That was late morning."

Crystal took the opportunity to mention her online search and wasn't surprised CID had checked whether Lucy Carter had ordered the glass Mr Argent had drunk cyanide from.

"They sell thousands of those glasses every year, both by direct mail order and as corporate gift packages."

"So it would have been easy to get hold of one?" Crystal asked.

"Yes, but that doesn't apply to the gift box. Only a small percentage are sold singly, and the design was changed to the pattern Mr Argent received, just before Christmas. It wouldn't be easy for an employee to take one, so this was almost certainly ordered."

"But not by Lucy – at least not in her name, nor to her home address?"

"No, and when buying online it's not easy to be anonymous. The name has to match the bank card used, and you have to give a billing address if it's different from the delivery one."

"Can you get a list of people who ordered single glasses since they changed the boxes and who gave different addresses for billing and delivery? It doesn't sound as though there would be many people in that category."

"You're almost correct. There's nobody who fits those criteria."

Crystal should have known the answer wouldn't have been so obvious – and that CID wouldn't have neglected to ask the question. "So, it was either someone else entirely or Lucy Carter possibly had an accomplice who placed the order. They'd have to be involved or someone she trusted not to say anything once they heard about Mr Argent's murder. She may have hoped it would be considered a natural death, but if someone ordered it for her, I don't think they did do so innocently."

"That seems unlikely," the DI agreed.

"Then it must be a partner who'd be sharing the inheritance with her…"

"Or someone who has agreed to help in exchange for payment, or someone she has some kind of hold over. Or someone else killed him for a reason other than inheriting his house."

Crystal sighed. "You don't have a suspect who fits any of those scenarios." If he had, she was sure the DI would have said so in his update on the investigation at the start of their conversation. "If you get a suspect other than Lucy, you'll be able to find out if they ordered a glass and if they did, that would be extremely strong circumstantial evidence against them?"

"Precisely."

"No one else with a motive, sir?"

"None we've discovered. It seems he didn't begin the competitions until he'd retired and moved here, so that slightly limits the field."

"I should think anyone who knew him well enough to want to kill him probably knew."

"Yes."

"This is frustrating. Are cases usually like this, with no leads and no real suspects?"

"Often by this time we have a pretty good idea who did it and the real job is gathering the evidence to prove it, and double checking we've not overlooked anything or anyone."

"It must be worrying for Lucy, if she is innocent. She'll have guessed that, because she's due to inherit, she'll be a suspect."

"Her past doesn't help. She was previously left property by another man who died suddenly."

"What!"

The DI grinned. "Don't get excited. He died in a car crash. As she'd been working for him, as well as living in the flat with him, it isn't surprising she inherited."

Crystal finished her coffee. "Does the fact she had one inheritance make it less likely she'd kill for another?"

"Hard to say. To keep the flat above, she had to sell the shop and take out a small mortgage. The shop was described as selling and restoring jewellery and antiques, but in reality they dealt in junk and a bit of repair work. It was thought Lucy Carter's lover may have handled stolen goods, but he died before that could be investigated."

"It's not proof of anything, but if she was happy to live with someone who broke the law, it hints she might not worry about breaking it herself."

"I agree, but murder is a big leap."

Crystal's phone buzzed to indicate she'd received a Facebook message. As she rarely used the site, but had recently suggested Jason contact her that way, there was a good chance it was him.

"Is there anything else you can share about the case, sir?"

"Not at the moment."

"Then I won't take up any more of your time." She finished her coffee. "See you around, sir."

As soon as she was out of sight of the coffee shop, Crystal checked her phone. Sadly it wasn't Jason getting in touch, but a widowed five star American general who thought she had a lovely smile and that they could have a beautiful friendship. Did anyone ever fall for that?

She checked her profile, to see if it gave the impression of being needy and gullible, and realised her status was 'in a relationship'. The latest pictures weren't recent at all, as they showed Crystal and her ex. It wasn't what she'd want Jason to see if he looked her up. She quickly sorted it, by updating her status to single and scrolling through her phone to find some innocuous snaps to post.

Tuesday 17th April

Crystal and Trevor's first task that day was to speak to a couple who'd reported vandalism to their property. They'd come home late at night to discover someone damaging their garage door. As soon as Crystal and Trevor arrived, they saw it might be more than that.

"There have been several burglaries recently in which the property was accessed via an integral garage," Trevor informed the homeowners.

"We heard about that, but it didn't look as though he was trying to get in," the woman said.

"He was whacking the door with a big hammer – which he dropped."

That further convinced Crystal and Trevor this had been a failed attempt by the same person. He tended to cause unnecessary amounts of damage. The police psychologist suspected anger issues and had warned he could be violent.

"Can you describe the person?" Crystal asked.

The couple did their best, but it had been dark and he'd been wearing a hoodie and gloves. That meant the hammer was unlikely to reveal his identity, but Crystal bagged it and put it in the patrol car anyway.

"We'll get him eventually, lass," Trevor said, as though sensing her despondency.

"Maybe, but a person who might be male, is possibly white, and maybe a bit taller than average isn't a lot to go on."

"There's progress on the Argent case though. DI Shortfellow had news for you."

"Not really." Crystal updated Trevor with the few things she'd learned from the DI. "Seems as though they've come to a dead end. I'm sure they won't just give up so soon, but I suppose that sometimes they have to."

"I don't think that's the official line. Even cold cases get looked at again, if there are potential leads, or similar cases."

She knew that. "Guess I was thinking about me giving up personally."

"Your photographer?"

"Very much not mine." She explained about not wanting to ruin a friendship, and then leaving the note when she had nothing to lose, and getting no response at all.

"When you say nothing, what do you mean?"

"Absolutely zero. I gave him my social media handles and I've not had a single friend request."

"Maybe he doesn't use those sites?"

"Yeah he does. He's most active on Instagram, but that's all work stuff. That's why I put the others, in case he preferred to be more professional on there. I overdid it and scared him off, didn't I?"

"I doubt that. Single men are rarely going to mind if their attractive female friend seems to want more than just friendship."

"That's sort of what I thought. You know, it is odd there was nothing at all… "

"He ignored your friend requests, blocked you, what?"

"I didn't send any requests. Not all the sites work like that anyway. Oh, am I sending mixed messages?" She'd wanted to follow him everywhere when she first got to know him, but worried she might come across a bit stalkerish, then after a while it seemed too late.

"This note, he definitely got it?"

"I put it in his mail box. It was fairly full at the time – he goes away on assignments sometimes. Don't look like that, he's been back, because when I went to check if there was any mail for me, there was nothing sticking out of his box."

"But you've not seen him, or heard from him at all?"

"No."

"You have his phone number?"

"Yes. And he's got mine."

"You're a police officer. Your neighbour hasn't been seen in a while and is acting out of character. It's not unreasonable to be concerned."

"You think I should ask the landlord if he's away?"

"No, idiot girl. You could call him to check he's OK."

Crystal studied her finger nails for a few moments. "I have been an idiot," she agreed. She didn't call though, she went to Instagram and liked Jason's most recent photos, which had been taken in Sweden. Scrolling through she saw the previous batch were city scapes in Manchester. If the dates of posting were a guide, he wouldn't have been home for long between assignments. It was possible he'd taken in his mail but not had time to go through it and not even seen her note.

She tried calling. She was half disappointed and half relieved to get voicemail. "Hi, it's Crystal. Um... Not seen you around lately so I just thought I'd say hi. Which I just did, so I suppose that's it then. Bye." Well, if that oratory triumph didn't get him calling begging for a date... she wouldn't be in the least bit surprised.

Chapter 8

Tuesday 21st April

When Arnold finished raking up the few blades of cut grass which had strayed onto the churchyard path, he went into the vicarage for coffee. As usual he called out a greeting in case Reverend Jerry Grande was in and free to join him, then switched on the kettle.

"Morning, Arnold. How are you? Everything alright?"

"I'm fine thank you." He wondered if he looked ill. Jerry often came to chat and they discussed a wide variety of topics, but the vicar didn't usually enquire after his health. "I hope the same is true of you," he added in case it was anything about Jerry's own medical condition he wished to talk about.

"Oh yes, thank you." It looked as though he was going to say something else, but the kettle had come to the boil and Jerry busied himself making their drinks, and inviting Arnold to cut them a slice from whatever was in the cake tin.

"Jerry, I'm applying for the alcohol licence for the new hall. There are two options. We can either apply for a temporary event licence, for the party on the third of June, which costs twenty-one pounds, or we can spend five times the amount on an annual licence. If we chose the temporary option I'm happy to do it in my name, but if it's to be the annual one, I think it would be better to include more people."

"I agree. Shall we opt for temporary this time and reconsider if and when we get further bookings?"

"Yes. I think that will be best." Arnold took a mouthful of rich, moist sponge. After swallowing he said, "This isn't Muriel Grahame's usual recipe,"

"It's not her recipe at all. This is from Agnes Patterson."

"But… it's coffee and walnut."

"Is there something wrong with it? I thought it very nice, but now you mention it Crystal did apologise in advance in case it wasn't as good as her aunt's usual offerings, as she'd helped with it."

"Agnes didn't actually make it? That's OK then."

"Is there something I should know about Agnes? Is her health failing or…?"

"No, no. She's doing wonderfully well. It's just that she doesn't make you a coffee and walnut. Muriel Grahame does those."

"You make it sound like there's a rota!" He ate and drank for a few moments and then asked how work on the new hall was progressing.

"Not as well as I'd hoped. I'd made contact with a plumber and electrician who'd both offered to do a good deal, but I'm sorry to say they now seem to want to go back on their promises. They've been quite uncooperative, almost as though they're pretending not to know what I'm talking about. "

"Let me guess – you telephoned them?"

"Not initially. I explained via email what we wanted done and about it being a community project and suggesting we provide them with publicity in exchange for a discount. That was very successful, but when I called to try to arrange a date, it was a very different story."

Jerry nodded and handed Arnold a piece of paper with several words on. "Does this mean anything to you?"

Arnold read, *'booking, cash, strange, but good incentive'*. The words did seem familiar. As he finished his slice of cake the answer came to him. "They relate to our conversation about the booking for the mystery party."

"Can you be more specific?"

"Sorry, no, except… These are the points which struck me as most important. Are you having concerns about the booking?"

"Not concerns exactly, although the more I think about it, the odder it seems. But that's not the point. Arnold, those words, and only those words, were what you said to me after receiving that strange letter and the money."

Oh dear. "I thought I'd explained. You gave the impression you understood… not that I'm blaming you."

"I did have a good idea what you were talking about. That's because I was reading the one sent to Martin, at the time."

"I hoped I was getting better." He didn't understand why, but he'd always found it difficult to communicate clearly by telephone. The more he tried, the more tongue tied he became, so he said as little as possible. He was aware and saddened that some people considered him abrupt to the point of rudeness, but thought he'd at least found a way to get his message across.

"Arnold, please don't be upset. I thought it best you know."

Arnold nodded. He knew Jerry would never be deliberately unkind. "It is, or it would be if I knew what to do about it."

"I suppose it's easy for me to say, but I suggest you try to speak slowly and in complete sentences if you must use the phone – better yet, send a text!"

"Oh! I'll try. Thank you." Could it really be that simple?

"Is everything else alright? No worries or anything you'd like to talk about?"

So he'd been right. There was something, something other than his abrupt telephone manner, which Jerry thought was amiss.

"I'm fine. Just the same as usual. Do I look ill?"

"Not at all. But sometimes you don't seem entirely happy."

"Is anyone always entirely happy?"

"I suppose not. Arnold, remember that although we're all different, God loves us all. Accepts us all. Be kind to yourself."

Arnold smiled. He might be accepted, but he wasn't excepted from the less pleasant aspects of God's work. "That will have to wait."

"Oh?"

"The rest of my working day will be spent clearing the gutters. A very necessary job, but hard work and not kind on the nose!"

Jerry smiled. "I'm very grateful I have you to take care of such matters for me."

The job was as tiring and unpleasant as Arnold had feared, but it was accomplished safely thanks to Old Bert Grahame's help. He stood on the bottom rung of the ladder to keep it steady, and insisted it was moved on a couple of feet each time a small section was cleared, so Arnold never over-stretched. Once Arnold supplied a hat, Bert was also accepting of smelly, stagnant water and decomposing foliage occasionally landing on him. That meant Arnold could drop the detritus straight to the ground, rather than grappling with a bucket.

Old Bert wasn't uncomplaining exactly, but he was patient, and worked for nothing more than the promise of a pint next time the two men happened to be in the Crown and Anchor. Although he was far from wealthy, it wasn't so much that he couldn't afford to buy himself a drink, as that the sister he lived with wouldn't let him. A pint bought by someone respectable, and Arnold seemed to be included in that category, was OK, but Muriel didn't like him to buy his own or drink at home.

Village opinion was that Muriel knew what was good for Bert. Come to think about it, her rule was also good for Arnold's social life as he sometimes went to the pub mainly to buy Bert the pint he'd promised.

On his way home Arnold decided he needed something beautiful and fragrant to counteract the work he'd just done. He stopped at Paula's Posies to buy flowers for his dear mum, which he often did, and some for himself, which he'd never done before. He'd sometimes bought Mum's the day before and put them in water to keep them fresh until he visited her. He'd enjoyed seeing them, especially when he came back home from work.

"Hello, Arnold," either Liz or Dawn said cheerfully as he entered the florist shop. Although they didn't look more than superficially alike, he wasn't sure which was which, as both the regular assistants had been introduced together as though they were a couple. For a time he'd assumed they were. They tended to speak for each other and converse like a tag team.

When he'd found just one of them in the shop, he'd said, "I hope your partner isn't unwell?" in the hope of being assured that Liz or Dawn was fine, and thus discovering her name. Instead he'd learned they weren't a couple, it was funny how many people thought that, she couldn't think why, that her friend was healthy and had a husband called Dave who liked looking at planes but not going in them.

A while later he'd asked the other woman if her friend was on holiday and learned she never took one these days because of Chiz, but she had been to Canada once 'before all that'. Whether Chiz was a husband, parent, child or possibly other than human was still a mystery, but Arnold knew they were a martyr to their feet and that, "You've got nothing if you've not got your health, have you?" Arnold had agreed and after a few more similar attempts decided not to try to gain further information from either lady. He could have asked Paula Roth, the shop's owner, whom he knew fairly well. It was she who'd carried out the joint introduction, which made it more awkward. He didn't want to be thought of as the sort of person who didn't take notice of a shop assistant's name when told it, so resigned himself to never knowing.

"So, carnations as usual is it?" Liz or Dawn asked. "We've got some of those speckled ones you like."

"Yes please, and I'd like something scented too."

"Freesias are lovely, but they don't last long. The lilies do, and they've got a real strong perfume once they open, but they cost more."

"I'd like lilies, please. If the scent is strong I'll be able to enjoy them anywhere in my flat." Just as it was difficult not to be told things by Liz and Dawn, it was difficult not to share something with them. He couldn't help wondering what kind of picture they might be building of him.

"Unless it's a really big flat, three stems will be enough."

"Thank you. I'll take three."

"So, when they open you might want to cut the stamens off so they don't drop pollen. Dawn and I always tell people that. You have to do it if you've got dogs or cats, 'cause it's poisonous to them, but I think it's a shame otherwise. Just be careful if it gets on anything. Don't rub it in – shake it off, or dab it with Sellotape."

"Thank you, Liz. That's a very good tip."

Chapter 9

Saturday 16th May

Ellie slowed her jog as she noticed Mike by the area adjacent to the pub which, until a few days ago, had been a neglected eyesore of a fallen down Nissan hut, brambles, sycamore saplings, nettles and all kinds of discarded junk and blown litter. It had been the one blemish in the otherwise picture perfect Main Street of Little Mallow. It was still far from pretty, but the ground had been cleared and levelled and the structures which were to be used as the village hall were installed and equipped with plumbing and electricity.

"I can't believe it," Mike said, when she reached him. "Last time I was here Uncle Jerry was frustrated that after six months of meetings the new hall committee hadn't agreed on a single thing other than that a new hall might be quite a good idea in theory."

"Actually it was even more maddening than that. Everyone did agree on pretty much everything, they just couldn't quite bring themselves to actually commit to anything."

Mike chuckled. "Not good for a committee!"

"No. We've sorted it out now though. Everyone who was on the original committee plus a few more are the supporters club, and the committee is a much smaller, and more decisive group."

"Including you, I hear, Miss Jenkins?"

Ellie hoped she wasn't blushing at the news Mike might have been asking about her. "Only because I happened to be in the right place at the right time when Arnold got things moving. He's been incredible. Instead of paying someone to clear that old hut he managed to sell it for scrap metal. That brought in enough to pay for the fuel used by the digger which cleared up everything else. The operator does serious landscaping projects and was persuaded to do the work for just the fuel cost in return for an advert in the Little Mag and his sign staying up for six months."

"Impressive," Mike said.

"Yep. And Arnold bought the cabins and had them erected and everything. Like you, I can hardly believe it's all happened so fast."

"I can, now you've explained it's all down to Arnold."

"Oh? Saw his hidden depths, did you?" Ellie felt a little ashamed that she'd previously dismissed the verger as a rather weak man with little personality who kept the church and grounds neat but hadn't the talent for much else.

"I can't say I had. I was thinking he must have had to make a lot of these arrangements over the phone."

"I hadn't thought of that. It must have been difficult for him."

"And created a real sense of urgency in whoever he spoke to?"

"If they understood him at all, which presumably they did, they'd certainly have got the impression there was no time to lose." Like many people in the village, Ellie knew of Arnold's unease with the telephone. Whether it was the chicken or the egg situation she didn't know, but it couldn't help that he only made a call as a last resort and therefore often really was in something of a panic.

Mike gestured to the wall of contractor's boards. "Are all these sponsors of the hall?"

"Sort of. They've all given money, goods or services, or taken something off their bill."

"What's happening today?"

"The fun stuff! We're laying out the garden. The digger driver uncovered a largish concrete area still in good condition, right behind where the new hall is now. We decided to leave that in place to provide a seating area. We're going to instal smooth wide paths, with a gentle slope to the doorways to make it as accessible as possible. The rest of the area will be planted up to be attractive to both people and wildlife."

It was the planting which Ellie was eager to help with. Two members of the hall's new committee suggested making the area low maintenance, but Ellie had vetoed that idea. She knew that low maintenance was often treated as no maintenance and the area would be in danger of returning to something not too far from its former neglected state. She was also aware that many of the supporters club were, like her, very keen gardeners who'd be happy both to supply and plant appropriate flowers and shrubs, and to maintain them over the years to come.

"There's time for breakfast before all the helpers and deliveries arrive," Ellie said. "A couple of landscape gardening firms are supplying surplus paving slabs and turf, and we're expecting sand, gravel and cement as well as top soil and plants."

"I'd better get back. Uncle Jerry said he's doing a fry up and he'll have started now."

"See you later then." She'd been about to offer to make him an omelette but was glad he'd pre-empted that. She couldn't compete with sausages and bacon, but would still have been hurt when he declined.

As Ellie stepped out of the shower, Mike phoned. "Ellie, I need your help. Please say you won't let me face it alone."

"Face what?"

"The breakfast mountain in Uncle Jerry's kitchen."

"I don't know how much help I'll be, but I'll do my best."

As always, when expected at the vicarage, Ellie let herself in. The unmistakeable aroma of full English preparations would have told her where to head even if she hadn't known her way. When she arrived in the kitchen her first comment was, "We'll need reinforcements."

"They're coming, Miss Jenkins, don't worry," Jerry told her. "And I've cooked breakfast for a few of them."

Ellie shared a grin with Mike over the misunderstanding about what the help was for. Then as others joined them she said 'good morning, verger' to Arnold, and 'hello, Martin' to the publican. Then 'hello, Adam' to one of her more precocious pupils who was in the care of his grandfather. The Milligans ran the post office and village store which was open that day, meaning "Granny couldn't come, so I'm going to do her jobs."

Jerry, Mike, Martin and Arnold had the full works of sausage, baked beans, bacon, mushrooms, tomatoes, fried bread and two eggs. Ellie accepted an egg and mushroom bap, followed by an almond croissant. That was more carbs than she'd usually consume all day, but she was hopeful she'd be active enough to offset that.

Mr Milligan said they'd already eaten, but was persuaded to accept a bacon sandwich and Adam got through a plate of everything which was left and which would have fed Ellie and several dogs for a week. That should see them all nicely through to eleven, when no doubt there would be tea brewed in the new hall's brand new kitchen and an excessive quantity of home made cakes on offer.

It had been warm in the vicarage kitchen due to the kettle, grill, hob and oven all working at maximum capacity. It was even hotter outside where the sea breeze had dropped and the sun burnt through the wispy clouds. Ellie was pleased to see the heat wasn't deterring the volunteers. Quite a crowd was already waiting and more people arriving. Among them was Crystal, pushing a wheelbarrow containing a camping stove and two old fashioned aluminium kettles.

"I thought you had to work today?" Ellie said.

"I do, but I'm on lates so can do a couple of hours first. I didn't want to say in case you were relying on me for more than a token effort."

"Tea making?"

"I'll leave that to Aunty and her chums, but first I have to report back about the kitchen facilities here."

"Limited! There's plenty of worktop space to set things up and enough crockery for today, but only two electric sockets on an extension lead and I think that will be needed outside for the cement mixer. I'm afraid the only tap is outside too."

"That's better than I thought. We were imagining having to lug bottles of water. That's mainly why I brought the barrow."

"It will still be useful. Most of that," she gestured to an assortment of hard landscaping materials which had materialised during breakfast, "will be needed out the back."

"Count me in for some of that. I know nothing about building or gardening, but I can push a barrow with the best of them – and then push off once everything's where it needs to be."

"Any response from Jason?"

Crystal shrugged. "He accepted my Facebook friend request, plus sent a message saying he had very patchy internet and phone signal where he was and he'd call in a couple of days. He didn't, just sent another message saying he was crazy busy, but would definitely call when he was home."

"On the plus side, it doesn't sound as though you've scared off a friend."

"Yeah, there is that, but clearly friends is all it's going to be."

"You're OK with that?"

"Yeah. A bit disappointed, but kind of what I was expecting. Was that Mike you walked down with?"

"Mmm hmm. I had breakfast at the vicarage."

"Ooooh."

"Along with the vicar of course, and the verger, publican, postmaster and a small child."

"Oh."

Shortly after they'd all agreed with the other volunteers who was to do what, a small van pulled up. The driver explained he was a tree surgeon and wondered if they had a use for the wood chippings he had in the back. "When I've got a load like this Old Bert sometimes has it for his allotment and he said you were sorting out the garden here."

By then Bert himself had left off directing Adam and the other children in their tasks and come over. "It's good for paths, or as a mulch to stop the weeds growing through," he explained.

"We're having solid paths, but the mulch idea sounds great," Ellie said. As well as stopping the weeds it would conserve moisture until it rotted down to enrich the soil.

"I'm doing a job today, I can bring you more later," the tree surgeon offered.

"Can't ever have too much mulch," one of the other helpers said.

The tree surgeon had to tip the load out, which was inconvenient as they weren't ready to use it, but it didn't completely block the road and in any case, half the village was there for the day, not attempting to drive past.

As expected, eleven o'clock saw the arrival of more people, mainly elderly ladies, bearing cake tins. They disappeared into the tiny kitchen area of the new hall, leaving the florist, Paula Roth, with an armful of plant pots and more at her feet. They were supposed to be early bulbs and spring bedding which had gone past its best – that's what she'd promised, but these were early summer flowerers, all in prime condition.

"Some village children are helping my husband with the rest, but I thought these would look cheerful in the big pots."

Ellie's assigned role was to oversee both the planting of the flower border alongside the road and the front path, and to co-ordinate deliveries and direct any more helpers to where they'd be most useful. The village's oldest residents, Agnes Patterson and Muriel Grahame, were supervising the planting of the back garden. They managed to do that from conveniently positioned deck chairs. Muriel's brother Bert had a more hands on approach as he organised the shrubbery and trees on either side of the hall. He'd had the nice idea of including fruiting bushes and trees, to be underplanted with strawberries and herbs. That would look, smell, and taste, wonderful and he'd assured everyone it would be as good for wildlife and at providing a bit of a barrier to wind and noise as either native or purely ornamental trees.

With only a few stops for tea and cake, work continued all day. The concrete area was extended with a border of paving slabs on three sides and decorated with flower filled pots. From there paths extended to both the front and back doors. Those walkways and the one from the road to the front door were carefully constructed from the random mixture of donated materials which someone had laid out brilliantly to create a repeated pattern. Honestly, if she'd not known how it had come about she'd have assumed it had been planned long in advance, with each part of the pattern deliberately sourced.

"Who laid it out like that?" Ellie asked.

"Young Adam and his friends," Arnold said. "It was hard work for them, but they enjoyed it, said it was like a jigsaw puzzle. Do you think it looks OK?"

"It's fantastic." Clever though Adam was, Ellie was sure she was currently praising the person who'd ultimately been responsible for the design.

While her attention was distracted, the tree surgeon returned with his third load of wood chip. This time in a huge lorry, not a small van. With a press of his hydraulic switch it became a road-full before her eyes. Although by then tired, and thinking they'd just about finished for the day, everyone pitched in to spread it over the newly planted area.

"I've told him we've got enough now," Arnold assured everyone.

The sun was beginning to set, and the air cool, by the time they'd done all they could.

"Will there be an official opening?" Mike asked.

"Yes, but not until midsummer, when your uncle will bless the hall in a small ceremony for the committee and supporters club."

"That's over a month away. Isn't it going to be used before then for some mystery party? I'd have expected him to conduct the blessing before that."

"He wanted to, but it's not as though it's a church hall where the decisions are down to him. The committee couldn't find a suitable date. Not because of any lack of decisiveness this time, there just isn't time. We've got electric and water into the building, but it still has to be connected to taps and sockets and there are a few other things which won't be finished until just before the first booking. There's a danger that whoever organised the party will think their first guests have come as tradesmen."

Once the hall was locked and the road swept clear of debris, people went home or down the pub. Jerry was in the latter group and invited Crystal to join him, Mike and the others.

"As I'm at the seaside I fancy fish and chips, which probably aren't on the menu in the Crown and Anchor," Mike said. "Want to join me for a picnic supper on the beach, Ellie?"

If fish and chips weren't on the menu at the Crown and Anchor it would probably be the first time since Raleigh introduced potatoes to the country, which suggested Mike's fancy wasn't entirely focussed on the food.

Ellie decided she'd burned off enough calories to justify accepting. Then she remembered the huge breakfast she'd eaten – and accepted anyway.

Chapter 10

Saturday 16th May

"You're looking mighty fine today, Crystal," Sergeant Dil Dylan said.

"Thanks." She smiled, waiting for the punchline.

"Your hair is very… hairy."

She suppressed a giggle as she imagined what he'd be like if he were trying to chat someone up. "I like that about it."

"So do I. I like pizza. Do you like pizza?"

Oh crikey. Maybe he actually was trying to chat her up? Trevor had hinted Dil was interested in her that way, but she'd thought he was teasing.

"Who doesn't like pizza?" she said. "Jason and I prefer Luigi's in Blake Road. Do you know it?" She watched the change on the sergeant's face as she spoke. He had been about to ask her out. Crisis averted she hoped. She attempted to cheer him up by telling him about Luigi's special offers and the option to have a spicy sauce instead of the traditional herb and tomato. That did seem to help, and she was able to make her escape leaving him not exactly joyful, but less crestfallen than when she'd made it clear she didn't want a date.

It was true she and Jason had used Luigi's pizza shop more than any other. It was the closest to their flats and they regularly received leaflets advertising special offers. When it was for a buy-one-get-one-free they'd sometimes eaten together. That was how their friendship started.

Crystal had gone down to collect her mail at the same time as Jason, and they'd both had an offer leaflet.

"It's a really good deal, if you want more than one pizza," Jason had said.

Crystal was about to say she sometimes bought two and had one the following day, but wondered if that made her sound like a sad, lonely slob. Instead she said, "I love pizza, let me know if you want to go halves on that offer sometime."

"This evening?"

"I'm working until ten. Tomorrow?"

"Yeah, great. Sevenish?"

"Perfect."

At ten to seven she realised she hadn't told him her door number and was wondering if she should go across to his, when he knocked. They'd chatted easily as they walked to Luigi's, waited for their pizzas and carried them home. As they'd planned to eat while watching the same TV show it seemed natural to do that together. They'd done the same thing each time they were both home for another two-for-one offer. Sometimes they ate at hers, sometimes his.

Crystal missed him so much. She was an idiot not to have done something to encourage him when she'd had the chance. And had she learned from that? Of course not. Jason's recent messages made it clear he still wanted to be friends. She wanted that too but was just waiting for him to contact her. Ellie would probably think she was behaving like some Victorian maiden not wanting to seem like a right strumpet for speaking to a gentleman acquaintance until she was spoken to.

Crystal messaged Jason saying, '*I miss you – and not just for the offers at Luigi's!*'

Was that too much? And why hadn't she asked herself that before she sent it? She followed it with, '*But I miss the pizzas too – split one when you're free?*' That was better. It sounded as though she was happy carrying on as they had before, which she sort of was.

So it didn't seem quite so obvious she'd only resumed her social media usage because of Jason she posted a photo of the cake Agnes made for that morning's volunteer session to sort out the outside areas at the new hall. Crystal included the comment that she'd be attempting to make one herself and taking it to work. '*Wish my colleagues luck!*' Baking a cake and making sure sergeant Dylan got a share might show she liked him – just not like that. He really had been kind to her and she thought that was genuinely him being nice, not an act because he fancied her.

Sergeant Dil Dylan's love of carbs was a standing joke in Gosport police station. Along with all the other similar jokes it was a wildly exaggerated version of the truth. Last year Imani Freedman had been filling out some kind of form on her birthday. It asked for her age and she'd said she should have completed it the previous day, and been in the lower range. It had immediately become established fact she was sensitive about her age.

If any of the officers or support staff brought in food to share, Dil Dylan always helped himself – just like everyone else. He was never the one to take the least, but he didn't usually take more than other people. Or not much more. What he did do was make a point of mentioning if one piece was bigger than the others and say, "Obviously that one's mine." And if there was anything left on the plate when everyone who wanted had taken some he'd say, "Better clear this up, it won't keep!" and start eating it before the inevitable reply of, "Not with you around!"

When Crystal had tried to cheer Sergeant Dylan up after cutting off his presumed attempt to ask her out by talking about pizza it had seemed to work. If it wasn't because he was carb obsessed then it was because she'd stayed to chat for a minute. She would like to be friends with him, with all her colleagues. It would be a really good idea to get better at showing her willingness to be friends, and her unwillingness to be more – where that was the case.

Her opportunity to make a start came seconds later, when Dil approached her to say a police dog handler who'd been due to visit a school that coming Friday had to cancel. "Didn't know if you'd want to offer to step in or not, so thought I'd give you a head's up."

"Thanks. I'll speak to Trevor. Sarge, can I ask you something?"

"Sure."

"I was wondering about your nickname. Are you just called Dil because your surname is Dylan?"

"No. Because my first name is."

"What?" Dylan was most definitely his actual surname.

"It's spelled D I, double L, O N. DI on its own would be confusing, so it's Dil."

"You're having me on!"

"I'm not. Honest."

"Yeah, right."

"If I explain, do you promise not to let on?"

"OK."

"I was originally Dillon Watkins. Mum wasn't married so I had her surname. Then she met Andy Dylan and eventually married him. He's the only dad I've ever known and a great bloke. When he became my stepdad Mum wanted me to change my name to his, but he said it wasn't fair as I'd get teased."

"But you did it anyway?"

"Some things are more important than what a bunch of twelve-year-olds think, you know?"

She agreed completely, but very much doubted she'd have done so when she was that age. Crystal had been the kind of kid who really thought she'd 'literally die of embarrassment' if her parents didn't buy her the pricey trainers 'everyone' else wore.

Crystal's enthusiasm level for the school visit wasn't sky high but it was far higher than Trevor's. He agreed they'd do it if that was the only alternative to letting the kids down. Two minutes later they learned from Sergeant Freedman that was the case, and that the school was St Symeon's – where Ellie taught.

"We should start thinking about what we're going to do for it," she told Trevor when they'd confirmed the timing and gone out on patrol.

"I'd rather not think about it at all," he grumbled.

"Come on, it'll be fun."

"That's what you said when we were told about that sudden death."

"I did not! I was interested, that's all."

She decided not to try to interpret his expression and instead asked, "Have you done school visits before?"

"Every time I couldn't get out of it."

"I'm friends with a teacher at that school. Do you mind if I call her and discuss ideas?"

"As long as one of those ideas is to have me sitting quietly making notes about how brilliantly you're handling it all, and working out how many boxes on your SOLAP we can get ticked off on the strength of it."

"Seriously? You'll let me lead on this?"

"Never been more serious in my entire life, lass."

Chapter 11

Saturday 16th May

"I'm exhausted," Ellie told Mike as they drove to the nearest chip shop, which was in the adjacent town of Lee-on-the-Solent. Her teaching job could be tiring mentally, even emotionally at times, but wasn't particularly demanding physically. She sometimes worked hard in her garden, but that only tested her muscles. Her role in helping sort out the garden at the new community hall had been tiring in all kinds of ways, including the energy needed for bouts of almost hysterical laughter. And she'd been on the go for nearly twelve hours with just a couple of tea breaks. If it hadn't been for wanting to spend more time with Mike, she'd be soaking in a bath right now, and looking forward to going to bed with a book straight after.

"You don't look tired," Mike said. "In fact you look even better than you did at seven this morning."

"Thanks. Maybe it's because I'm tired in a good way? Not stress or lack of sleep, just honest work?" Or because she was so happy Mike wanted to spend time with just her?

"Probably," Mike agreed. "I didn't mind lending a hand, but hadn't expected it to be so much fun."

"The tasks were divided out well with people doing things they were suited to, which helped, and it was a positive experience. We were so obviously making a big improvement and it's a nice feeling to be doing something for others as well as yourself. And to be part of a team."

"Little Mallow is like that. You don't all agree on absolutely everything, but you're all basically on the same side," Mike said.

"We're neighbours and we all want the village to be a happy, safe and beautiful place to live."

"Easy to tell you've always lived here!"

"If there are places which aren't like that, I don't want to go to them."

"Good. I like Little Mallow and you, to always be here, always the same, whenever I visit."

"Nothing stays the same forever, Mike."

"No? You're not going to say, 'I don't want many chips, so let's split a large portion,' and then eat at least as many as me, then?"

"Of course I am!" It had been so long since they'd done that.

"I've missed you, Ellie."

"I haven't been anywhere, at least not since Uni." As she'd studied in Durham he'd been close enough to visit her regularly, and for her to spend the occasional weekend with his family. Maybe that's what he meant? The drive to Little Mallow was around six hours. The advantage, from her point of view, was that it meant he usually came for a few days and they always spent some of that time together, which probably wouldn't be the case if he was only visiting his uncle for an hour or two. The disadvantage was that he couldn't just pop down on a whim.

"And it's not been just us since then, has it?" he said. "Remember how, when we were kids, we used to sneak into the castle and pretend we lived there, or you were trapped and I had to save you?"

"I do. I'm slightly ashamed now about the little girl who wanted to be a princess and was content to wait around for the prince to save her."

"I wasn't always a prince. Sometimes I was a king or a dragon."

"I remember that! You scorched my hair and I had a terrible short fringe… Oh, that can't have really happened. Funny how your mind plays tricks."

"I can remember you having a haircut you didn't like, but if I was responsible for it I've repressed the memory."

"What about the time you were a flying dragon and got caught in the pigeon netting?"

"Yep, repressed that too, and if you love me you'll do the same."

Ellie changed the subject by pointing out a good place to park.

They ordered an extra large cod and chips and a pea fritter. It was all done up in one parcel, which meant they had to sit close together on the bench, looking out to sea and watching the sunset as they ate. Ellie didn't mind – the light breeze from the sea was cool, so it was nice to feel the warmth of Mike's body against her own.

"You were right about things changing in Little Mallow," Mike said. "Change can be good, can't it?"

Ellie nodded. If their friendship changed into what most people thought of by a relationship, that might well be a good thing. "Like the new hall? We'd got used to the mess that was there before and kind of took it for granted without seeing it could become something so much better."

"From what Uncle Jerry said, I'd got the impression some people were against it."

"Oh? Of course some people were more in favour than others, but I don't think anyone was actively against it. Besides, the land was given for the benefit of the community as a whole, so there was a limit to what could be done. We're lucky to have plenty of green spaces round here, so although that would have been fairly easy and cheap, it wouldn't be a huge advantage."

Mike had used her long speech to eat most of the fish. He put the thin, crispy end of batter into his mouth, chewed, swallowed and said, "I can see the hall being more useful. Uncle Jerry's sometimes said the only fault with St Symeon's church is a lack of somewhere suitable for local groups to meet. I suppose that's why he was so frustrated about how long it took to get started."

"Thank goodness for the booking in June."

"Arnold's mystery party?"

"Yes, but it's not Arnold's doing. We don't know who's behind it, but it's certainly spurred people into action, him particularly."

"And you. You did a brilliant job of delegating tasks and directing people and deliveries just where they were needed."

Ellie smiled at the compliment. "You're giving me too much credit. I did tell people where to go, but just because I was in the front garden and saw them arrive. It wasn't me who worked it all out."

"Arnold?"

"See, you do see his hidden depths!"

"I suppose so," Mike agreed. "He must know everyone quite well. Putting you out front was a genius idea. Being a teacher gives you a note of authority, but nobody would call you bossy or officious, so if you directed them to do something it wouldn't put their backs up, it would just strike them as the right thing to do."

Ellie liked Mike thinking that about her, and that he clearly did think about her. If she suggested he kiss her right now, embark on a madly romantic whirlwind romance, get married, have seven kids and live happily ever after, would he decide that was the right thing to do? There was no point even thinking about it, as she'd never have the nerve to ask.

"Maybe it's Arnold's party? He could have realised what was needed to get the ball rolling," Mike suggested.

"I don't think so… Realising it would work, yes I can see that, and the wanting to stir people into action. If I'd thought of a way to do that I'd have been prepared to use a bit of subterfuge. I don't know if Arnold would, but I can imagine he's good at keeping secrets."

"Yeah, he would be."

Ellie wasn't sure what made them both think that, but she was glad she and Mike were on the same wavelength. "Organising a surprise party doesn't seem an Arnold kind of thing to do. Not like this."

"I was thinking there might not be a real party. He might have been planning to make a donation anyway, or decided the hundred and fifty pounds was worth it to get things moving."

"It's a lot more than a hundred and fifty, Mike. Martin Blackman has an order for food and drink, which has been paid for. That was a thousand pounds. Arnold doesn't strike me as likely to have that kind of amount spare."

"I'm amazed he can even live on what he earns. Did you know he's officially only part time and does the magazine and other stuff for nothing?"

"No, I didn't." Ellie was surprised – Arnold must do a lot of the work in his own time.

"Maybe I shouldn't either, but Uncle Jerry sometimes gets me to help with computer stuff and I get to see parish records. Arnold's wages aren't generous, even if you only count the hours he's contracted for."

"He doesn't seem to spend a great deal," Ellie said. Of course those on low incomes couldn't but, although restrained, Arnold did pay for a few luxuries such as flowers and was generous to others. He bought more pints than he drank and always donated to good causes.

"That's true. No car for example and he could have a private income we don't know about. There's something slightly mysterious about Arnold."

Ellie nodded. "Hmm, I know what you mean. I speak to him frequently and he's always pleasant, but I don't feel I really know him. Even so he seems like a good person and sensible. If he did have money to spare, surely he'd not use it for food which would go to waste?"

"Nobody sensible would do that."

They ate the last of the chips.

"The date must be significant," Mike said. "It wouldn't be on a Wednesday otherwise. Do you think we'll have to wait until it actually happens to find out who's behind it and why?"

"I think so. Nobody has mentioned a single theory to me."

"In that case it's obvious." Mike grinned.

"You think I'm the one organising it?"

"No – the guest of honour. Think about it, who's usually the only person who doesn't know about a surprise party?"

"Brilliant theory. Just one tiny snag," Ellie said.

"Your birthday is in January?"

"That, plus the fact I've not been invited!"

"Who has?"

"Absolutely no idea. That's odd too – it's the kind of thing I'd expect to hear about in the Post Office or at a committee meeting."

When they walked back along the shingle beach to where they'd parked the car, Ellie stumbled slightly, making contact with Mike. "Sorry, more tired than I realised."

"Here, lean on me." He put his arm around her waist and pulled her close against him.

Ellie was so tired, and so full of chips, and so warm in the car she almost fell asleep on the drive home. She was so sleepy her inner feminist didn't wake up to protest she was quite capable of getting herself indoors when Mike scooped her out of the seat and carried her into her cottage.

He was too much of a gentleman to do anything more than kiss her cheek and wish her a good night.

Chapter 12

Friday 22nd May

Crystal tried teasing Trevor that she wanted him to impersonate the police dog the children were expecting, but ruined it by laughing at the idea before she'd uttered more than a few words. "Actually I got through to Ellie and we decided she'd just tell the kids the dog handler had to cancel. That way, instead of being disappointed it's just people, it will be a nice surprise they're getting an alternative visit."

"Smart thinking."

"Thanks. That one was mine. Ellie, or Miss Jenkins as I suppose we'd better call her, had an equally good one."

"Miss Jenkins from Little Mallow?"

"Yes. Oh, of course, you're friends with the vicar. I'd forgotten."

"He probably has as well. It's long past time we shared a pint. Anyway, Miss Jenkins being involved has cheered me up. I don't suppose she'll let her little darlings eat me."

"I'm pretty sure cannibalism isn't on the curriculum! Her good idea is to take them on a nature walk first. She says that will help with getting them to sit still for a little while this afternoon."

As they'd arranged, Ellie left Crystal to introduce herself and Trevor. She did that by saying Constable Trevor Harris was a very experienced officer and she was very lucky that he'd been training her. "Would you like to try some of the things I've learned?"

There were a few nods, and Adam Milligan called out, "Yes please!" For once she was delighted with his eagerness, as the rest of the class seemed on the shy side.

Crystal produced her handcuffs. "Miss Jenkins, if I may?"

Ellie stepped forward with her arms held out in front of her. That produced a few giggles, then gasps as Crystal cuffed the teacher.

"Anyone like to try?"

When every hand shot up, Crystal's nerves completely vanished. She was even happier when Trevor came to join them at the front of the class and held up his own cuffs. Perhaps she should have seen his next move coming, but she was totally unprepared for him saying, "OK, everyone who wants a go, get into two lines."

The lines quickly formed, one in front of Ellie and the other in front of Crystal. Not a single child remained seated, not even the little girl with crutches. Trevor took Crystal's cuffs off Ellie and handed them to the first child in line. "What's your name?"

"I'm Adam, Mr police officer sir."

"You can call me PC Trevor. Now, Adam, I want you to watch carefully and copy me. I'm going to put these cuffs back on Miss Jenkins, and you're going to put those on PC Crystal. OK?"

"Yay!"

Adam very quickly got the hang of it, earning Trevor's praise. He then uncuffed Crystal and helped the next child in line to repeat his actions as Trevor supervised the kid giving Ellie the same treatment.

"You were right, this is fun," he told Crystal when she'd been cuffed for the fifteenth time. To add to his amusement, he took a photo on his phone of her with manacled wrists. No doubt it'd be printed and pinned up in the station.

That hadn't gone entirely as Crystal had expected, but it was great that every child had the opportunity to use the cuffs. Even better – Trevor hadn't resumed his seat at the back. She needed him for the next step.

"What's next, PC Crystal?" Trevor asked.

"We're going to try to solve a mystery. What I'd like us to do is to get into three groups. Each group will have an object which they'll wipe clean and then just one person will handle it. Then we'll try to work out who that person was in the other groups."

"How will we do that, PC Crystal?" a sweet little girl asked.

"I know! I know!"

"Yes, Adam?"

"Fingerprints!"

"That's right."

"Oh." The little girl sounded disappointed.

"Were you hoping to question people? We can do that too."

"And waterboarding?"

"Um, no. The police don't do that."

Ellie's group had the eraser for the dry marker board, Trevor's a paper knife, and Crystal's object was a glass. It was a tumbler borrowed from the teacher's staff room, not a whisky glass, but she'd chosen it in case it gave her an idea about Mr Argent's case. Setting up the evidence was a little chaotic in Crystal's case, as everyone wanted to be involved and each time she'd thought the glass was clean another child picked it up. If the other groups successfully identified the fingerprints, they'd catch a whole gang of criminals.

The attempts to get clear fingerprints from each child had mixed success, but the class clearly enjoyed it and the results were good enough to prove that fingerprints varied and, with trained professionals using the right equipment, it would be possible to tell which individual had touched a particular object. Crystal soon gave up on getting them to actually do that – she'd over-estimated their attention span when it came to sitting still staring at pieces of paper.

As the kids found their own sets of prints to take home, they decided the three objects were all evidence in gruesome murders.

"Was the eraser used to rub out clues?" one boy asked.

"Maybe."

"The person wrote on the board who killed them, in their own blood. It was in code and only the teacher understood, and when she saw it she rubbed it out before anyone could work out she did the murdering," the angelic looking waterboarding enthusiast claimed.

Crystal thought it a lot more likely that even a completely fictitious murder victim would have the presence of mind to write their murderer's name in a way which would be understood by people other than the guilty party, but she didn't want to dampen anyone's enthusiasm for solving crimes. She knew how she'd feel if DI Shortfellow were to publicly point out massive holes in one of her theories.

"What do you think the other things were used for?" she asked.

"The dagger was used to stab someone and there was buckets of blood EVERYWHERE!"

"Nice," Crystal said, hoping they weren't going to have nightmares which she'd be blamed for.

"And the glass had poison," Adam said. "Look, there's a bit left."

What he could see was a slight mark, almost certainly the residue from the local hard water having been left to evaporate. What Crystal saw was a possible breakthrough in the case of Mr Argent's murder.

It wasn't appropriate to pull out her phone and Google 'how much cyanide kills' during a talk to primary school children, no matter how bloodthirsty they might be. That meant Crystal's theory had to wait until she and Trevor had been asked an extremely diverse range of questions and listened to some random stuff which not only wasn't phrased as questions but had no relevance to policing. Those included quite a lot about a cat which looked like a dog, and perhaps was one, the remark, "See him? His mum can't eat cheese," and a complaint about having to share grandparents with a sibling. After that Crystal and Trevor were thanked by Ellie and received a very long and loud round of applause.

Crystal asked Trevor to drive back to the station from the school, so she could make her online search. Just under a message offering help with suicidal thoughts was her answer. It didn't need much cyanide at all, especially for such a slight man as Colin Argent. He'd owned spectacles which he wasn't wearing when they'd found him and the room had been dim. If the liquid cyanide had been applied to the inside of the glass and allowed to dry before being sent to him, there was a good chance he wouldn't have noticed any residue which resulted. That made it possible for the killer to be elsewhere when he died. A nightclub in Chichester for example.

"Are you still being an idiot, lass?"

"Still?"

"Your photographer. Have you phoned him, or done something daft like trying to get another shift to check up on him?"

"What? I called him, left a voicemail message and sent him a friend request. He eventually accepted that and said he'd been away on a job and would be in touch when he got back."

"OK, good. My mistake."

"Not very good, as I've heard nothing since. What's that about getting him checked up on?"

"Dil Dylan asked about him. It did cross my mind you might have asked someone to make enquiries about when he'd last been seen or something like that."

"That wouldn't be very professional now, would it?" Crystal pointed out.

"No."

"Actually I asked the building supervisor myself – but as a concerned neighbour, not a police officer. Jason's been working away a lot lately and asked the supervisor to take in and keep a delivery safe for him and hasn't come to collect it yet."

"So Dil had no reason to be interested?"

"Sort of, but not a professional one. You were right about him liking me – like that. When he tried to ask me out I mentioned Jason."

"Ooops."

"What?"

"When Dil asked who he was, I said just a neighbour. Sorry, but I played down you having any personal interest just in case. Sorry."

"It's fine. I'll sort it."

Crystal spotted Dil Dylan studying a noticeboard and quickly executed an about turn to avoid him. She almost collided with Sergeant Freedman.

"Skip, can I have a word about Dil Dylan?" Crystal spoke plenty loud enough for the other sergeant to hear. She was counting on natural curiosity keeping him out of sight, but within earshot.

"Sure. Do you want to go somewhere quiet?"

"Here's fine. I just wanted a bit of advice. Dil is always very nice to me."

"I'd noticed." Imani Freedman said that in the same way she responded when someone came in absolutely drenched and informed her it was raining. "Is he bothering you?"

"No, not at all. Absolutely not. The thing is, he's an excellent police officer and really great bloke and I like him a lot."

"You do?" She looked a little sceptical, and even more so when Crystal nodded in a super serious manner.

"Yes, but I've got so much going on in my life now with Aunty needing me so much, and moving house and there's Jason my old neighbour. He's, well, it's complicated and Dil, that could be complicated too, with him being a sergeant and me not yet an independent officer. I'd hate him to get into trouble, if anyone thought… anything."

"I see."

Only recently they'd had a chat in which Crystal had confirmed her official address was now permanently in Little Mallow with Great Aunt Agnes and the skipper had asked about the old lady's health and been informed it was her looking after Crystal now, not the other way around. The skipper must have realised the conversation wasn't quite what it seemed on the surface.

"I'll try to have a tactful word."

"Thank you," Crystal said, pointing in the direction she was sure Dil Dylan was still to be found.

Sergeant Freedman took two steps in that direction, then turned back. "DI Longfellow left a message asking you to contact him."

"Right, I will."

"That's not going to be complicated, I hope?"

"It won't be, no." Nothing could happen between them, because of what she'd just said about Dil Dylan, her preference to keep her love life and job separate, and the fact he probably didn't fancy her anyway.

In the unlikely event he did, and was foolish enough to try to do something about it, Crystal felt confident both that she could resist her own crush and tactfully remind him there were rules about that kind of thing. If that wasn't enough to dissuade him, he wasn't the man she thought he was and she'd have no hesitation in taking whatever formal steps might be necessary to resolve the situation.

With that thought in mind, she was very formal when she phoned him, identifying herself as student officer Clere and saying 'sir' as often as a group of schoolgirls said 'like', 'so' and 'OMG'.

"Has there been a development in the Argent case, sir?"

"Indeed there has, Officer Clere. A neighbour has come forward with new information about a visitor the victim had on the evening he died."

"That's great!... sir. Does it help, sir?"

"It does open up a new and unexpected line of enquiry. The witness, Mrs Owen, says she was discussing the man's death with her sister, who remarked that she was nearly the last person to see him alive. Apparently she'd been visiting Mrs Owen, and as she was about to drive away saw someone knock on his door and be let in."

"That's interesting... sir."

"Not as interesting as her description of the person who knocked. A young woman in police uniform. Now, Officer Clere, I can't help wondering if you were so keen to become involved in a murder investigation, you were the cause of it."

Chapter 13

Friday 22nd May

When Ellie got home after the fun of Crystal and Trevor's visit to her class, she found what looked like an unseasonal birthday card waiting for her. It was addressed to Miss D. Jenkins. Could it be something to do with Mike? He knew her real first name, sometimes called her Miss Jenkins and when they discussed the mystery party he'd mentioned it wasn't her birthday. So, thinking he'd sent her a card made no sense at all and was simply due to the fact she thought about him far more than was sensible.

Inside the envelope was a thick sheet of bright pink card on which was printed, *You are invited to a party in the Little Mallow community hall, Wednesday 3rd June at 7.30. Free food and drink. Bring a friend! Come in disguise!*

The invitation was almost as peculiar as the letters Arnold and Martin had received in order to arrange the party. There wasn't much notice and no way for her to accept or decline. So far she'd not heard about anyone else receiving an invitation. Maybe it was a joke of Mike's after all? She could phone and ask him. In fact she would, after she'd attempted a little information gathering.

Ellie walked down to the combined post office and village store to buy a meringue to go with the ripe strawberries from her garden. She'd be going to the gym later and meringues were mostly air. The Milligans offered an extraordinary range, but customers didn't always come just for the goods and services on offer. It was also an excellent source of information and gossip.

114

Without that the post office probably wouldn't be half so busy. And if it wasn't half so busy it wouldn't be such a good source of gossip. That afternoon it was very busy indeed.

One of the customers had been told by her neighbour that the person who came to do her mother's nails had been invited to a mystery party in the new hall. "Fancy dress it is, and free drinks."

"I like the sound of that. I wonder if I'll get an invitation?"

"There was nothing in the post for me this morning, nor Cherry next door."

Ellie loitered long enough to hear the story repeated twice for new arrivals. Despite a great deal of speculation, everything Ellie learned was of a negative nature. Nobody else who came into the shop said they'd been invited, the Milligans hadn't sold an unusually large amount of stamps to anyone, nor were the invitations handed over for collection in the post office.

As Mike had said, attending would be the best way to find out who was hosting the event and why. She called him even before she reached home. "Guess what I've been invited to?"

"The grand opening of the castle?"

"No." Restoration of that had been going on so long it was hard to recall how much of it there had been before work started and there was clearly a lot still to do.

"A concert by the heavy metal band Arnold has just joined."

"No."

"I give up."

"You have to have three guesses."

"That's harsh, Miss Jenkins. What idiot made that a rule?"

"Can't remember, but he's got a vicar as an uncle."

"The mystery party in the new hall."

"Yes."

"No way."

"Why did you say it if you didn't believe it?" Ellie asked as she let herself into her cottage.

"I refer you to my guess about Arnold."

"Oh yeah. He's more musical than Jerry, but... Hang on a sec, I'll read you the invitation." She did that adding, "Do you want to be my plus one?"

"Of course!"

"Enthusiasm like that, a girl could get flattered."

"It *will* be nice to see you again so soon."

"But that's not why you're so keen to come to this party?" Ellie asked.

"It's not the only reason. It's probably all going to be fine, but the whole thing does seem odd. Uncle Jerry is a bit concerned – he even suggested I gatecrash to find out what's going on. Mostly though, I wouldn't be at all happy about you going on your own."

"That's pretty sexist!"

"Really? Don't you ever worry about a friend doing something you're not quite sure about and go along to check everything is OK?"

She had of course. At Uni whenever one of her crowd was meeting someone new a couple of others would also be in the bar or wherever. If the date showed up, they'd go and say hello and hang around until the friend gave a sign she was comfortable enough for them to leave. And if it was a no show, they'd all go out in a group. "That's different."

"Am I uninvited now?"

Was she supposed to apologise for not being grateful that a big strong man was willing to protect little helpless girlie her at a party in the hall of the quiet village where she lived? No way. But she did want him to come and if he didn't she'd have to go to the stupid thing on her own, just to prove he wasn't the only reason she'd considered attending.

"Please come, Mike. It will be more fun with someone I know and it'll save you gatecrashing."

"You don't know anyone who's going?"

"I only got the invite today. Presumably they were all sent at once so it's a bit early to have heard who's going."

"Don't you need anything from the post office?"

Ellie laughed. "OK, I did try there. Someone had heard of someone else who received an invitation today. Mary Milligan knew nothing about it, so the invitations weren't posted from Little Mallow. Now you know as much as me."

"We'll find out more. And Ellie, it really will be nice to see you again so soon."

After that conversation she rang Crystal and said, "When you get a date with Jason, don't mess it up by being a complete idiot."

"Has something happened between you and Mike?"

"No because, yet again, I messed up."

"Come on then, spill," Crystal demanded.

"I got an invite for that mystery party in the new hall."

"Oh! Is it still a mystery who's behind it?"

"Yes. It sounds very odd. Mike loves a mystery, so I phoned him and asked him to come to the party with me," Ellie said.

"That doesn't sound at all stupid. If you don't know who's behind it you'd be best not to go alone… "

"I know! That part was sensible. Mostly it was just an excuse to see him, but I'm curious too and didn't fancy going on my own. It worked. But then, because he said he wanted to see me, was curious about the event and didn't think I should go alone I snapped at him for being sexist."

"Oh dear."

"Why do I always pick these fights with the wrong people? I remember being incensed when the head at the first school I taught in referred to me as Miss Jenkins. Thinking he was being sexist I lectured him about harmful stereotypes. I still cringe when I think about it."

"Oh dear."

Ellie didn't feel Crystal realised the full extent of her stupidity. "Who makes an idiot of themselves like that on their first day?"

"Aren't we more likely to do it when we're new? We're so keen to show what kind of person we are and we don't know what the others are like."

"Maybe."

"It's not the same, but I made a fool of myself soon after I started at Gosport station."

"Go on."

"A man came in, claiming to know who was behind a recent spate of burglaries. Everyone else was dismissive of him and told me to take no notice. I didn't listen, thinking they were prejudiced because he was homeless, and spent ages getting a statement from him. He claimed to have masterminded the crimes and pretended to be homeless so as to mostly be ignored, but now his accomplices had turned on him, so he was spilling the beans. I was so excited to have solved dozens of cases in one go."

"But he wasn't really involved?" Ellie guessed.

"Worse. None of the crimes actually happened and the people he named didn't exist. All he was guilty of was wasting police time so he could get a warm bed on an especially cold night."

"Oh dear," Ellie couldn't resist saying. "What happened then?"

"Everyone had a good laugh at me. Fortunately I soon saw the funny side and joined in. They hardly ever tease me about it now. What happened to you? Did they stop calling you Miss?"

"The head explained the perfectly good reasons all the female staff, married or otherwise, were called Miss. He said that even so he appreciated my reluctance, and invited me to adopt whichever title I felt would be more suitable. Half an hour later I was standing in front of the whiteboard, introducing myself to the class as Miss Jenkins." Ellie was the only one who ever brought it up, but only mentally to berate herself for jumping to conclusions and insulting or pushing away those she'd hoped to get closer to.

She now cheerfully accepted Mike, and some of the residents of Little Mallow, referring to her as Miss Jenkins. She saw they meant it as an acknowledgement, perhaps even praise, for her role as teacher, not horror that she wasn't safely married to a man who made sure she knew her place. That was progress, wasn't it?

Chapter 14

Friday 22nd May

"Sir, no!" Crystal exclaimed. "I didn't, I wouldn't." Did he seriously think she was evil enough to murder a stranger for entertainment and stupid enough to get spotted, in uniform, going into the victim's home?

"I'm sorry, I was teasing. Of course I don't think you killed Mr Argent."

"Right." Trevor sometimes teased her, in fact it was just the kind of remark he might have made, but he was a friend and equal. It didn't feel right coming from the DI.

"It is true about the report though. And now Mrs Owen has spoken to her sister she's realised she didn't tell us Mr Argent had a delivery on the evening he died. Perhaps we could meet up over a drink and I could update you?"

A drink, not coffee? Technically coffee was a drink, but not when a handsome DI was suggesting it to an impressionable student officer.

"Of course I'm very interested to hear all the latest information, sir. I'll check with Trevor when he's free."

"Actually, there's not much else new."

"Right. Sir, was it definitely a police officer who called?"

"That's what the witness said, but she was unable to give any detail beyond that."

"His cousin is a traffic warden, maybe it was her who called? Lucy Carter told us she visited earlier that day. Either she or the witness could be wrong about the timing, or maybe Lucy went back later and didn't like to tell us in case she incriminated herself, with or without cause."

"Most likely. People don't often see beyond the uniform and they don't always look too closely at that."

"Lucy was wearing hers when she called in on her cousin?"

"She was on the visit she's admitted to, yes."

"Natural mistake I should think. Mr Argent didn't own a car, and you wouldn't expect a traffic warden to come to the house…"

"Quite."

"What about that evening delivery driver, sir? Could that have been the cousin come back?"

"Unlikely. She's shortish and curvy. Mrs Owens said she didn't think it was the usual chap, as this man was a bit taller."

"Ah. Was there anything else, sir?"

"No. Actually yes. It would have been natural to assume that my suggestion of meeting for a drink wasn't entirely because I wanted to pass on that piece of information."

"Ah. Sir, I… " She hoped the pause conveyed everything she felt even though it wasn't entirely clear in her own head.

"If you'd thought that, you wouldn't have been mistaken."

She didn't even risk a 'sir' in case that did convey all her emotions.

"It was an attempt to see you socially. Please believe me when I say I didn't mean to put you in an awkward position. Sadly, this case appears to have stalled. That happens. I didn't want you to feel not being updated meant you were being kept out of the loop. I genuinely feel you will be a tremendous asset to CID and your obvious enthusiasm for solving crimes has reminded me of everything I love about my job at a time I was feeling a little jaded."

"Sir, I understand perfectly. I'm very flattered and look forward to working with you soon."

Everything he'd said was true, she was sure of that – just as she was sure he found her attractive in the same slightly inappropriate way she felt about him. She was also pretty confident that they'd keep things strictly professional from now on.

When Crystal got home she asked Aunt Agnes if she could have another cookery lesson. "Cake seems to be the answer to most of life's problems."

"That's what I've always thought. It helps in different ways. Eating it is comforting, sharing it with others brings a different kind of comfort and, if you're good and cross, bashing the mixture as hard as possible with the biggest wooden spoon you can find works wonders."

"I like that!" Crystal said.

"What shall we make then?"

"I'm not cross, but I quite fancy something which needs a good bash, rather than gentle sifting and folding. I'd like it to be something to take in to work and share with my colleagues. Anything will do, Dil Dylan isn't a fussy eater."

"You want it for a man you're trying to encourage?"

"No, discourage – not that your cake will do that obviously. It's to let him down gently."

"I suppose you know what you're doing?"

Crystal thought she did.

"How about a yeast dough? I've not made any for a while because the kneading is hard work, but I have all the ingredients and it sounds as though you might enjoy it."

"What sort of cake do you make with yeast dough?"

"Lardy cake, Chelsea or cinnamon buns, tea cakes, babka, savarin, doughnuts, panettone, bara brith, brioche."

"Wow!"

"Let's start with buns. They're not too difficult and will be easy to share."

"Perfect."

The cinnamon buns were a great success. As they waited for the dried yeast to activate, Crystal tried to persuade her great aunt to accept more in the way of keep than half the food bill and additional council tax incurred now there was more than one person living in the cottage.

"No. I want you here, child, but I don't want your money."

"And I want to be here." She really did, but it might become far longer term than she'd initially thought when she decided not to renew the lease on her flat. Aunty had fully recovered from her operation, but she was ninety-two. There were things she struggled to do and she'd told Crystal so many times how nice it was to have company that it was obvious if Crystal moved out it would be a blow.

Crystal knew Agnes had very little in the way of savings and her state pension was her only income. She'd learned that when, shortly before her operation, Agnes gathered together Crystal's mum, aunts and cousins. She'd explained the covenant affecting most of the village meant selling it wouldn't raise as much as they might expect. The rules meant only those living in Little Mallow already could buy property there, but anyone could inherit and take up residence.

"It's all I have to leave, so it's going jointly to the seven of you. Sell it if you like, but please give thought to keeping it. I'd like it to stay in the family."

"We'll think of something, Aunty," Crystal's older cousin Yvonne had said.

"Of course we will," Mum had added. "We all love this house and have happy memories of staying here with you. We want that for our children and grandchildren."

Agnes had relaxed so much at that, and even more when Crystal suggested she stay with her aunt until after the operation. Crystal had imagined a stay of around two months. Six weeks was what her quick internet search suggested was the usual period before which people could return to work. As Aunty Agnes was ninety-two Crystal had allowed a little longer. Aunty was doing brilliantly, but there was no getting away from the fact she was an old lady. The two months had long since passed and now looked as though it might extend for the remainder of Agnes's life. Crystal was going to have to be firm.

"I'm going to set up a payment for half the electric and water and things."

"No, love… "

"Aunty, if I don't pay my way I won't be comfortable staying here and will get a flat in Portsmouth after all. I'd much prefer to stay living here rent free and save for a deposit so I can buy somewhere eventually, but it's up to you."

Agnes agreed just in time for them to stop the frothy yeast mixture escaping from the jug they'd started it in.

Crystal wasn't annoyed or anxious, but she could tell kneading would be a great stress reliever. Shaping the dough into neat balls was relaxing and seeing them prove to be twice their size with, in most cases, not losing their shape was satisfying.

Just the smell of them cooking would have been worth the effort. The sight of them, all shiny on top, as they came out of the oven and the first taste were an added bonus. As were the likes and comments when she shared a photo on social media.

Saturday 23rd May

Crystal took two tubs of buns into work. "Sergeant Dylan, I remembered how much you enjoyed the hot cross buns at Easter, so I hope you like these," she said as she placed one tub on the desk in front of him.

He expressed his gratitude and seemed quite touched she'd made them with him in mind. "I sort of have something to give you in return. Information."

"Oh?"

"Trevor said you were asking how Portsmouth got the nickname Pompey?"

"Yes. Even Aunty doesn't know."

"I don't either, but I know some of the theories. One is that it comes from a ship called *La Pompie* which was involved in a mutiny out at Spithead, another that it comes from the French for firemen because the Royal Artillery formed the football team. The maddest one is that it looks like Bombay. The one I think is most likely is that it's from a Shakespeare play that says Pompey is strong at sea. You can imagine Nelson liking that one, can't you?"

"Yeah, I reckon that must be it," said Crystal who had known Nelson was a naval hero with local connections, but couldn't have picked him out in a line up, let alone got inside his head. "Thanks for the info."

She shared the second lot of buns round discretely, so everyone who wanted to could try one even after Dil Dylan had helped himself to the others. There was only one left when Jason phoned.

"Hi, Crystal. Sorry, I didn't know when you'd be at work. Is this a good time to talk?"

"I am at work, but on a break so I've got a couple of minutes."

"OK. Maybe we can meet up sometime? I've not seen you for ages."

"You've been in Switzerland I saw. Great photos."

"Thanks. I flew back from there and then out to Denmark on the same day and then went over to Shetland. There was rubbish signal where I was in Denmark and I had power issues in Shetland, so I've been out of touch for a while."

"That explains you not replying to my note." Damn, she wasn't going to mention that.

"What note?"

Ah. "To say I've moved out of the flat permanently."

"I knew you had, but I somehow missed the note. Sorry, I think it may have got mixed up with the junk mail. The couple of times I've come back there's been tons of it and I've just flicked through and ditched it."

"No problem. I just said it would be nice to stay in touch and gave you my insta handle." Well, not just that but she didn't want to alarm him.

"OK, great. So you're up for meeting up sometime?"

"Deffo. I could pick up a pizza from Luigi's on my way home from work, if you'll be in and hungry about two-thirty?"

"Yeah, I'll be here." He didn't sound too sure.

Oops. She'd been too pushy.

"Look, Crystal… The thing is… "

"It's OK, we can do it another time if you're busy."

"I'm not. Well I am, but it's not that. Please come."

"Double pepperoni?"

"Of course… and as you're getting this, will you let me take you to dinner one evening?"

That sounded a lot like he was asking her out. "You might be able to talk me into it."

"I'll practise my most persuasive lines."

His, "I've missed you so much," the moment he opened the door did the trick. But then him asking if it was still raining would have worked just as well.

They chatted like the good friends they were as they ate pizza and Crystal wondered if his suggestion of dinner really had been him asking her out, or he just wanted something other than pizza for a change. That was until he awkwardly suggested they meet at Sapori, the Italian restaurant in Lee-on-the-Solent. She pretended not to notice the blush creeping up his neck or hesitancy of speech and simply agreed that was a good plan. The small town was between Gosport and Little Mallow, meaning a short drive for Jason and reasonable walk for Crystal. Even before they'd agreed a time, she'd decided to walk so that having two different cars there didn't make it a forgone conclusion they'd go their separate ways after coffee and limoncello.

"Sorry, I've lost track of your shifts. When have you next got a free evening?"

Jason tried to keep track of her shifts? "The day after tomorrow."

"Shall we do it then? That's if it's not too soon after this." He gestured to their empty pizza boxes.

She wasn't entirely sure if he meant his company or Italian food but that didn't matter as the answer was the same for both. "You can't have too much of a good thing."

Chapter 15

Saturday 23rd May

After her late lunch of pizza with Jason, Crystal asked Ellie to come and look through her clothes and make suggestions. It was more for a girlie chat than for fashion advice. Crystal took little notice of fashion and, from what she'd seen, neither did Ellie. That's where the similarity in their clothing ended. Crystal liked bright colours, bold patterns and showing off her figure. Ellie seemed to prefer hiding away behind pastel prints.

"I'll be right over," Ellie said.

"While I'm waiting, I'll get out everything I have which might be suitable for a first date in a classy restaurant."

When Ellie arrived, Crystal had nothing except a bottle of her favourite shade of nail varnish to show her new friend.

"Shopping then?" Ellie suggested.

"Have you got time now?"

"I have. When you rang I was half thinking of going to Southampton to see if I could find a new cardigan."

As Crystal drove, Ellie explained, "Cardis are a kind of uniform with me – when I first qualified I found dressing like a stereotypical teacher made me feel the part and gave me confidence. Now it's easiest to carry on the same. Then when I get home I can take it off and stop being Miss Jenkins and become Ellie. Oh, what am I saying? Of course you know all about uniforms."

"Yeah I do, and I get you deciding to invent one. It's nice not to have to think about what to wear and whether it's appropriate or not. At my previous job I always felt my clothes were being judged. They had to have been because what everyone else wore was discussed at length. The boss wore smart clothes so was mutton dressed as lamb. Other older ladies dressed for comfort and were dowdy and had let themselves go. Younger ones who looked attractive were tarts. Nobody could win. Must be a nightmare being a young, attractive teacher."

"I don't feel the other staff judge what I wear. Perhaps that's because it's always a variation on the same mumsy theme?"

Ellie bought a lilac cardigan with mother of pearl buttons and a thin strip of velvet trim down the front and around the cuffs of the three-quarter length sleeves. Despite it seeming old fashioned and a bit twee, Crystal had to admit it was pretty. "Very suitable for a teacher who wants to look pleasant but not sexy."

"A look which is no good for you – not for dinner with Jason."

There was no problem finding clothes more suitable for dates than the classroom, and they challenged each other to try on some of the more extreme examples. It was a laugh.

"I've not done this kind of thing in years," Crystal said. "My parents moved away from Gloucester just after I finished school. I keep in touch with some old friends a bit, but we rarely meet up and since coming here I've not made many friends outside of work."

"What made you move here? Work or your great aunt?"

"A bloke. It didn't work out – obviously – but by the time I'd realised it wouldn't I was already training with Hampshire police. We used to come and stay with Aunty when I was a kid, so I sort of felt at home here. How about you? You've always lived near here, haven't you?"

"Yes. My parents had a hardware shop where Paula's Posies is now. We lived in the flat above, which is why I was able to buy property in Little Mallow. They now have a flat in Lee-on-the-Solent but they're never there. They're both award-winning ballroom dancers and teach on cruise ships."

"Nice!"

Ellie found a brilliant dress. "It would look fab on you if you don't think it's a bit revealing or as though you're trying too hard."

Crystal wanted to look like she'd made an effort, so tried on the ankle length, wine red dress. It was classy, but sexy too as there was a slit up one thigh and another plunging down from the high neckline.

"You look fantastic," Ellie said.

"Really works, doesn't it? You should try one."

"I couldn't. It's not me at all."

"Not this colour, no. Did they have others?"

"Black," Ellie said.

"Nah, don't think so. Any others?"

"Maybe. I didn't look further once I'd seen the red. I knew it would suit you."

Crystal found the dress in a deep green and made Ellie try it. As she'd guessed it looked fab on her. "I'll buy the red if you get the green."

"I don't think… Where would I wear it? Not a parent teacher's evening!"

"No. Mike wouldn't be at that, would he?"

"I wonder what he'd think if he saw me in this?" She sashayed provocatively in front of the mirror and then laughed at herself.

"Something X rated? If you want him to stop seeing the little girl he's known since you were both kids and see a gorgeous potential girlfriend, that's the dress to do it."

Crystal took hers to the counter and asked if they'd get a discount if her friend bought one too.

"I can give you 5%."

"That's enough for a bottle of prosecco in the Crown and Anchor," Crystal pointed out, making it a done deal.

"Do you have shoes?" Ellie asked as they left the shop.

"Black stilettos – hardly worn because I hardly ever wear heels." She could walk in them OK, they just didn't seem appropriate for most of the places she went.

"Black will work perfectly. Bag? Jacket?"

"Nothing that does justice to this dress."

They tried several shops without success. All the jackets of the right weight and style were in light summer colours which would look silly with the deep red dress. All the handbags were either reasonably priced but cheap looking, or cost more than Crystal had spent on clothes since she'd joined the police.

"I've got both I could lend you. Hardly used because I hardly ever wear black. Don't feel you have to…"

"That would be great, thanks." Crystal had been considering asking Aunty Agnes if she could borrow her smartest bag, and would still have that option as a fall back if needed.

Monday 25th May

Crystal got to the restaurant early. She couldn't decide whether to wait inside or out on the street. She went in, then came out because there was more chance of greeting each other with a hug or kiss outside.

After a cringeworthy exchange of, "Here you are! "Glad you could make it." "You look nice." "So do you," followed by a few moments where they just stood there not quite looking at each other, she did get her hug. Quite a long one and it seemed she wasn't the only one wondering whether to go in for a kiss. They both made up their minds at the same moment and ended up bumping noses. They tried again and found each other's mouth rather than cheek and instantly sprang apart.

They were shown to a table. The candle was lit for them, they ordered drinks and were given menus.

Jason put his aside. "You know the really good thing about dating a friend?"

Crystal was too relieved to learn she'd not got it wrong and this really was a date to come up with a clever reply. Besides it sounded as if the answer might be a kind of punchline. "Go on."

"It's not at all awkward."

"Thank goodness for that. Can you imagine how awful it would be if neither of us knew what to do or say?"

"Terrible."

"Hideous."

"I might do something stupid like say you look nice when actually... Wow, Crystal. You look amazing."

"Thank you," she said with a grin. "That's the effect I was aiming for. Talking of which, you've posted some amazing photos. Is the Lake District really as good as you've made it look?"

"Incredible – in parts at least and when the weather played ball." The sun might not have always shone on his subjects, but his enthusiasm for his work and the travel it involved lit up his face as he described the trip.

It was clear that however together they might become figuratively, they'd often be apart physically. Her own job currently involved shift-work and, once she joined CID, it would be demanding with very unpredictable hours. Would them both having jobs which made arranging time together be an added problem, or help them see things from the other's point of view?

"You're looking thoughtful," Jason said.

Telling him she was contemplating possible difficulties in their long-term relationship before they'd even ordered food on their first date might alarm him so she decided to lighten the mood. "You obviously love travel so much, I was just wondering if I'd need to use handcuffs to keep you at home."

"Not more than three times a week, I shouldn't think." He pulled a comically lecherous expression, making her laugh. "Seriously though, I do enjoy the travel, but that's really because I enjoy fresh challenges. One of the best things about being self employed is that I get to pick and choose which jobs I accept. At the moment it's pretty much all of them, but in theory I'm in control of where I go and when. In the future that should become more of a reality."

"My job isn't going to be like that."

"You'll have to go to where the bad guys are doing bad stuff, whenever they're doing it?"

"Pretty much, yeah. But at least it's mostly going to be local."

"Local with handcuffs – sounds OK to me!"

After that, conversation was easy and fun. The food was delicious, the wine rich and heady. The atmosphere created by soft lighting, gentle music and discreet staff, intimate and romantic. Crystal tried really hard to properly enjoy it all and not mentally fast forward until they left the restaurant and...

"I nearly forgot, I've got some post for you," Jason said as the waiter removed their coffee cups and liqueur glasses. "The people in your flat have had it a while because they didn't realise it was for you and have been asking everyone in the building if it's theirs.

"Why didn't they... Oh." It was addressed to Cynthia and if she'd been mentioned to the new people at all it would be as Crystal. She ripped it open, pulled out the pink card and read, *You are invited to a party in the Little Mallow community hall, Saturday June ³ʳᵈ at 7.30. Free food and drink. Bring a friend! Come in disguise!*

"This is odd," she said. She let Jason read the invitation and then said she'd heard about the party from her friend Ellie but didn't know why she'd been invited or who by.

"If your friend knew about it before you, maybe she's organised it for you. It's not your birthday, is it?"

"It's not, but she does know my real name." Almost nobody did. Certainly nobody who'd be likely to invite her to a party.

"How did you meet Ellie?"

"In the pub in Little Mallow. When I went in she was sitting with the vicar, the verger and the landlord and they'd been talking about this party. Then she saw me on my own and joined me."

"Sounds innocent enough. Maybe it's a strange local tradition?"

"Like cheese rolling?"

"What?"

"They do that where I come from. Someone pushes a cheese down a hill and people chase it and break legs and things."

"Oddly it's not much of a thing round here."

"Too flat I suppose. But it can't be that, can it? If I'm being invited because I live in Little Mallow the invite would have gone to Aunty's house in Little Mallow where I actually live, not the flat I used to occupy in Gosport."

"Fair point."

They were both quiet for a moment. Crystal thought of ringing Ellie to see if she'd found out anything else about the party. If it hadn't sounded particularly interesting she quite likely wouldn't have mentioned it, especially as she didn't know Crystal was also invited. It was late though and she was on a date. It could wait.

"Are you going to the party?" Jason asked.

"Of course! It's a mystery and I'm going to solve it. Want to come with me?"

"Yes, but I've got a job that day." He checked his phone. "I should be able to make part of it, if I meet you there."

"Great. Oh look, we're the only ones here. I suppose we'd better ask for the bill."

"Already taken care of."

He hadn't forgotten about her post at all, he'd timed giving it to her so she was distracted when the bill arrived. Sneaky, but if he wanted to play the gentleman she'd let him – at least until their second date. That would be the party, she discovered as he drove her home, because he was fully booked up until then, except for one evening when she was on nights.

"You work too hard."

"You're right. Like I said, I'm taking on almost everything I'm offered. Part of that is because I'm trying to build up a client base and good reputation, but it's also been because I didn't have much of a life outside work. I can't not do the things I've committed myself too, but I can start saying no to a few things from now on."

Her disappointment that his lovely goodnight kiss was very brief and not followed by another was partly compensated for by his clear indication that he did now have something in his life more important than work – his relationship with her.

Chapter 16

Wednesday 3rd June

Although, as he wasn't a guest, Arnold didn't really need to wear a disguise to the mystery party, he thought wearing ordinary clothes might draw more attention to him than if he put on a costume of some kind. He dressed in his loosest trousers, a white shirt pulled open to the third button, and buckled shoes. He covered these with his burgundy satin dressing gown and topped it all off by draping a flowing silk scarf in light turquoise artistically around his neck. He'd not been awfully successful in coaxing his hair into curls, but overall was quite pleased with the effect.

He arrived at the hall at six, to unlock and check the tables were set up ready to receive the food and drink which Martin Blackman would bring from the Crown and Anchor. They were, but he shuffled them into a slightly better position. He wasn't sure about the chairs. They'd been set against the walls. That would be best if the seventy people Martin had been asked to cater for were all to arrive close to the start time. If not, it might be better for the furniture to be arranged in groups so there wasn't such an expanse of empty space. He'd ask Martin what he thought when he arrived.

Arnold checked the toilets were spotless and had plenty of tissue and towels, which they did. Silly to worry really, as he'd put in the supplies himself only two days ago and nobody should have been in since, but he didn't want any mistakes or oversights cutting the event short.

He checked the fire alarms and lights again and then walked out to the seating area in the rear. The climbing plants which Old Bert Graham and the others had planted smelled very good. The pots and borders already looked attractive. When the sun sank a little lower and the solar powered fairy lights took over, it would be magical.

"Hello!" Martin called.

"Coming!" Arnold went through to meet Martin and saw he had an assistant in the form of Adam Milligan. The boy eagerly carried plates of food and bags of ice as Martin shifted the heavier cases of wine and soft drinks. Arnold helped by bringing in the boxes of glasses and setting out the delicious looking selection of finger food. Martin Blackman had brought wine as requested. Sensibly he'd limited it to a choice of just red or white in not overly generous quantities and included lots of non alcoholic alternatives – sophisticated looking fruit juice mixes, elderflower spritzer, ginger cordial, plus jugs of iced water. It was still hot, so that might be welcome.

When Arnold mentioned the chairs, Adam said, "I can move them for you, Mr Stewart," but as Martin's advice was to leave them as they were, Arnold declined the offer. Not giving the boy jobs always felt to Arnold as though he was letting him down, so he attempted compensation.

"Why don't you try some of the food and a glass of juice to check they're OK?"

As Adam carefully peeled back some of the coverings and helped himself to a mini ham salad wrap, tiny red pepper quiche and handful of crisps, Arnold decided it was a job for two people. He sampled a little piece of spicy chicken, bite sized broccoli and stilton tart, and a stuffed egg. He'd have liked a glass of wine with it, but he didn't want to either gulp it down before any guests arrived, or be seen to be drinking alone when they did.

"Really good," was his verdict about the food.

Adam's was, "Yum."

"Good to know," Martin Blackman said.

Oh dear. Arnold hoped Martin didn't think he'd asked Adam to check the food was OK because of any doubts on that score.

"I'll be back at closing time to clear up. Come on young man, better get you back to your Gran and Grandad."

"I could stay and help Mr Stewart with the party."

"'Fraid not, adults only," Martin said, much to Arnold's relief.

The first guests arrived very soon after Martin and Adam left. Miss Jenkins was one of the few people Arnold knew had been invited and she'd offered to come early in case there was anything Arnold needed help with. She was dressed as an unlikely nurse, and had brought Mike, Reverend Jerry Grande's nephew, who was wearing something vaguely nautical.

"Has all been revealed yet?" asked Mike.

"If you mean about what's behind the party, then no. I assume the person who made the booking will arrive soon and explain everything."

That didn't happen.

The next couple arrived at seven-thirty precisely. Both wore pyjamas, slippers, and black wool knitted into figure of eight shapes over their eyes. "Hello. Our host not here yet then?" the man said.

"He's not," Mike said. "Who is he?"

"No idea."

"Then how do you know it isn't one of us three?" Ellie enquired.

"Because I don't know you. It would be odd to be invited to a party by someone we don't know, wouldn't it?"

They all agreed that was the case.

"I suppose we must have something in common," the man said. "I'm Davy Holbrook, like the place, and this is my wife Sue. We run the Knitted Tea Cosy café in Gosport. Perhaps you know it?"

Arnold said he was sorry he didn't, despite that not being relevant because he wasn't among those invited. "Unusual name," he added.

"It's a gimmick really," Sue Holbrook said. "There are several tea rooms and we wanted to stand out."

"Our cakes are first rate, but 'the place with the good cakes' isn't so easy to identify as 'the place with the crazy tea cosies," Davy said. "So we put a brightly patterned cosy on every tea and coffee pot. I like making them and we sell a few too."

"You make them?" Ellie asked. "That's excellent."

"I used to be a submariner."

"Ah!"

Arnold smiled at the exchange. When he'd first moved to Little Mallow he'd heard the fact that someone served with the submarine service used to explain their uncommon behaviours. It had taken him some time to realise that was simply because those who spent months in an underwater boat tended to develop hobbies which could be enjoyed in a small space without annoyance to the rest of the crew. Now, understanding such comments made him feel like he belonged.

"Hello, verger," one of a couple both draped in sheets, who'd just arrived, said. "What's it all about then?"

"Sleep masks!"

"Sorry?"

"Your sheets made me realise… " He gestured towards the figure of eight shapes the Holbrook's had on their faces. "Sleep masks, I believe?"

"Yes! They don't look right with the holes, but we had to see where we're going."

"Of course."

"I think our ghostly friends here are wondering about the reason for the party?" Davy said.

"Someone's birthday, is it?"

Arnold was still explaining he couldn't answer that, introducing everyone and learning they couldn't find anything in common, when more people arrived. He repeated the whole rigmarole numerous times. After almost an hour Arnold went to fetch himself a glass of wine, which he enjoyed in the seating area behind the hall. As he'd imagined, the area did look quite magical, with the sparkling lights and white flowers much more obvious now the sun had sunk lower. It was wonderfully quiet out there, with nobody asking him whose party it was and why it was being held. Perhaps with it being quite dark, people hadn't realised the seats were there? He'd speak to the committee about an additional light source. The motion activated security light they'd installed could be switched permanently off, as it was now, or permanently on if good visibility was required, but it was far too harsh to be relaxing. The door had been shut when he came out and he'd pulled it closed behind him.

He went back inside. The hall was very full – either all of those invited must have attended and found someone to bring, or there were gatecrashers. Perhaps both. Quite a few people asked him if he knew whose party it was, but now he wasn't stationed by the door greeting new arrivals at least they didn't act as though he should know.

When his circuits of the two connected structures which comprised the hall brought him back to the refreshment area he manoeuvred through the crowd to see how supplies were holding out. He found Miss Jenkins re-arranging what was left so there were fewer, better filled, platters on the table.

"I've put the empties underneath," she explained.

"Thank you. That looks tidier. Do you think there's enough left?"

"Plenty. I'm sure it won't last much longer, but everyone has had time to take some. Same with the wine. There are plenty of soft drinks left."

"That's good. Is Mike still here?"

"Yes, he's off sleuthing. I assume you've not found out who made the booking?"

"I'm beginning to think we'll never know. Perhaps I made a mistake in accepting." At the time he'd known very little about running a hall, including the fact that whoever booked should have filled out paperwork for legal and insurance purposes. Still, he hadn't made the decision alone, but he had urged Miss Jenkins to make up the quorum and proposed the motion.

"You couldn't have known it would remain a mystery – we all thought the cat would be out the bag within days. Besides, it was the push we needed to get the hall up and running and it's a very nice party. Because everyone is trying to find out if they have things in common with other guests they're all getting to know people and making friends."

"Yes, that's true." He wasn't always completely comfortable in social situations, but he'd been chatting relatively effortlessly all evening to a wide range of people. True being asked the same thing over and over was a smidge monotonous, but then all small talk tended to be.

Arnold poured himself a second glass of wine to go with the wraps, quiche and cheese pastry he'd picked up, and began to circulate. He challenged himself to approach people who weren't already deep in conversation and try to talk to them about something other than their elusive host. Whether it was due to the wine he'd consumed, or what other people had drunk, he didn't know, but he was fairly successful. Generally, after the initial approach, the other people did most of the talking, but they seemed to enjoy that.

He began to feel himself watched, so made his excuses to the couple who'd been joking with him about the chances of some person he'd never heard of doing well in a sporting competition of some kind, and turned to see who wanted him.

"Hello, I'm Cameron Pollock." An attractive man spoke with an equally attractive Scottish accent and offered his hand. He was a little older than Arnold – perhaps forty.

As Arnold shook hands with the oddly dressed vampire he felt like a film character walking towards danger rather than running from it. "Arnold Stewart, pleased to meet you."

"My name doesn't mean anything to you, does it?"

"I'm sorry, it doesn't. I don't watch much television or get involved with politics." Even with the unfamiliar uniform and fake fangs, the man looked like he was somebody.

Cameron chuckled. "What must you think of me? Other than that I may be an actor or politician of course. I assure you that wasn't a 'don't you know who I am?' It's just that I've noticed you entertaining a large number of the guests and you have an air of being in control, so I assumed you must be our host."

Arnold was very flattered by the air of being in control comment and hoped he didn't ruin it with, "Nobody seems to know who that is. I'm only here because I hold the alcohol licence and accepted the booking."

"Now that's intriguing. How did it come about, if you don't mind me asking?"

Arnold explained the mystery booking and how it had prompted them to get the hall ready in time. Somehow the topic no longer seemed stale.

"You're worried, aren't you?" Cameron asked.

"A little. I wasn't, as I thought I'd learn the truth tonight, but it really doesn't look as though that's going to happen."

Cameron placed his hand sympathetically on Arnold's arm. "I agree with you – but there must be a reason. Perhaps the event can accomplish its aim without anyone being aware of it?"

"I don't see how."

"Someone sent out the invitations and must have had a reason, or reasons, for selecting the people they invited. Perhaps they wanted to get certain people together? I doubt you and I would have met otherwise. Would you say that's the same for others here?"

"Yes. Most are quite local, yet surprisingly few know each other."

"Now we have met, let's not return to being strangers. It seems like providence for a master and a lord to meet against a backdrop of mystery." Cameron took a card from his pocket and tucked it into the one in Arnold's dressing gown. "Give me a call sometime."

Despite his dislike of the telephone, Arnold found himself nodding. Maybe it was because Cameron was the only person who'd realised he'd come as Lord Byron.

"Are you poetic, Arnold?" Cameron asked.

"No. That is to say I enjoy reading poetry, but can't write anything except sentimental doggerel. I'm sorry, but I can't quite place your costume. A master?"

"Station master. Trains, you know?"

"Ah! Yes of course. The fangs put me off."

"Then I shall remove them." He did so.

To Arnold it seemed as though Cameron had done more than change the appearance of his mouth – everything about him suddenly seemed subtly different.

"This uniform is my own," Cameron explained. "I have a model railway and wear this when I run it. To me the little landscape my tracks run through is a real place. A happy one where things can be just as I want them. The sun always shines, the flowers always bloom, the trains take people to places they want to go." He shrugged. "Some people think it silly and I'm a little sensitive about the matter, so I added the fangs. To disguise the fact that sometimes this is the real me."

"I don't think it's silly." Arnold really didn't. To him it seemed that if one was going to have a hobby it made sense to get really involved and enjoy it. He was rather charmed that Cameron had shared his enthusiasm. Cameron's words about his hobby were at odds with his confident introduction, suggesting he didn't tell everyone. "I can understand you being sensitive about it. I have a hobby which I don't tell many people about." In fact he'd never told anyone.

"Am I to be one of the chosen few?"

"I make jewellery. Not with diamonds and gold. I use found objects. Sea glass, old coins, lost or broken trinkets."

"How interesting."

The words reminded Arnold the late Queen had reputedly said that when bored. Cameron's tone suggested sincerity. Arnold tried to ignore the thought that her Majesty's had most likely done the same.

"I think so. I enjoy creating beauty from that which was damaged or dismissed. It's detailed, precise work, creating collars for the items or attaching bales to suspend them from chains or earring mounts, soldering pieces together or hammering silver. I find it contemplative, almost a meditation."

"Mindful upscaling then?"

"It sounds modern and innovative if you put it like that, but really a lot of people have been doing it for a long time. The difference is that most of them have bare feet, long flowing hair and seven children, or they're students, or live off grid, or... well, they're not church vergers going a little thin on top."

"There's nothing wrong... " The rest of the sentence was drowned out by a scream which disproved those first three words.

Chapter 17

Wednesday 3rd June

Crystal pulled on a deerstalker hat, tied the belt of the trench coat around her waist and set off for the party. Less than a minute later she was back in front of her hallway mirror, fixing a curly black moustache under her nose. She'd bought it with the hat, as it was only a couple of pounds and made her laugh, but decided against wearing it on what was sort of her second date with Jason. However, the invitation had said 'come in disguise', and without the face fungus she was only wearing fancy dress. She could take it off before Jason got there – or as soon as he'd arrived and had a laugh at her expense.

Nobody looking at Crystal would be able to tell whether she was supposed to be Sherlock Holmes or Poirot. Her well-polished uniform shoes and crisply ironed dark trousers, plus the hat and a borrowed tweed jacket, made her outfit a kind of hybrid between the two. Anyone who knew her well would probably still recognise her, and her choice of outfit would be a clue, as everyone who knew anything about Crystal knew her profession.

Outside the hall there were no clues as to the reason behind the party. No banners saying happy birthday, or 125th anniversary of some organisation. Inside it was almost the same story. Quite a few outfits seemed to be leftover from hallowe'en. There were at least two witches, several ghosts and a cheeky devil. Good job it was a warm evening as the pointy horns on Lucifer's headband were the most substantial part of her outfit. One person looked familiar, until Crystal realised she'd come as that artist with the huge monobrow who was always doing unflattering self-portraits.

Crystal attempted to get a glass of wine, but there was such a queue she gave up and did a circuit of the hall. There were a few faces she recognised, but nobody she actually knew. From the bits of conversation she overheard, not knowing other guests, and uncertainty about the reason for the party, were common.

"Crystal?" Ellie asked. The hint of doubt in her voice proved Crystal's disguise was fairly effective. Ellie was dressed as a slightly saucy nurse. It wasn't a disguise exactly, but Ellie most definitely hadn't come as herself.

"That's me! You look fab."

"Thanks. You look like a detective!"

"It's a double bluff."

An attractive man of about thirty, dressed not very convincingly as a sailor, and holding two glasses of white wine, appeared at Ellie's side.

"Thanks," Ellie said taking one. "This is Mike. Mike, meet my friend Crystal."

"Hello, Crystal. White or can I get you a red or soft drink?"

"White's great, thanks."

He handed it over and went off, presumably to get another for himself.

"Nice," Crystal said, nodding in his direction.

"I did tell you! Have you found out anything about what all this is in aid of?"

"No. I'm guessing you haven't either."

"It's weird," Ellie said.

"Yeah. I was thinking, when you found me you weren't entirely sure it was me and there are quite a few people here with better disguises. Maybe someone has a reason to want to be here, but not to be recognised?"

"Could be. We once had a father desperate to see his kid in the school play, when he and his wife were going through a nasty divorce. Not his fault but nobody wanted there to be a scene which would spoil the evening and upset the kids. We let him come in late, and stand at the back in disguise."

"Did it work?" Crystal asked.

"Yes. Close up the disguise wouldn't have fooled anyone who knew him, but of course everyone was looking in the opposite direction and he left while everyone else was still clapping."

Mike returned and asked Crystal if she knew anything about the reason for the party.

"Ellie and I were wondering if it could be someone who wants to be here but not recognised."

"Because they faked their own death, but now miss their neighbours?" Mike suggested.

"That's one theory!" Certainly one Crystal hadn't considered.

"Or maybe this party is an alibi? They're off robbing a bank, but will say they were here and nobody will be sure they weren't."

"The police would want something a bit more convincing than that," Crystal pointed out.

"Like a police officer speaking up for them?"

"You think there's a corrupt officer here?"

"Before you answer," Ellie said, "Maybe I should remind you what Crystal does for a living."

"Ah." He sipped his wine. "The burglar has a web cam in here. He'll say he saw you drinking white wine and chatting to a sailor and a nurse, and they were also here as a nurse. Ellie, can you demonstrate?"

"Do what? Oh!" She put on a surgical mask.

Crystal definitely wouldn't have recognised Ellie if she'd been wearing that and hadn't come up to chat. Mike's theory sounded mad, but it wasn't totally impossible. She decided she liked him a lot.

"Are you on your own?" Ellie asked.

Crystal didn't know how to respond. If she made it obvious she and Ellie had talked about Jason, Mike might think they'd discussed him – which they had.

"My boyfriend was working away today, so is going to meet me here as soon as he finishes." To Mike she said, "Jason is a photographer and often away on assignments."

"I'm looking forward to meeting him," Ellie said.

Crystal said, "I'm looking forward to finding out what's behind this party. You both want to know too, don't you?"

They agreed.

"Shall we circulate and regroup in twenty minutes by the food table?"

"Excellent plan," Mike said. "But first, tell me what you think Arnold has come as."

Crystal looked in the direction Mike indicated. "Love his scarf, but no, I give up."

"Well, detective, please add that to your list of things to solve. Unless he's doing something messy, the verger usually dresses like a Jehovah's Witness, so he's wearing that on purpose."

"How do Jehovah's Witnesses dress?" Crystal asked. She often thought she recognised couples as Witnesses, but was never quite sure what gave them away.

Maybe the same was true of Mike as he took a moment to answer. "Neatly… Quite formal, but kind of subdued."

That did sum up Arnold's usual look pretty well, and couldn't apply to his current outfit. "It's elementary, my dear Mike. Arnold's always wanted to wear… whatever he's wearing, in public and organised this whole thing just so he could."

"You could be onto something there," Ellie said. "I like Arnold, but he is a bit of a mystery and usually he's a stickler for the rules. If anything I'd have expected him to speak against this party, not for it."

"Have rules been broken?" Crystal asked.

"It turns out whoever booked the hall should have signed some form that nobody knew about until we got insurance. I'm not blaming Arnold for that. Not for anything, it's just all very odd. Like the person behind it paying in cash for the drinks and everything."

"When we met you joked about money laundering," Crystal said. Arnold and Martin Blackman being paid in used ten pound notes, was very odd. Maybe there really was something illegal behind it. Crystal remembered thinking the late Mr Argent's stored packing materials were being used for some kind of scam. As his killer still hadn't been arrested the motive behind his death wasn't known, so that was still a vague possibility.

"How much cash are we talking?" Crystal asked.

"Over a thousand pounds."

"That's not enough for money laundering."

"Trial run?" Mike suggested. "Or they're counterfeits. I assume it's been spent now?"

"Probably," Ellie agreed. "I know most of the booking fee was paid into the bank… by Arnold. Honestly though, I can't believe he'd go to all the trouble of organising a mystery party too… Well, not for any illegal reason."

"No, far too law abiding and sensible," Mike said. "If he was a master criminal he wouldn't draw attention to what he was doing like this. He could easily slip a few dodgy notes into the collection each Sunday to test them out."

"Mike!" Ellie slapped his arm.

"Sorry. Crystal, for the record, I don't think my uncle Jerry's verger is a master criminal."

Neither did Crystal, but perhaps the party was a front for some kind of scam? Maybe it was a way to get people out of their homes so they could be burgled? No, as Mike said it would draw too much attention and no gang would be targeting so many properties at once and, if they were, her old flat wasn't likely to be on the list.

"I'm going to circulate, see what I can find out," Crystal said. She also didn't want to crowd the couple, now Ellie had Mike to herself.

As soon as Crystal moved away, the witch approached her. "Great moustache!"

"Thanks." Crystal was about to compliment the woman on her outfit but fortunately was interrupted.

"I wish I'd realised everyone was going to dress up. I'd have done the same myself."

So the mad hair, all over purple and mismatched eyeshadow weren't a costume? Right... "Some people have gone to a lot of trouble." She indicated a particularly flamboyant pirate. The flamingo on her shoulder and vibrant pink boa were perhaps not quite as convincing as the missing leg, but overall the effect was pretty spectacular.

"Do you know who's behind this evening?" the accidental witch asked.

"No idea. It's weird."

"Fun though – and free wine!"

As Crystal continued her circuit of the hall she had to agree with crazy hair lady's assessment. The mystery about the party was a good ice breaker. The free wine didn't hurt either. Crystal had no new information to report when she regrouped with Ellie and Mike, who'd had the same lack of success. Everyone seemed to be a guest and to have no idea why they were there.

Jason arrived then, dressed as a cartoon burglar complete with mask over his eyes. Crystal had no trouble recognising him and, as she made her way over, it was clear he'd spotted her. But then she'd been looking out for him, and he'd come especially to meet her. Had they not expected the other to be there they might never have noticed their presence. And had one of them wished to remain unobserved, the way the hall was really two interconnected spaces would have made that easy. For a moment Crystal thought she was close to deducing the reason for the party, but as she reached Jason she realised it made little sense. If someone didn't want to be seen there, the easiest and surest way would be to not organise a party.

"Oh no!" Jason said with mock horror. "The detective is onto me!"

"I'm not a detective yet, but you needn't think that will stop me taking you into custody later," she said.

"Just as long as you're not too gentle with me!"

She grinned at that, then remembered her moustache. "I can't believe you saw through my cunning disguise. At least, I hope you did," she added and quickly removed it.

"Afraid so. Did you solve the mystery behind the party as quickly? I have to admit, it's not obvious to me."

"Nor me, or anyone I've spoken to. Anyway, come and say hello to Ellie and Mike."

After the introductions and everyone had collected food and drink, Crystal said, "Let's try brainstorming. Why might someone hold a party, without letting anyone know who they were or giving any kind of reason?"

"Maybe it is a birthday or something like that, but can't be celebrated properly. The person could be dead and they're holding it in their memory, or maybe someone left money for a party in their will?" Ellie said.

That made some sense to Crystal. It being on a Wednesday made a birthday or anniversary most likely. If the reason wasn't tied to a date then a Friday or Saturday would probably have been chosen. And them being dead would explain them not making themselves known now, but... "Why the secrecy before? They can't have been dead when they made the booking."

"They could have known they were dying?"

"That would work," Mike said. "Maybe they didn't want to make it a sad occasion, by making people think of their death?"

"Do you know of anyone who has died in the right time frame?" Crystal asked. "I don't."

"Nor me," Ellie said. "And would they have invited random strangers? That seems to be what most guests are to each other. Crystal and I didn't know each other until after the booking was made and we seem to be about the only people who have friends here."

Mike nodded. "Fair point."

"Someone is just being nice?" Jason suggested.

"To random strangers?" Crystal asked.

"It's possible."

"Almost anything is possible," Crystal admitted. "If you had spare money and wanted to be nice anonymously, what would you do?

"Donate to charity, send flowers or gifts, perhaps leave books or money for them to find, get vouchers for a coffee shop and give to homeless people…"

Crystal really liked that Jason could think of lots of ways of being nice and she was certain he'd actually done some of them.

"Maybe it's an experiment?" Mike suggested. "Seeing how people react to the situation?"

"Or to test the food and see which people prefer?" Jason said.

"It was all supplied by the landlord of the Crown And Anchor," Ellie said. "He could have done it, but… "

"Ellie's right," Mike said. "Martin is a very straightforward bloke and he could easily and far more cheaply have put plates out in the pub and asked people which they liked. Could it be something else along those lines… scent in some areas to see if people congregate there or avoid it. Or perhaps it's aliens, wanting a good look at us in a social situation?"

"That'd explain the disguises," Jason said. "They're walking among us, learning to blend in. See that guy dressed as an angel?"

"Where? Oh yeah, so obvious!" Mike agreed. "That halo is actually his antenna."

Laughing, Crystal and Ellie edged away.

"They're getting on well," Ellie observed. "I was thinking about what you…"

Crystal felt something was wrong, even before she heard a scream coming from the garden area.

"Police, let me through," Crystal shouted as she pushed her way through the crush of people.

Chapter 18

Wednesday 3rd June

Inside the hall people made way. When Crystal reached the doorway, her exit was blocked by people who were clustered around. "Police! Stand aside please!"

Nobody stepped forward into the outside seating area. Instead they tried to move backward and were hampered by those behind who wanted to see what was going on. When Crystal finally got outside she smelled vomit and saw a priest attempting to save a nun from having the life sucked out of her by a zombie.

That explained the screaming.

Except it couldn't really be happening. A combination of the unsettled feeling from not knowing the purpose of the party, Mike and Jason's crazy theories, the dim lighting and the costumes the three people wore had put that idea in her head.

She glanced behind her and saw Arnold pushing through the crowd. "I need more light," she called to him.

As Arnold stepped through the doorway he reached up and instantly the area was brilliantly illuminated.

The reality of the scene wasn't a whole lot more pleasant than Crystal's initial impression. One party guest was performing CPR on another, as a third got in the way. What Crystal had initially seen was a pause in the zombie's efforts as she put her face close to the nun's face, to check for breathing. The zombie continued performing the life saving technique in the correct manner. The priest was urging them to, "Help her, for God's sake help her."

"Has anyone called the emergency services?" Crystal demanded.

Her answer came from someone saying, "Ambulance please," into their phone.

"You, you and you, go out the front to make sure the ambulance driver finds the right place. What are you going to do?"

"Go out front and make sure the ambulance stops here."

"Good. Go."

Crystal heard the person on the phone describing the situation, then the zombie said, "Say patient is woman... early forties... possibly experienced anaphylactic shock." The zombie didn't stop her steady rate of chest compressions.

Confident the right information would get through, Crystal instructed several people to spread out along the path to the entrance. "Keep it clear. If anyone comes out, tell them to go back inside. When the ambulance arrives, direct them along the path." She checked they understood what was required and sent them to do her bidding.

"Everyone else, please stay inside. Jason, Mike, Ellie, can you see they do? Tell people a lady has been taken ill, is receiving first aid and an ambulance is on the way and to please stay where they are, so as not to get in the way."

The man dressed as a priest wasn't exactly hampering the zombie first aider, but he was crowding her.

"Please go inside, sir," Crystal said. When he made no response she placed a hand firmly on his shoulder and repeated her request.

He grabbed at Crystal. "She's my wife! I can't leave her!"

"OK. Let's move back a little and give her some space." She coaxed him to stand and take a couple of paces back, then had to catch him as he collapsed. Clearly he was in shock. Crystal helped him to a bench, gently pushed his head between his knees and opened the door back into the hall. As well as Jason and Mike, Arnold the verger was there.

"A man is in shock. Are there any blankets?"

"I'll find something," Arnold said.

Crystal returned to where the zombie was still working on her unresponsive patient. "I'm a police officer," she said. "I'm trained in CPR, so if you want me to take over… "

"I'm trained too and have done it for real before. I'm fine for a bit."

Crystal was relieved, not least because she'd only ever performed CPR on a dummy. She'd definitely have taken over if needed, but then wouldn't have been able to help in any other way. "Do you know what happened?"

The answer came in stages, as the zombie continued her routine of two breaths followed by thirty chest compressions. "No. The husband asked if there was a doctor… A friend fetched me… said she was having a fit… Her name is Paula… was fine when they arrived… stopped breathing before I got out here… he became hysterical."

"He's in shock. Someone's getting blankets. Back in a mo." She returned to the back door.

"Ellie's going round telling people everything is OK. Is it?" Jason asked.

"I don't know. But officially yes, all under control."

Arnold returned with an armful of material. "Dust sheets from the decorating. Will they do?"

"Perfect. Can you come and help?" Arnold was totally calm, the ideal person to sit with the shocked man.

"Of course."

"Keep him warm and talk to him. Find out what happened if you can, but don't distress him."

Arnold nodded. "Come on, Michael, let's get this around you," he said to the man.

"You still OK?" she asked the zombie.

"I'll carry on if you need to call this in."

"Thanks." Crystal moved away a little and telephoned the control room, giving all the information she had. She was asked more questions than she could answer.

"Sir," she asked the man Arnold was comforting. "I'm Crystal. I'm a police officer. Can you tell me your name?"

"Michael Roth." He spoke very quietly.

"And the lady who isn't well?"

"She's my wife. Paula."

The florist? "Does Paula have any medical conditions, allergies or anything like that?"

"Not really. There are things she can't eat, but they wouldn't do that. It was horrible, she was being sick and started having a fit. I didn't know what to do, it was… " His voice got louder and shriller and he tried to get up.

"Michael," Arnold spoke firmly. "Michael, look at me. It's OK. Paula's being looked after now."

That did the trick, so Crystal continued her questions. The more information she could give the ambulance crew, the better their chances of helping Paula. "Can you remember what happened just before Paula felt ill?"

"We came out to look at the garden."

"Was anyone else here?"

"No. We weren't sure if we should come out, but Paula had donated flowers. Someone brought us drinks, and it looked and smelled nice and was quiet, so we sat down to drink our wine out here. Then she said she didn't feel well and… and… "

Alcohol could react badly with medication, or there could have been traces of detergent on the glass which triggered a reaction. Leaving Arnold to work his soothing magic, Crystal called the control room with an update. As she spoke she looked for the glasses the Roths had been drinking from. By shining the torch on her phone into the dark corners she found them. Both were standing upright and still contained wine. Not much in the case of the one with a lipstick mark.

The ambulance crew arrived at that moment and Crystal was aware Michael Roth had again tried to get up. The sheets and Arnold's arm around his shoulder prevented him doing so and he became agitated. "Best to let them do their work," Arnold murmured persuasively.

Crystal greeted the crew. "No allergies or medical conditions according to the husband. She was OK when they came out here, then began to vomit and have seizures. She had been drinking wine, but probably not very much. It's possible something was introduced to her glass without her knowledge. Do you have something I can put them in?" This seemed an unlikely place for it to happen, but another possibility for Paula's sudden reaction was that her drink had been spiked. If that was the case, analysing the contents of the glass would help with her treatment.

Once she'd dealt with the glasses, Crystal returned to Michael. "Who brought you the wine?"

"I don't know."

"A waiter?" Crystal knew there weren't any catering staff hired for the party, but hoped to prompt a description.

"I think he was a guest. He was dressed up like everyone else."

One of the ambulance crew approached. "We're taking her to QA." That was no surprise. Queen Alexandria was the closest hospital with an accident and emergency department.

Michael Roth, assisted by Arnold, followed the stretcher. As soon as he'd left, Crystal properly introduced herself to the zombie and thanked her for her efforts.

"I'm Chrissie Batt and I'm very glad you were here."

"Likewise. How did your patient seem when they took her away?"

"Dead. Sorry to be blunt, but she didn't look good."

"This might sound mad, but could it have been cyanide?"

"No idea, sorry. I'm not a doctor. I'm a football coach. We have first aid training in case of injuries and I know some medical stuff because of my job, that's why my friend called me to help. You think she was poisoned?"

Did Crystal think that? She should certainly be careful what she said. "We have to consider every possibility until we know the truth."

"Can I go in now? My wife will be worried."

"Yes, of course. I'll just take a contact number."

The woman, looking even more like a zombie than it was likely she'd done at the start of the evening, gave the required details. "Can you let me know?"

"I will," Crystal promised. She really hoped she'd be able to report Paula made a full recovery, but wasn't hopeful.

The door didn't shut behind Chrissie, because Jason immediately came out to ask if everyone could go home. "Some went as soon as the ambulance arrived, maybe some before that, but others are asking permission."

"I don't have the authority to stop them." She wasn't sure if she had cause either. "Don't let anyone come out here though – and can you bring me a couple of wine glasses?"

"Um, yeah."

"Empty is fine."

Crystal took photographs of the scene. She had no idea if Paula's collapse was anything other than an allergic reaction or result of an undiagnosed medical condition, but it seemed likely someone might need to investigate. If she died, that was a certainty. When Jason brought out the glasses she placed them exactly as the others had been when she discovered them, and took more photos. She'd done all she could on her own and suddenly felt really cold.

"Crystal, are you OK?" Jason put his arms around her.

That helped a lot. So, in a different way, did the arrival of DI Shortfellow.

At least it did until he said, "Officer Clere and another sudden death. We must stop meeting like this."

"Sir, I… "

"A thorough briefing in as few words as possible, please."

Crystal complied.

"Thank you. This must have been an unpleasant experience for you."

"It wasn't fun. Sir, you said death?" Crystal hadn't really expected the florist to recover, but she had hoped.

"Paula Roth was pronounced dead on arrival at the hospital. It was nicotine poisoning. Massive quantities were found in both glasses. The husband is unwell, but his symptoms aren't life threatening."

"It's murder, then?"

"That's certainly one line of enquiry and I'm aware you're not officially on duty, but I assume you're happy to work under me tonight?" His smile suggested both that he realised it was an innuendo and that she'd say yes.

Chapter 19

Thursday 4th June

Crystal awoke from a dream in which she'd solved the double murder of Mr Argent and Paula Roth. It had been really simple once she'd known the same person was responsible for both. Perhaps it was just as well she couldn't remember who that person was as she'd have found it very difficult not to spend all her free time stalking them.

"Are you OK, love?" Aunty Agnes asked when Crystal came downstairs.

"Yes, I'm fine. Sorry, did I disturb you when I came back last night?"

"Didn't hear a thing and I was up before the calls started this morning."

"Calls?"

"You left your mobile by the sink and that's been buzzing. I didn't try to answer it, but I took messages from everyone who called the house phone. I take it something happened at the party?"

"You could say that."

When she'd got in last night, Crystal had intended to call Jason to apologise for abandoning him when the DI arrived, but saw it was far too late. When she got upstairs with her glass of water and realised she didn't have the phone she'd decided not to go back down and risk disturbing her great aunt. Besides, she was far too tired to be of any use to anyone who might ring.

Crystal filled the kettle and checked her phone as she waited for it to boil. Oh dear, dozens of messages and missed calls. She tried calling Jason, got a message that his phone was switched off and sent a brief text instead.

She read Aunty's notes. Martin Blackman from the pub, and Arnold the verger both wanted to know if they could go into the hall and clear up, and sergeant Dylan said 'you're not to go on shift, but get epic as soon as you're up – you'll know the fellow'.

"I didn't quite understand the sergeant… "

"EPIC is what the CID building in Pompey is called."

"Because they do epic work?" Aunty asked with a grin.

"That and the fact it stands for Eastern Police Investigation Centre. It sounds as though I'll be working there with DI Shortfellow today, instead of my usual duties with Trevor." She sipped the tea Aunty had made.

"Crystal, love? Did something bad happen at the party?"

What to tell her? She'd soon be having inquisitive visitors. It wasn't fair to ask her to keep secrets from them, nor for her to be on the receiving end of a lot of gossip and have nothing to say. It didn't help that Crystal wasn't sure what information had been officially released. "Someone was taken seriously ill last night…"

"Oh! Who is it?"

"Paula Roth, the florist."

"Poor girl. I do hope she'll be OK."

"I'll make some calls," Crystal said. Aunty would think she was finding out how Paula was doing, not asking if she could say the woman was dead.

"Shall I make you some breakfast, love?"

"Yes please." The food would be welcome and the sound of frying bacon would drown out Crystal's conversations.

The post arrived. Crystal went to fetch it and phoned from the hallway. She brought back an envelope addressed to Aunty in the old lady's handwriting.

"That's come quick," she said. "I only sent off for the pattern two days ago."

The speed was explained by the fact she'd got mixed up and put the order form and envelope addressed to the supplier inside her self addressed envelope.

"Silly me. I've wasted two stamps and envelopes for nothing."

"You could try again."

"I don't think I will. I've already got plenty of patterns and only sent off for that one because it was free and so easy to do."

Crystal nodded – it would be just as easy to drop a booking request, food order or party invitation into a post box, and receive it a few days later, just as though it had been sent by someone else.

By the time the eggs were done, Crystal had failed to reach Jason and texted him another apology for running out on him, promising to make amends. She knew Martin and Arnold already had their answers, agreed to tell Ellie 'everything' as soon as she could, assured DI Shortfellow she'd be in Portsmouth within an hour, and knew what she could tell Aunty and have circulated around Little Mallow.

"How's the nice florist girl?" Agnes asked.

"I'm afraid she died. At first we didn't know what was wrong. A lady who was there as a guest tried hard to save her, and the ambulance came quickly, but nothing could be done. Somehow nicotine got into the glasses she and her husband were drinking from. He's not well, but is recovering."

"Oh, I am sorry. They don't have children, do they?"

"I don't think so."

"The nicotine, would that have come from cigarettes?"

"I don't think it would be easy to extract it so it didn't have any colour or flavour. Sorry, I have to go. Shall I ask someone to come round?"

"I'll have plenty of visitors, don't you worry!"

DI Shortfellow thanked Crystal for her help the previous evening and for coming in that morning.

"I'm happy to be part of the investigation, sir."

"Crystal, you are here as a witness. A very valuable witness who will be a huge help to this investigation, but you're not a detective and won't continue to be actively involved. I'm sorry, but you will join Trevor and the rest of the neighbourhood team with their patrols and routine enquiries once we've finished here."

"That's not fair. I was …"

"You'll be given time off in lieu for the hours you put in when not on duty."

"That's not what I meant."

"I didn't think so. Tell me, did Trevor mention the incident with the students filming?"

"Briefly – he promised me the long, dramatic and funny version, but hasn't got round to it."

"If it hadn't coincided with a CID raid it probably would have been funny, at least in retrospect and for others more than Trevor. But it would have been a funny mistake, not an avoidable error of judgement."

"But?"

"It did coincide with something we were doing and which we didn't notify uniform about. We should have done so and I'm as guilty as anyone that it didn't happen."

"Anyone can make a mistake," Crystal said. She hoped it was something he'd remember when she messed up which, being human, she was bound to do at some point.

"Indeed they can. I made more than one. At the time I was angry and looking for someone to blame. I accused Trevor of having forgotten about our op and lying about not being informed. And did so publicly. At the time I believed that to be true. Even so, the way I treated him was unforgivable…"

"Sir, Trevor only told me because I specifically asked how you know him. He hadn't said a word until you took the shout about Mr Argent's death. He'd had plenty of chances before, if he'd wanted to speak against you."

"He's a good man."

"He is and, like you, thinks sticking to procedure is important. There's plenty of reasons for that. Not letting a criminal go free because of our mistake is the big one. I get that I can't officially investigate this case. I realise I might go too far and then miss things because of my lack of experience or knowledge."

"But?"

"But, sir, a murderer invited me to his weird party and then killed someone practically right in front of me!"

He nodded. "That does make a difference. I promise you'll be involved as much as is possible whilst following correct procedures. You understand?"

"Yes. Sorry, sir. I should mention that I broke the news to Chrissie Batt who performed CPR on Paula Roth that she'd died. I promised her I would and I knew news would soon get out."

"What did you tell her about the cause?"

"Nothing. I said CID would be in touch soon and asked her not to discuss it with anyone before then. I thought it would be best if her memory wasn't coloured by other people's speculation."

"You're right. I'll just check that's attended to as a priority."

When he returned he began the interview with, "You said the murderer invited you to the party?"

"It can't be coincidence... OK, it could be. There was definitely something dodgy about it, but it's possible the nut... the individual who organised and paid for the party did so for another reason and the murderer took advantage of it. That doesn't seem likely. He'd have to have come prepared."

"You received your invitation when?"

"A week ago, but mine was delayed because it went to my old address. I believe most arrived on the twenty-second of May."

"The killer would have known about it then."

"Yes, even if he wasn't a guest he'd have known soon after the invitations came out. It's likely people who had one would have talked about it, tried to find out what it was for and who else was going. I did."

"As did the victim. She mentioned it to staff, relatives and friends."

Crystal realised this wasn't any ordinary interview. DI Shortfellow was sharing information in a way he wouldn't do with a member of the public. "OK. I get that the killer knew there was a party, but he wouldn't know what kind. It was a weird invitation. I was thinking maybe there wouldn't be a party when I got there and it was a joke or some kind of mystery for people to solve."

"And you couldn't resist that!"

"No. Even so, I told people where I was going and I wouldn't have just walked in if it hadn't been obvious there really was a party."

Chapter 20

Thursday 4ᵗʰ June

"You went alone?" DI Shortfellow asked.

"The invite said plus one, so I asked… someone," Crystal replied.

The DI glanced at his notes. "Mr Jason Blythe." Of course, even when interviewing a colleague rather than a suspect, he wouldn't restrict himself to only asking questions to which he didn't know the answer.

"He didn't know what time he could make it, so we arranged that we'd meet there, or next door in the Crown and Anchor if it turned out the whole thing was a hoax. That's what I meant about the killer coming prepared. I didn't know the victim had been invited, presumably he did and thought he'd have the chance to act. Plus he was either invited, or knew he'd be able to just walk in anyway. It suggests he knew more than I did. My invite was in my bag in case I was asked to show it."

"I agree with you that the killer probably had some prior knowledge of the party, other than an invitation."

"I'm sure he planned the whole thing, but if he didn't there's still a big mystery behind that."

"I agree. How many of the guests did you know?"

"Only Ellie. I sort of know the verger, through living in the village a little while, but he wasn't technically a guest. I recognised the victim as being the local florist and another as a witness in a minor incident. I've seen some of the others around, perhaps spoken to them. It's hard to say, because of the disguises."

"Was there anything the majority of them had in common?"

"It didn't seem so. Lots of people were asking – trying to work out the reason behind the party."

DI Shortfellow asked Crystal to go through the events from when she got to the party until he arrived, in detail. She tried to stick to pure facts, not speculate. It took a long time, some of which was taken up with the DI reminding Crystal he was the one who was supposed to be asking the questions, and a little with him answering a few of hers.

After repeating what Michael Roth had said about the person who'd given him and his wife glasses of wine, she'd asked if CID had obtained a better description.

"I was coming to that." The DI checked his notes. "I interviewed Mr Roth in hospital. He said the person was 'about my height, maybe a bit thinner.' He believed the person to be male, but said he couldn't be completely sure as their face was covered and he'd not taken much notice."

"And he's what, six feet? And quite slim, so the killer is tall and skinny."

"And was wearing lime green gloves, clingy dark blue trousers with a red stripe down the side, a baggy top like a painter's smock and had something tied around his face. Did you notice anyone dressed like that?"

"I didn't and I'm not sure he did. It was pretty dark out there. Too dark to distinguish colours. Mr Roth's outfit looked all black until Arnold switched on the security light. It was really maroon."

"The light would have been better inside, where the drinks table was."

"Much better. I thought the drinks were brought out to him. Did he tell you it was inside?"

"He says there was a queue at the drinks table. While he was waiting someone slightly bumped into him, apologised and said if he was waiting for white wine to take his. Mr Roth accepted, which of course he now bitterly regrets."

Crystal recalled Mike handing her the drink he'd got for himself when he brought Ellie hers. "Something similar happened to me and I accepted a drink from someone I'd not previously met."

"Why did you think Roth had been given the drinks outside?"

"Sorry, I can't remember exactly what he said. I recall asking him if it was a waiter who'd brought them out. I don't know why I did that... anyway he said he didn't think so, but the person was in fancy dress like everyone else." She thought for a moment. "OK, yes. I was thinking waiter in terms of someone bringing him the drinks, but he could have thought I was referring to the costumes. I did think of people as being a witch, zombie, pirate or whatever. If it happened inside it sounds more like a random killing... or maybe the person who gave away his drinks was the intended victim?"

"Or?"

"Mr Roth was lying."

"About?"

"Where he was given the drinks, or the fact anyone gave them to him at all. Does he have a motive for killing his wife?"

"Nothing jumps out," DI Shortfellow said. "Mr Roth says he and his wife were on good terms with no money or other problems. He states he's wealthy in his own right and his wife's business was a hobby which barely broke even. Her life was insured, as was his. Apparently, the policies were taken out when they married, as a kind of package with the mortgage, and kept up but not increased ever since. They made wills in each other's favour at the same time; over ten years ago."

Those things wouldn't be taken on face value – but it wasn't Crystal who'd investigate whether they were true. The only information she'd have was what she could extract from DI Shortfellow. "Did Roth think anyone else had a motive?"

"That was interesting. He claims to believe they were either both targeted, or the spiked drinks were given to them randomly, which may well be the case. However, when I put that question to him he mentioned an employee of his wife's who'd recently been sacked and might hold a grudge, although he made a point of saying he didn't think she'd have done anything like that. When I asked if he had ever sacked anyone from his own firm he said of course he had, but couldn't supply any names."

"Was the sacked florist at the party?"

"He thought so but wasn't sure. He couldn't recall what costume she, if it was her, wore. What did you go as?"

"Is that relevant to the investigation, sir?"

"It might be, you never know."

She found a selfie, complete with moustache, on her phone and showed him.

He gave that sudden burst of laughter of his. "Hiding in plain sight, eh?"

The fact he already thought of her as a detective was more than enough to forgive him his amusement.

"How can I help, sir?"

"You already are. I've found it interesting discussing both this case and that of Mr Argent with you. We think along similar lines, but not exactly the same. I'm going to enjoy working with you, Officer Clere."

"Thank you, sir but I meant getting involved. Are there any routine enquiries I can make? I know you'll have to request them through the official channels, but I'm sure Sergeant Freedman, and Sergeant Dylan come to that, will ensure as many as possible come my way."

"There are, yes. Some, as you say, will come as official taskings, but others might be better dealt with more informally."

"Like someone who was at the party chatting to other people who were there?"

"Indeed. If you can tactfully find out who booked the party and why, the entire guest list, what connection if any they have to each other or the deceased, and if anyone was wearing the outfit Mr Roth described, that would be helpful."

"'I'll do my best."

He laughed again, properly this time. "I should have expected that. Now I've said it there'll be no stopping you, will there?"

"I wouldn't go against a direct order." Please don't issue a direct order not to get involved, she said – but only silently.

He was quiet for a few moments and Crystal feared the worst until he said, "Please don't ask outright. You're a party guest wondering what happened, not a member of CID conducting interviews. If anyone seems likely to confess or incriminate themselves, try not to let them until we can get them cautioned and on record. And don't react if you hear anything potentially incriminating. I don't want either you or the investigation put at any risk."

"I understand, sir. Everyone was already curious about the reason for the party and asking about it, me included. It would be natural for that to continue and for people to speculate about the murder. Oh, what's the official line? Do I say it looks like murder? Or try to play it down so as not to alarm people?"

"Use your judgement. We won't be able to keep it quiet and the murderer will already be alarmed."

"Could it have been an accident? People will ask me that."

"Officially we're looking into that. Realistically no. The nicotine came from vape refills and several would have been needed for the quantities in each glass. Suicide is unlikely too. There's no hint of a reason she'd want to take her own life, and Mr Roth said she started drinking the moment she was handed the glass. He felt sure she couldn't have put anything into either of them."

"That's a point against him being the murderer then. He could easily have described her as upset and made up something which would have given her an opportunity to tamper with them – putting them down to adjust her outfit perhaps... Oh. No, it's gone but that triggered something."

"What was your immediate impression when you arrived on the scene?"

"I saw a zombie trying to suck the life out of a nun and a vicar trying to save her... That's wrong, isn't it? If Michael Roth was trying to save Paula, he wouldn't be trying to stop the first aider, Chrissie Batt, give CPR."

"He says he didn't immediately realise what was happening. Because he couldn't accept his wife had stopped breathing he thought the other woman was harming her. He was confused and upset and it was dark."

"He certainly acted upset. He could have been putting that on, but I'm sure his shock was genuine. He was sweating, seemed completely stunned and weak."

"Those symptoms are the same as mild nicotine poisoning."

"All of them?"

He tapped on his tablet. "Symptoms of nicotine ingestion include burning in the mouth and throat, nausea, vomiting, confusion, dizziness, weakness and sweating. There may be features including tachycardia, tachypnoea, hypertension and agitation followed by bradycardia, systemic hypotension and respiratory depression. Severe poisoning can lead to arrhythmias including atrial fibrillation, coma, convulsions and respiratory and cardiac arrest."

"That doesn't sound as though it's very quick."

"It depends on the dose. The autopsy will tell us that and how long it would have been from drinking it to death. You're right though, it sounds as though it would be slow. If her husband administered it I imagine he'd have been shocked to see such a rapid and severe reaction, especially as he'd drunk some of it himself."

"Or he could be in shock because he took his wife to what he thought would be a nice party and they left in an ambulance with her not breathing."

"True. I did take that possibility into account when interviewing him."

"I didn't mean... He's going to be OK, is he, sir?"

"The doctor said the shock and grief are affecting him more than the nicotine poisoning, and he'll probably be discharged later today or tomorrow morning."

"Could the cases be linked?"

"Which cases?"

"This one and Mr Argent's. Last night I had a confused dream and in that I knew they were committed by the same person. Don't worry, I'm not claiming sixth sense or anything, it's just that this isn't a murder hotspot so two only a couple of months apart seems like more than coincidence."

"I can see why you think that, but the time frame actually makes it less likely they're linked. Murder draws attention to itself. Unless there was a pressing need to act quickly, a clever killer wouldn't commit a second murder while the police were so actively and obviously searching for them – and in both cases it does seem as though someone fairly intelligent is behind the deaths."

"That's not the only similarity. Both victims were poisoned with a drink of alcohol."

"That's not particularly unusual."

"No and it's probably coincidence… unless Lucy Carter was there? I didn't see her, but she easily could have been."

"If she was, that fact will be of considerable interest, but remember there's currently nothing known to indicate a link between the cases and no direct proof Carter did kill her cousin."

"You don't think she did?" Crystal asked.

"I think it's entirely possible, but I'm far from convinced to the point we're ignoring other lines of enquiry."

She thought for a moment. "Mr Argent was the second person she inherited property from. It included an antique's shop which did repair work…"

DI Shortfellow shook his head, but smiled too. "Which you know because I told you, which means it's something we're looking at."

"Of course you are, sir. I was thinking more about what her former lover did while he was alive."

"And whether it involved the use of cyanide?"

She felt her face glow. "Sorry, I'm being an idiot." If she could use Google to discover cyanide was sometimes used in the repair of antique jewellery then so could CID.

"You're not," he said. "It's rare, but cases have fallen apart because something, which in retrospect seemed obvious, was overlooked. It's happened to me once and I'd far rather six people were to say, 'Oi, did you check if the person who gained by the death ever had access to what killed the victim', or 'anyone let uniform know about the op, so they don't accidentally walk in and wreck it' than everyone assume it must have been done."

"Thank you, sir. You can rely on me to be the seventh person to ask the same thing and, if it will help, state the obvious at regular intervals."

"I look forward to it – very much."

That compliment had her blushing again. It was just professional pride, nothing to do with the DI's good looks and wicked smile.

Chapter 21

Thursday 4th June

"I've been invited to visit the Eastern Police Investigation Centre in Portsmouth to answer a few questions," Arnold told the vicar. "I got the distinct impression the invitation was one I have no choice but to accept."

"No, of course you must go. Do you need someone to drive you? Unfortunately, I can't this morning, but I'm sure Mike wouldn't mind," Reverend Jerry Grande replied.

"I can get a bus… "

"Let's see what he's doing." Jerry stuck his head outside the kitchen door and called his nephew's name.

"You want me?" Mike said a few moments later.

"I was wondering what you intended to do this morning."

"I was thinking of going round to Pompey, have a look at the shops in Gunwharf Quay, but it's not urgent if… "

"Splendid, splendid. Now if you'll excuse me, I must get going."

"Do you have any idea what I've just volunteered for?" Mike asked Arnold.

"Driving me to the CID centre. I can get the bus… "

"I'll be happy to take you, Arnold – as long as you know where it is."

"Airport Service Road, Hilsea, I understand."

"My SATNAV will know where that is. Do you want to go straight away?"

"There's some paperwork I'd like to collect from home first and… Do you think I should have a solicitor?"

"I wouldn't have thought so. Not if you're just answering questions about the booking and what happened last night."

"That's what they said."

"Is there anything in particular you're worried about?"

"No, no. I just feel responsible. I accepted the booking… "

"You didn't decide anything on your own, Arnold. Ellie and Uncle Jerry both agreed. They wouldn't have if they'd thought anything was wrong."

"That's true."

"Give me a call when you've finished and I'll pick you up."

"I don't know how long I'll be." Or if he'd be let out at all. "Perhaps I had better take the bus back."

"You just need to say 'ready' and I'll know it's you and where to come. If I'm not ready I'll say and you can decide whether to wait for me. If they keep you hanging about for hours and I've not heard from you by the time I want to come back, I'll call you and we'll work out what to do, OK?"

"OK. Thank you."

As Arnold put all the paperwork he thought CID might possibly ask to see into a folder, he wondered about adding clean underwear and a toothbrush to his briefcase. He decided against it.

During the drive Mike, as he often did, chatted to Arnold. As always Arnold was embarrassed and felt awkward about his short and vague responses. He liked

Mike, but they had so little in common. Arnold never knew what to say about sports he didn't follow, television programmes he'd not watched, or countries he'd never visited.

Arnold's bag was searched on his way in to be interviewed, so he'd made the right decision in not bringing his toothbrush and underwear. It would have sent quite the wrong message if it seemed he was expecting to be kept in custody.

He was told someone would soon come to fetch him, so when he saw Crystal approach he thought that was why she was there and wondered whether or not her big smile was a good sign. As he stepped forward she seemed surprised to see him.

"Hello, Arnold. Thanks for your help last night. I hope you got some sleep?"

"I did, thank you. Now I'm here to help again, with your enquiries this time." His feeble joke did nothing to cheer him up, but Crystal's response did.

"There are a lot of people CID need to talk to. I expect someone will be out soon."

He wasn't a key suspect then, just a witness. He felt even better when another officer, who walked him to an interview room, offered a cup of tea.

Once they were settled with drinks, DI Shortfellow thanked Arnold for coming in, introduced a female detective constable whose name Arnold didn't catch and said, "I'm sorry that we'll be going over much of the same ground as last night, but it's important we get everything straight and correctly recorded."

"I understand."

The female officer asked for Arnold's full name, address and date of birth. "You're thirty-six?" she clarified.

"That's right." Although some assumed he was older and some younger, people often seemed surprised when they learned his age.

Arnold was asked about his job.

"I'm verger at St Symeon's Church."

"Is that a paid role?"

"It is, yes." Although not the whole truth, that was perfectly true.

"And taking bookings for the hall is part of that job?"

"It's not in my job description, but yes, I suppose so." He explained the hall was new and a community project rather than belonging to the church. "However, I'm on the committee which brought it into being and my duties include assisting the vicar to care for the needs of the parish, both spiritual and secular."

"How was the letter making the booking addressed. To you personally?"

"I have it here. I'm sorry, it's been handled by several people."

"Were you surprised it came to your home address?" It was DI Shortfellow who asked that. Arnold hadn't noticed any sign he would take over the questioning, but presumably there was one as the female officer showed no surprise

"No. It's common knowledge. I print it in Little Mallow's Little Mag so that people can send in contributions and it's displayed on the church noticeboard for emergencies."

Neither police officer responded. In fact the constable sat back a little as though aware she'd played her part.

"I wouldn't necessarily have expected post about the hall to come directly to me, but as the hall didn't exist at that time it couldn't go there. I can't think of anywhere else it could have been sent."

"The church?"

"It's not actually a church hall." Had he not already explained that?

"I see. The magazine you mentioned, you're the editor?"

"That's right."

"Another part of your job?"

"Not really. It's not a parish publication in that it's produced by, or on behalf of, the church, but it is something for the whole village. My predecessor set it up and I kind of inherited the job."

"Would it be fair to say you work more hours than you're paid for?"

"I suppose, but it's my choice and I enjoy it. I don't quite see how this is relevant."

"I'm just trying to get the background. Did anything strike you as unusual about the booking?"

"All of it! I wish now I hadn't persuaded the others to agree." He explained about the quorum with Jerry, Martin and Ellie Jenkins, and pushing forward with the plans. How the peculiar letter had seemed like an answer to his prayers.

"And the actual letter?"

"Yes, that was odd… but it seemed like a fun puzzle and I was sure the mystery would soon be solved."

"What was a puzzle?"

"Look at the wording. He's made some unusual choices. Eventide, diminutive and expedite for example. I thought perhaps they might spell out his name. I enjoy word games and spent quite a bit of time trying to work it out. The difficulty of course was knowing which words were clues. I made a copy, highlighting those I thought might be."

He produced that version.

Dear Arnold Stewart,

I **desire** to make a booking for the new hall for the **eventide** of 3rd June, for a surprise social gathering. The event itself is to **occupy** the time from 8 until 11 and I would like an additional hour **preceding** and afterwards to allow caterers to set up and for removal of **trash**.

I request you supply 50 chairs, or as near to that number as possible, arranged with an **adequate** quantity of **diminutive** tables in informal groups. In addition, a lesser amount of larger tables on which to place a buffet and drinks sufficient for 70 people.

In order to preserve the **roguish** surprise element of this event, I must remain entirely anonymous. To that end, I enclose payment in cash. I trust it is more than sufficient. The surplus is to be used to **expedite** preparations of a **habitable** hall.

To confirm this booking, please place a **missive** in the next issue of Little Mag saying precisely, 'The new hall has received its first booking! The first of many we hope!!'

Regards,

Mystery Party Planner

"I found that by taking the first letter of each of those words, and rearranging them, I could create what appears to be a relevant phrase."

DI Shortfellow took the photocopy from Arnold and placed it on the desk so that he and his colleague could study it together.

Chapter 22

Thursday 4th June

"Hi, I've been trying to get hold of you," Crystal said when Jason finally answered his phone.

"I know and I was just about to call you back, honestly. I switch my phone off when I'm working."

"Me too, mostly. I wasn't nagging – honest! I just wanted to apologise for last night. Once I saw what was happening… "

"You selfishly stopped drinking wine and speculating as to the reason behind the party and instead did everything in your power to stop it becoming a tragedy?"

"I wouldn't have put it quite like that. I didn't even give that poor woman a break from the CPR."

"Crystal, you were magnificent. Apart from that one person nobody had a clue what to do. You took charge and got people being useful instead of just getting in the way. I'm so proud of you."

"Right." Magnificent? She'd just been doing her job and a woman had died practically on her watch.

"How is she, do you know?"

"Dead."

"I'm sorry, that's awful. Whatever the reason for the party and whoever was behind it, they can't have wanted that. What was it, allergic reaction to a wasp sting?"

"Murder." Gosh, she was getting good at breaking bad news gently!

"No! But… no."

"It seems very unlikely to be anything else. What made you think of wasp stings?"

"Several people heard the first aider lady say anaphylactic shock and, as there were no peanuts in the food, guessed that's what it was. Could you commit murder by wasp?"

That made Crystal smile. "If anyone does they won't fool me as, now you've said that, it'll be the first thing I check for with any unexplained death. That's not what happened here though; she was poisoned."

"So… Was that the reason for the party?"

"To quote the DI that's a possibility we're investigating, but yeah, I reckon it must be. That's off the record."

"I'm glad you feel able to trust me."

It would soon be public knowledge if it wasn't already, but Crystal did trust him. "There's something you might be able to help me with. What did you think of Ellie and Mike?"

"Please tell me they're not suspects."

"They're not suspects. At least no more than you and I. We were all together when we heard the scream." Actually that didn't totally clear them as Crystal didn't know how long prior to that the poisoned drinks were handed over, but CID would get that information and if she was a truly terrible judge of character and her friends were killers, they'd be caught. "Oh!"

"What?"

"I'm wondering who screamed."

"No idea. Is it important?"

"It could be. Anything could be."

"Is that why you asked about Mike and Ellie?"

"No, that's got nothing to do with murder."

"I like them both a lot."

"Good because I'd like your help in getting them together."

"Aren't they already? They seemed close," Jason said.

"Old friends. I'd like to give them a chance to be more."

"Count me in. Do you have a plan?"

"Yeah, but it's sneaky."

"Go on."

"I was thinking that Ellie could tell Mike she wants to help us get together and is having a dinner party or something and he's also invited."

"Sorry, that's probably not going to work. Mike and I were chatting and… "

"And what? What did you say about me?"

"I can't remember, but I probably gave the impression we were together."

"OK." With any luck Mike told Ellie and Ellie would tell her. "Did Mike say anything about Ellie?"

"He likes her. I think that's pretty obvious, but I don't know if he… Sorry."

If Mike was equally unhelpful in passing on information, maybe she wasn't going to find out what Jason had said about her. Oh well, she didn't need to be a detective to work out they were no longer 'just good friends'.

"How about this dinner party is to discuss the murder and you want the four of us because we were there together and discussing theories about the party?"

"That could work," Crystal said.

"Because it's true?"

"You know me a bit too well for two dates!"

"Better arrange a third then, hadn't we?"

The shift briefing at Gosport police station began with the news that a string of burglaries had apparently been solved by colleagues on C shift, when a member of their neighbourhood team responded to complaints about a dog barking all night. Two officers had called at the property in the early hours of the morning and literally bumped into the owner returning with his loot.

That information got a cheer. The thief always gained entry by forcing the doors on integral garages and caused a great deal of damage looking for valuable items. Several times he'd been surprised and had punched his victims before making his escape. The last time, the elderly lady he'd hit had spent three days in hospital with concussion.

The skipper then gave an outline of the events from the party and some of the things CID were interested to know. The news that Trevor and Crystal would be handling most of the routine enquiries didn't displease anyone. It wasn't that they didn't want to help, just that they all had plenty of work already.

Imani Freedman gestured for Crystal and Trevor to stay behind, as everyone dispersed to their various duties.

"Crystal, are you OK? It must have been a shock," she said.

"It was, but I'm fine, honestly. It's probably good in a way that I had a late night, as I slept OK."

"That's good. I did expect you to cope, but remember that just because it's your job doesn't mean you won't react like other people. It's OK to be upset, sad, frightened, angry, any of that. And it's more than OK to ask for help dealing with that if you need to. A broken cup can't bail out the boat as my, admittedly crazy, grandmother used to say."

"Thank you. I'll remember." She should do, she'd been given a version of this pep talk in different forms by numerous people, including the sergeant and Trevor, since she first applied to join the police. It was repeated because it was important.

"I take it you'd like to do your bit to make sure Little Mallow benefits from a visible police presence while this case is solved?"

"No… Oh, I hadn't thought. I'd intended to ask around in my own time to see what I can find out. Two officers in uniform might not encourage people to talk, but those with nothing to hide will probably find it reassuring to see us."

"That's my thought too. Obviously you can't neglect anything else, but when you're supposed to be on patrol I'd like you to spend at least some time in the Little Mallow area."

"Sure thing, Skip," Trevor answered for them.

"What do you think then, lass?" he asked as they left the station.

"It depends when you ask me. While the DI was interviewing me I changed my mind several times. There's a lot to think about."

"What I meant was, what do you think about walking the beat in Little Mallow?"

"Oh, right. Yes, let's do that."

"You can fill me in on everything on the way."

Crystal fully briefed Trevor with all the facts, wild theories and everything else she could think to mention. Quite a few people were about in the vicinity of Little Mallow community hall but, by the time Crystal had parked the police car, all those people were walking away in different directions. Crime scene tape was in evidence, but no officers.

"Anyone who wants a look can see through the railings," Crystal pointed out. That's what they did, but it didn't add anything to their understanding of events.

"What now, boss?" Trevor asked.

"We slowly walk up and down the High Street and then Main Street looking like the kind of people you want to give useful information to?"

"Worth a try. Maybe we'll get lucky like C shift and the murderer will bump into us, clutching armfuls of evidence."

"I doubt it will be that easy! Where is Jester Road anyway? I've never heard of it."

"That's because you were so sick with envy at not making the collar yourself that you didn't listen properly. It was Jessie Road, not Jester."

"That's right near where Mr Argent lived... I'd better ring the DI."

"Why?"

"Jessie Road is very close to Mr Argent's home. The owner had a dog. If Mr Argent had been asked to look after it, he might have seen some of the stolen items and if the thief realised that, maybe he decided to shut him up."

"Would someone who left their dog barking all night worry about getting someone to walk it in the day?"

"If the service was free, they might. And maybe it only started the barking because it doesn't get taken out in the evening now Argent is dead?"

"There's lots of ifs and maybes in there, lass."

Crystal sighed. What had, a few seconds ago, seemed a strong lead now looked like a long shot, but it was still possible there was a connection. "Isn't it better I say something and be wrong than keep quiet about a potential suspect?"

When Trevor nodded, Crystal pulled out her phone and called the DI. "Sir, I'm not sure if you're aware of the arrest in Jessie Road last night?"

"Don't tell me they've put you straight onto nights."

"No, no, I wasn't on duty. I heard about it at this morning's briefing and realised there's a possible connection with the Argent case." She explained her reasoning.

"There's a big difference between burglary and premeditated murder."

"That's true, but he has been violent, sir."

"We'll look into it. Thank you for letting me know. Are you in the station now?"

"No, sir. Trevor and I are in Little Mallow, providing a reassuring police presence and keeping our eyes and ears open."

"And remembering what I said about not wanting you or the investigation put at risk, I hope? Don't let anyone confess or incriminate themselves until we can get them cautioned and on record. And don't react if you hear anything potentially incriminating."

"Got it."

They continued walking along Main Street, meeting no one, until they reached the junction with the High Street and turned that way. The High Street was really quiet. That was partly explained when they reached Paula's Posies and discovered that, despite the death of its owner, it was open for business. It seemed that everyone out shopping wanted to buy flowers. There was a hush as Crystal and Trevor walked in and all eyes swivelled in their direction.

Chapter 23

Thursday 4th June

After the two CID officers had studied the copy of the booking letter which Arnold had marked to indicate what could possibly be a code, he told them the phrase he'd created from the initial letters of the more unusual words. "Me P Roth Dead. Do you see?"

The officers nodded.

"I didn't spot it beforehand, but I looked again this morning and wondered if it could be a suicide note."

"That's something to consider."

"Could it be the other way round?" the female officer suggested. "Instead of a suicide note it's a warning from M. E."

"Is there anyone connected with the case who would fit?" the DI asked.

"Not that we're aware of, sir."

Arnold didn't wait to be asked directly. "I can't think of anyone in Little Mallow with those initials." He couldn't – Mike Ellison lived in Durham and although he often visited the village he was currently in Portsmouth, and Arnold knew the vicar's nephew hadn't committed the murder.

"Had you previously reached a conclusion about the letter's possible code?" the DI continued.

"Yes. That rather than being clues, those words are the opposite." Encouraged by the look of interest on DI Shortfellow's face, Arnold continued. "I thought he was attempting to disguise his usual style of writing. When I'm editing the magazine I sometimes notice a particular word is over used, or not quite the right one, and I use the computer's thesaurus function to change it. I very much hope it isn't the case, but it occurred to me that perhaps he contributed to the Little Mag and feared I'd recognise his style."

"That's certainly possible. You've constantly referred to the person behind the party as he. What makes you so sure it's a man?"

"I'm afraid that's just an assumption on my part. He, if it is a he, has assumed this booking will go ahead, but under the circumstances... I mean with the hall not even existing, that was by no means certain. I think it's a man who is perhaps used to giving orders and having them obeyed." Someone like DI Shortfellow he thought, but didn't say. The officer sitting next to him clearly knew her place.

"You say that, when you contacted the vicar, he already knew about the request?"

"Sort of. Martin Blackman, the publican at the Crown and Anchor, had received an order for food and drink. They were reading it when I called. I don't know if Martin still has it, but it was exactly the same kind of thing as the booking. No contact details, same style including unusual word choices, and just the minimum information. His had a lot more cash in. I don't know if it helps, but I have some of the money. We didn't pay it all into the bank in case cash was needed, but that's not been the case." He produced the notes he'd brought with him.

"Thank you. We'll give you a receipt of course."

The female officer rose and stepped out of the room. Presumably she relayed the request to someone else because she returned very quickly, empty handed.

"Can you tell me who attended this party?" the DI asked.

"I've made a list of everyone I can recall. It's not complete as there were a good many I didn't recognise nor converse with sufficiently to know their names." He was aware nerves were making him sound unnatural. That was silly as his list was as accurate as he could make it, including the addition of Cameron Pollock, the charming model train enthusiast he'd met that night.

As the DI scanned the list there was a knock at the door and someone passed Arnold's receipt to the constable. She gave it to Arnold, then picked up his list of attendees and studied it.

"As far as you're aware, was everyone who attended invited?" the DI asked.

"I wouldn't know if they weren't. I didn't ask or check invitations. Do you think it was a gatecrasher who…?"

"We are investigating a number of possibilities."

The DI asked Arnold to talk him through the events of the evening, starting from when he first arrived at the hall. This Arnold did, aided by occasional questions from DI Shortfellow, until he reached the point where, "I was talking to one of the guests about our costumes, when we heard the scream. I immediately made my way to the outdoor seating area."

"Do you know who screamed?"

"No. I think whoever it was had come back inside by the time I went out."

"Tell me what you saw when you got there."

"Paula Roth was lying on the ground and being given CPR by one of the guests. I don't know her, but she appeared competent and calm. Her husband, Paula's I mean, was there in quite a state. I recognised your colleague... I only know her Christian name is Crystal. She lives with her aunt, Agnes Patterson, so perhaps that's her surname?"

"I know who you mean. What was the officer doing?"

"Taking charge. Making sure the ambulance people would know where to go, that kind of thing. I helped as best I could by switching on the big light, encouraging those not involved to go inside and then standing by the door so nobody else could go out and get in the way. Then your colleague asked me to fetch a blanket for Mr Roth who was in shock." He explained about leaving Mike and a friend by the door, fetching the dust sheets, attempting to comfort Mr Roth and helping him into the ambulance when his wife was taken to hospital.

Arnold felt quite exhausted by that point and his throat was dry. He rarely talked so much and never about anything so difficult. "Might I have some water, please?"

"Of course," the constable said. "Or another tea?"

"Yes please."

"Sir?"

"Yes, thank you."

The constable went out to pass on the request. She returned promptly.

"You mentioned switching on a light, when you saw what was happening outside," the DI said.

"Yes. At Crystal's request. There are fairy lights, which look pretty but, as I noticed when I went out with my glass of wine earlier, they aren't quite bright enough to see properly. I switched on the big light as I went back in. Sorry, I thought I said."

"Perhaps you did."

Arnold was certain the DI could recall that better than Arnold could. "Oh, I see what you mean. I switched it on twice, meaning somebody switched it off at some point."

"Any idea who?"

"It could have been anyone, and I'm not surprised as it's a very harsh light and I imagine anyone else who wanted to sit there would prefer it darker. I really only put it on, the first time I mean, so people would know it was OK to go out there and would find the benches if they did."

"I see. Did others go out there?"

"After the scream, yes. Before that, I don't know. Anyone could have done, but perhaps they weren't aware they could or even that there was anything there. Actually that applies to the big security light. The switch is easily accessible, but there's no sign for it, so not everyone would know of its existence."

"Who did know?"

The arrival of the tea gave Arnold time to think about that. "A good many people would know about the garden and seating area. Many of the residents of Little Mallow helped with landscaping the area. I could probably make a list, but there would be more as anyone could walk in and take a look. Fewer would know about the light switch, but it wasn't a secret."

"How well did you know the deceased?"

"Quite well. She was on the new hall committee and I buy flowers from her shop. I found her to be pleasant and community spirited and have the impression she was generally well-liked. Is it certain she was deliberately targeted?"

"Nothing is certain at this stage."

Arnold was asked to go through everything again from the beginning, which he did without feeling he'd added much to what he'd already said. The female detective then read him his statement, repeatedly asking him to confirm it was accurate. It was a relief to finally sign it.

"Thank you for your time, Mr Stewart. You've been very helpful. Should you think of anything else, or learn anything which might be of interest, please don't hesitate to get in touch." She gave him a card with contact details on.

"Will I be called as a witness?"

"That's quite likely, yes. There will probably be an inquest fairly soon. Please don't worry, it will just be a case of answering questions as you've done today. Any trial isn't likely to happen for quite a while, but your statement can be used to remind you." She gave a reassuring smile.

As soon as he was outside the building, Arnold took his phone from his briefcase. He recalled the vicar's advice to either use complete sentences, or text. Arnold did both by typing, *'Hello, Mike. My interview is complete. Arnold.'* As he pressed send he thought he probably could have said that. Perhaps all that was needed was to plan his words in advance?

Knowing that even if Mike were ready to leave immediately it would take him some time to get to where

Arnold was waiting, he decided to go for a stroll. The area was an industrial estate and Arnold was pleased to find a little heap of metal pieces in hexagon shapes, which he guessed were the offcuts from something used nearby. They were on the footpath against a kind of kerb and looked as though they'd been there a very long time, so he felt no guilt in scooping them up and putting them in one of the paper bags he always had with him in case of interesting finds.

He saw a sign, and smelt fried onions, indicating a burger van, and was suddenly very hungry. He was considering whether there would be time for him to have something cooked and to consume it when Mike called back.

"Good timing, Arnold. I've just finished my lunch, so can come straight away. Probably be about twenty minutes, if that's OK?"

"Yes. Thank you." He felt so pleased with himself. Even after the stress of a very thorough police interview he'd managed a proper conversation by telephone.

As he ate a very good cheeseburger and drank a rich, fragrant coffee, Arnold thought over everything he'd said to DI Shortfellow and his colleague. He wished he'd thought to ask for a copy of his statement, but once they'd finished all he wanted to do was to get outside. Perhaps they wouldn't have given him one anyway? He'd never seen it happen on television.

Everything surrounding the booking of the party must have sounded very suspicious to the police. Arnold didn't know if he'd convinced them of his innocence, but couldn't see what more he could have said.

It was over and done with, he reminded himself. He couldn't change the past and should think instead of the future. Would that include Cameron Pollock? He'd really liked him and hoped he wanted to be a friend – Arnold didn't make friends terribly easily. He'd included the man's name on the list of those present, but not his telephone number. The DI hadn't asked for it, so that was OK. He'd learn it soon though, and Arnold had it already. He took out his phone.

What to say? 'I've just given the police your name to add to their list of suspects'? No. And he couldn't send that message by text—it might seem quite menacing. It would be better to tell him face to face. Much better, but it still meant Arnold had to telephone to arrange it. Cameron had urged him to call. Why would he have done that if he'd not wanted to see Arnold again? It would be fine to call, if he just thought about what to say first.

They would need to agree a location if they were to meet. Cameron lived in Gosport, so that would be most convenient for him. Arnold wouldn't feel right inviting himself to the man's home and didn't know anywhere suitable to suggest. The library was always so busy and noisy. Then he remembered.

Arnold extracted Cameron's card from his wallet and keyed the number into his phone. Then he took a deep breath and pressed the green symbol.

After just two rings, Cameron answered, "Hello?"

"Hello. This is Arnold from last night. I want to see you. Can we meet in the Knitted Cosy tea rooms as soon as possible?"

Chapter 24

Thursday 4th June

Most of the faces regarding Crystal and Trevor in Paula's Posies were curious. Those of the two members of staff were red and puffy.

"Is Mr Roth OK?" one of the staff asked. "We heard they're keeping him in hospital."

"He's expected to be discharged today or tomorrow morning," Crystal said.

"That's good. We didn't know what to do. We'd opened up before we heard and people kept coming in so we thought we should stay open."

Crystal wasn't sure if they wanted to be told they'd done the right thing or to be sent home, but they clearly wanted guidance of some kind. "Can you manage without Mrs Roth?"

"Today's no problem, it was her day off anyway," said the florist who'd not yet spoken.

"And we run the place when she's on holiday," her colleague added.

"Then it's probably best to carry on as you would in that situation until you hear any different."

They both looked towards Trevor as if for confirmation. That seemed odd, especially considering their boss was a woman. Maybe it was just because he was older than them and Crystal was younger.

"Quite right," Trevor said. "Don't let us keep you from your work. We just have a few routine questions about how the business operates."

The staff looked relieved. Most of the customers looked disappointed, until Trevor said they might be able help with something else. "We're trying to get a complete list of everyone who was at yesterday's party, and learn what they were wearing."

"Especially anyone who left early," Crystal added. "If they were gone before Paula was taken ill they may not have heard about that and so not know they should contact the police. We need to know so we can eliminate as many people as possible from our enquiries." Crystal was pleased with that. It would allow people to gossip about their neighbours and feel good about it rather than as though they were informing on them.

A very short lady who compensated for her lack of bodily height with impressively vertical hair began to speak, but was talked over by a red-faced woman who asked, "She was killed then?"

"We are investigating a number of possibilities." But she wanted to encourage gossip. "I can tell you it wasn't a natural death, and an accident looks to be unlikely." She couldn't swear anyone actually said 'ooooh' but it felt like it. Again the short lady tried to speak, but wasn't quick enough.

"I didn't go and I wasn't invited," said the red-faced woman who'd asked if Paula had been killed.

"You think someone went without an invitation?" Crystal asked.

"I heard my neighbour's son on the phone saying he was thinking of gatecrashing if whoever he was talking to was up for it. Don't get me wrong, he's a good lad and wouldn't have meant any harm. It's just teenagers and free drinks, you know?"

Crystal gave her most understanding nod. "It would be very tempting, and I expect he would have been curious about the party anyway. Do you know if he went?"

"Not for definite, but I saw him walk out the house about half seven dressed as a clown."

"I'd better take the details," Trevor said and noted the name and address of the lady and her neighbour.

"He did go. I saw a clown go in with a lad dressed to play football," said the short lady. "And Ellie Jenkins the schoolteacher did too. The vicar's nephew called for her, and they went over just after seven. I didn't know there was going to be a party until I saw what they were wearing and remarked on it. I live two doors down from Ellie, you see. She was a nurse and he was a sailor. Not a real one, but like the bath bubble bottles you used to get."

"Oh, I remember! Can you still get those?"

"No idea. I just have showers these days."

"And me. Not the same, is it?"

Trevor cleared his throat in a meaningful manner.

"They'd have told the police though," the short lady said. "They didn't come back until quite a while after the ambulance left and they'd know their duty."

"You're right. They've both given statements, but it's good to have information confirmed, so thank you for telling me. You must live close to the hall?" Crystal asked. Ellie lived almost opposite the pub. If she'd passed this lady's house on the way to the hall, she must live directly opposite.

"That's right. You're Agnes's niece who's staying with her?"

"Great niece actually." She gave what she hoped was an 'I'm one of you' smile to everyone.

"I thought you were. I did see quite a few people go in, but didn't recognise anyone else."

Not even Crystal evidently. "How about the costumes?"

"There was all sorts. Ghosts and witches and things like that."

Crystal and Trevor listened patiently and made notes as she listed all she could remember. None of the outfits she described included lime green gloves or trousers with red stripes. Crystal felt it better not to ask in case she put ideas in people's heads.

"You've been really helpful," Trevor said in his most charming manner. "When we have a suspect you might be able to identify them."

"You'll be bringing them to account, Aurora!" the red faced woman said and laughed as though that was hilarious.

The short lady looked thrilled at the idea, and gave her name, Aurora Evans, and contact details, but admitted she hadn't seen everyone come and go. "I saw someone delivering boxes of stuff and little Adam helping fetch and carry, so I wondered what was up. That's why I saw Ellie and the vicar's Mike, and after that I watched to see what people were wearing for a bit. After that I didn't take much notice until the ambulance came."

Nobody else admitted to having been invited to the party, nor to having attended or knowing for certain of anyone else who had. Most of them drifted away when they realised they'd got all the information they could, and that the police were going to stay put. As those who remained made their selections and paid, Crystal and Trevor learned the two employees were Dawn and Liz. Both worked five days a week which always included Saturdays. Dawn usually took Mondays off, Liz varied hers. There was also Miranda who mainly dealt with deliveries and Benjamin who did Saturdays and sometimes came in at other times if it was especially busy. "And Paula and Michael Roth of course."

No customers remained when Crystal said, "Paula didn't run the business herself?"

"She did mostly," Liz said.

"But Michael checked things and sorted out any problems," Dawn added.

That explained why the staff had looked to a man to tell them what to do – they were taking their cue from their boss.

"No other staff?" Crystal prompted.

"Not now," Liz said and glanced at Dawn who nodded. "There was Beth until she was sacked. That was horrible. We liked her and believed her when she said she hadn't done anything wrong."

"She might have made a mistake, but I don't think she'd steal. She was really upset when he said she had, and promised she never did."

"She was sacked with no proof?" Crystal asked.

"Well, technically not sacked," Liz said. "She was on trial here, but let go."

"She'd only been taken on for the Valentine rush to start with. Two people were. One didn't want to stay, but Beth did and Paula said she'd keep her on part time, until after Mother's day and Easter at the very least. We all started temporary – it was Paula's way of making sure we were suited."

"She didn't fit in?"

"Yes she did. She's lovely. Well, we thought she was. Gorgeous looking too."

"That's right. Much prettier than that Naomi Campbell, if you ask me. And none of her snarky attitude either."

"Dark as she is, Beth's an absolute ray of sunshine, or maybe a rainbow with all those bright colours she wears. And she's just… nice."

"She's got an adorable little boy. Do anything for him she would and it was all worked out so she could take him to nursery, work for the busiest part of the day, then go get him. Then some money went missing."

"That wasn't the start of it," Liz said. "There were a few problems with orders. A couple of people had paid for deliveries which never turned up and more than once some went out and it turned out they hadn't been paid for and we couldn't tell who ordered them. It hadn't happened before Beth started so we thought she was making mistakes. Paula gave her more training and tried to make sure she wasn't in the shop on her own and it stopped."

"Yeah, that's right. She's bright enough but it'd be easy to get mixed up and flustered if there's a few customers at once. Most are lovely, but some get cross if we're still putting stuff from the last one in the computer instead of serving them right away."

"But the money was different?"

"It was always short by ten pounds," Liz said.

"Always?" Crystal queried.

"Every time it was wrong, I mean."

"Anyone can make a mistake," Dawn said. "But that's not a likely one. If people pay in cash it's usually for a bunch which costs less than a tenner, so counting it wrong or giving ten pounds extra change... it wouldn't happen often."

"So, we still thought it was a mistake, or hoped so, but then Michael caught her at it."

"How?" Crystal asked.

"Don't know, it was just them here. We only found out when Paula said she'd had no choice but to let her go. Ever so upset she was."

"So, Beth texted us both after and said she didn't steal anything. I still think it could have been a mistake, but I can see why Paula couldn't keep her on."

"Understandable, if she was losing the shop money," Crystal said.

"Well, yeah but I meant it was Beth's word against Michael's. Paula didn't like to upset him – or anyone."

"Yes, that would be difficult. They got on well then, the Roths?" Crystal asked.

"Paula got on with everyone, she was lovely," Dawn said.

"He helped her a lot with the shop," Liz said.

"They were always very polite to each other."

Crystal glanced at Trevor. They'd both dealt very politely with plenty of members of the public they didn't particularly like, helped them too. On the other hand she was helpful, and usually fairly polite, to Aunty Agnes. All that Liz and Dawn's comments proved was they either didn't know much about the relationship between the Roths or weren't willing to openly speculate.

"Could you give us a general sense of how the business is run, who your biggest customers are, that kind of thing?" Crystal asked. She didn't expect to learn anything that would lead directly to Paula Roth's killer. More likely she'd get an idea whether Beth was likely to have been a thief. She wanted to know, even though it was unlikely she could do anything with the information. Paula couldn't now press charges or reinstate the girl and Michael Roth had far more serious concerns than whether or not Crystal believed he'd misjudged a former employee of his wife's.

Dawn and Liz explained how the flowers were obtained and treated on arrival and indicated how long it took to prepare orders. "If there's more than one funeral or wedding either we're both in, or one of the others comes in to serve."

"Do you use any chemicals to preserve the flowers?"

"Just bleach to keep everything clean," Dawn said. "Paula liked everything to be really clean."

"She joked she spent more on bleach, and gloves and hand cream for us all, than she did on flowers."

Both women looked close to tears as they mentioned their dead boss.

A customer came in. Probably just for gossip judging by their reaction to the presence of Crystal and Trevor, but they left with a small bunch of carnations, which gave Liz an opportunity to demonstrate how the till worked. It seemed clear to Crystal that taking money would be very easy, but doing so without a trace was impossible. The till recorded the type of sale, and even if the cash drawer was opened without a sale being made.

"The other main thing is taking orders," Dawn said. "We go through what customers want and have books of photos to help them decide and we've got these forms to make sure we know everything we need to know. Then we take payment, or a deposit which goes through on the till like I showed you, then we put all the details on the computer."

"Can you show us that?"

"If I put something in then it would be a real order."

"What if you enter something and the customer cancels or you realise you made a mistake?"

"We have to put in a cancellation. I suppose I… "

"That's OK," Crystal said. It wasn't likely to help advance the murder enquiry, she was just curious.

"Can everyone who works here use the computer?"

"We have to. All orders need to go in and it's supposed to be done right away by whoever took it. We often check what we've got coming up, especially when we want to book a day off. Paula usually decided which flowers to buy, but if she was on holiday we did it. Miranda prints off a list for her deliveries…'

"I see, thanks." There was such a thing as too much information. Crystal then thanked them both for their help, adding CID would probably come to speak to them too.

"Don't worry if they ask you the same questions – it won't mean you didn't do a great job answering ours," Trevor said.

"I hope you get whoever did for Paula."

"And throw away the key!"

Chapter 25

Thursday 4ᵗʰ June

"Quite a double act, weren't they?" Crystal said outside. "Not as good a team as us, but not bad."

"Was it useful?" Trevor asked as they walked along the street. "Other than for when you retire and open a florist shop, I mean."

"I haven't totally solved the murder yet. There were some questions I felt I should leave to CID."

"Excuses, excuses."

She knew he was teasing. "I think Beth was innocent."

"It's not a strong motive."

"Didn't mean the murder. Not that I think she did that either – well, I don't have any evidence about that. I meant of stealing from the shop."

"I agree, but I expect you want to tell me why you're right."

"Obvs! For a start, both Dawn and Liz liked her. They're good friends so might not take easily to someone new unless she was actually nice, and they're loyal to Paula so wouldn't accept anyone cheating her."

"Bad people can be charming."

"True. But those mistakes with orders – it sounds as though it would be easy to either forget to put one in or not remember to cancel something. The computer seemed to be in frequent use and they didn't mention logging in, so either they didn't need to or it was very easy. Maybe not all the mistakes were Beth's. And even if they were,

I'm sure they were mistakes. Paula's policy of starting staff on a temporary basis and seeing how they do suggests she was perfectly aware not everyone would be a reliable employee, yet she gave Beth several chances."

"Any clues about the murder?"

"It doesn't seem to be linked to Paula's job. Dawn and Liz obviously wanted to help. If they'd known of anyone with a serious grudge against Paula, or if she'd been afraid of anyone, I'm sure they'd have said. I'm not sure she was killed for herself, if you see what I mean. She doesn't seem the sort to make enemies."

"Can't argue there, but there's still a lot you don't know. I suppose I'm going to have to let you off not solving this yet."

She was no further forward after they'd completed a patrol of the rest of the High Street and returned to where they'd parked the car outside the new hall on Main Street. The few people they spoke to had questions, but no new answers. Those people mentioned as having been at the party were already on Crystal's list. Shock and dismay about the murder and kind words about Paula Roth were a common theme, as was the hope the killer was soon brought to justice.

"You know, I feel I've got a pretty good impression of the kind of person the dead florist was, just from talking to her staff, and I had an even clearer picture of Mr Argent from poking about in his house. Why are living people so much harder to read?" Crystal asked as she unlocked the patrol car.

"Trouble with the photographer?" Trevor asked.

"Actually no, things are good now we both realise we don't just want to be friends."

"Communication is a two way thing, lass."

"Yeah. I was looking for clues about how he felt, without giving him any myself."

With that in mind, Crystal called DI Shortfellow and told him what she and Trevor had learned so far. He didn't express surprise their visit to Paula's Posies hadn't revealed an obvious motive for murder and said they'd been right not to ask directly. He agreed it would be worth someone speaking to Aurora Evans, Ellie's next-door-but-one neighbour who'd seen some of the party arrivals and departures, and that Crystal and Trevor had again been right to not ask directly about anyone matching the description Mr Roth gave for the person who'd allegedly given him the poisoned wine.

"An official request for you to check something will be coming through."

"Happy to help, sir."

"I was counting on it. Another area of interest is who knew about the outside seating area behind the hall and the location of the switch for the security light."

"I think I got all that," Trevor said, after Crystal ended the call. "And now I reckon it's time we got something to eat."

"We could combine it with reassuring an elderly resident the police are working hard, certain in the knowledge she'll pass that around Little Mallow."

"I'd be delighted to drop in on your Aunty Agnes."

Agnes did indeed believe they were working hard – she saw that for herself when she got them chopping vegetables and beating eggs for a Spanish omelette. Crystal, following Agnes's instructions, did the cooking.

The three of them ate it, followed by a piece of chocolate brownie Crystal had previously baked. Crystal washed up and Trevor dried.

They'd hardly got back to the patrol car when the control room made a radio request for attendance at a park in Lee-on-the-Solent where teenagers were apparently drinking and causing damage to play equipment. As nobody from the response team was immediately free and they were so close, Crystal and Trevor took the shout.

The youths were a lot louder and more aggressive than those they'd almost caught drinking in Stanley Park a few weeks previously, but no older. There was no pretence of innocence, but a lot along the lines of, "What you going to do about it, pigs?"

"Confiscate your alcohol, take your names and addresses, explain the error of your ways, if necessary caution you and inform whoever is responsible for you." Trevor spoke in a neutral tone.

The group weren't very co-operative and at least some of the names given were most likely false, that is unless every teenager in Lee-on-the-Solent was named after a millionaire footballer. Fortunately the lads had the sense not to do more than moan and swear when Crystal and Trevor collected up all the bottles, cans, cigarettes, a lighter, and a vape device.

"You can't take the fags and that. I'm sixteen," said the boy who'd claimed to be Lionel Messi.

"And you have ID to prove it, I suppose?"

Crystal took the repetitive stream of swear words as a no. "Then it's all going to the station. If you want it back and can prove you're old enough to have it, you can come and get it when you've sobered up."

Crystal and Trevor photographed the slight fire damage to a swing seat and the haul of confiscated items. All the while Trevor delivered a lecture on the dangers of excessive drinking, the way they were making themselves vulnerable to accidents or the illegal activities of others, and the penalties possible for criminal damage. Crystal knew he had plenty more material, but the group decided they'd heard enough, claimed they were just having a laugh, wouldn't do it again and wanted to go home.

"Tell us where you got all this and you can go," Trevor said.

"We didn't nick it."

"We know that," said Crystal who'd recognised the carrier bags as being the same design as those holding the beer bought by the last lot of under-age drinkers they'd dealt with.

"And we're not bloody grasses!"

Crystal noticed a woman, wearing the bright green uniform which indicated she worked in an ASDA supermarket, striding towards them. It seemed likely she intended to either complain about the teenagers' behaviour, or the police response to it. Whatever she had in mind, it wouldn't stop Crystal and Trevor doing their job to the best of their ability.

"It's not grassing, it's doing a deal. You give us information and we don't take you back to your parents and give them a talking to before we officially caution you," Trevor explained.

"You don't have to take that one anywhere, officer," the woman in green said. "He's my son and if he doesn't co-operate I will."

"Mum!"

"I've told you before about drinking and hanging round with this lot. If I can't stop you maybe it's time to let the police have a go?"

"Alright, I'll tell you – but only so Mum don't grass up my mates."

The name of the shop was no surprise to Crystal and Trevor, who knew the owner had been warned after the last incident.

"We're going to need a statement," Trevor said.

"What! No way. You said if we said where we got it, we could go."

"A statement is just doing that formally," Crystal said, as much to the mother as the lad. "We're not going to arrest you or press charges."

"As long as you give us that statement," Trevor added.

As Trevor dealt with the electronic paperwork, the boy's mother spoke to Crystal. "It was me who called the police this evening," she said. "I called 101 but it took nearly twenty minutes just to get through to someone."

"I'm sorry about that. It's not ideal I know, but staff shortages…"

"I wasn't complaining, I just wondered if there was a quicker way to get a response. I'm really worried about Dom. Those boys seem to have some kind of hold over him and I suspect they get up to a lot worse than this."

"If a crime is actually being committed you can call 999," Crystal said. She realised the woman wouldn't be comfortable doing that unless she considered it a real emergency. "I'll give you my number. If you think they're drinking again, or worse, text me with the location and as many details as you have. If it's possible we'll come out. Obviously I can't guarantee that, or that I'll even see the message in time, so call 101 right after – and 999 if anyone seems to be in danger."

"Thank you. I really appreciate that. He's not a bad lad underneath."

"It feels like we're fighting a losing battle," Crystal said to Trevor, as they returned to the car.

"It might not seem like it, but it being the same shop is good news. We cut off that supply and we've made a difference. With what we have now they're going to lose the alcohol licence, maybe even do time."

"Really?"

"Really."

"That makes me feel better – and it might make other shop owners a bit more careful."

Friday 5th June

The next morning, Agnes said she wasn't sure she had the strength to deliver the Little Mag.

"Don't worry, I'll do it, but if your hip is still giving you trouble, you should tell the doctor."

Agnes chuckled. "It's not my hip, it's my ears!"

"Sorry?"

"Young Adam is going to help me."

"Ah."

"I can manage the walking again now. I was thinking of doing it over a few days and maybe stopping for a rest and cup of tea with a friend each time. It'll be easier with him going down the paths and up the steps and bending for low letterboxes, but listening to him… Oh well, better get ready, he'll be here soon."

Poor Aunty looked quite sorry for herself, which hadn't been the case even when she was waiting for her operation. It probably wasn't so much the boy's chatter as the fact that Agnes couldn't very well take him into other people's homes and expect him to be silent as she caught up on all the gossip.

"I've got a plan," Crystal said when Agnes reappeared. "I'll help too. If you get invited in for tea, or just want to stop for a rest, Adam and I will carry on and come back for you when we've finished."

"Thank you, love!"

At the third house, they were all invited to 'step inside for a moment'. It was clear to Crystal that Agnes hadn't expected it to happen at that address. What she couldn't tell was whether her aunt wished to accept. "Perhaps, we could… " she started to say.

"What a good idea," Agnes said, then turned to the homeowner. "My niece did suggest she continue if I got tired. She's a police officer and very good to me."

"You come and sit yourself down. I'll just pop the kettle on and I'll be with you."

"Come on then, Adam," Crystal said.

He looked as happy with the arrangement as Agnes did.

Wanting to give Aunty some time to chat, Crystal suggested they do all of the opposite side of the road, then cross back to do the rest and finish back where they'd left Aunty.

"How long have you been in the police?" Adam asked, once they'd stopped, looked, listened and crossed.

"Nearly three years."

"Are you a detective?"

"Not yet, but I will be."

"When?"

"By the start of the school holidays."

"Do you like being in the police?"

"Very much. Sometimes we have to do things we don't like, but it's rewarding because we help people."

"I like helping people."

"Yes." She gave him a magazine and pointed towards the next house.

"Do you like delivering magazines?" Adam asked when he'd delivered the one she'd given him.

'Not really, but it's saving Aunty from your questions' would have been honest but not tactful so, remembering her stint delivering to the street Lucy Carter lived in she said, "Sometimes it's a good way of finding out things about people."

"Like clues?"

"Sort of, yes." She gave him another magazine and he raced up the next path.

He was soon back. "Are you looking for clues now?"

That hadn't been her intention, but it might keep Adam amused and it was just possible they'd stumble across something useful. "Not clues exactly, just trying to find things out. Like, do any of these people smoke?"

"They shouldn't. Smoking is bad for you. Granny and Grandad sell things to help them give up."

Admittedly the chances of the boy having witnessed a sale of dozens of odourless vape refills to one person and therefore allowing Crystal to solve the case in under forty-eight hours were very slim, but she'd be stupid not to ask. "Do you know who buys them?"

"A bus driver did once. He left his bus and all the people on it and didn't turn the engine off. You're not supposed to do that, are you?"

"Sometimes people do things they shouldn't."

"I know. That's why I'm going to be a detective and stop them. Do you think I'll be good at that?"

"You've certainly got an enquiring mind."

"What does that mean?"

"You ask a lot of questions." She was handing him a magazine outside each house so he could run down the path and push it through a letterbox, but it wasn't doing anything to stop the bombardment.

"Yes, I do. And I'm good at noticing things. Like the people in the house we just delivered to have a cat. Do you want to know how I know?"

"Go on then."

"There's a cat flap on the door to the porch, to let it go in if it rains and there's a bowl of water and cat food in there. It smells of fish."

"It might not be for their cat."

"Do you think they're trying to get somebody else's to come and live with them?"

"You never know!"

As he set off with another magazine Crystal had a sudden image of the house being descended on by pitchfork wielding locals because a cat had gone missing and they'd acquired a reputation for enticing them away from their loving owners. When Adam returned she said, "I expect it is their cat. I just meant you can't rely on circumstantial evidence or let your imagination run away with you."

"What's circlestantial?"

"Circumstantial. It's like… suppose I had 50p which went missing and I saw you with 50p. I might think you'd stolen it because the circumstances looked that way, but really it was your 50p and I'd just dropped mine."

He looked thoughtful and then nodded.

"Can you think of one?"

It took him three deliveries to come up with an answer. "When my dad parked at the supermarket someone dented his car a little bit. That's because they're a very rude word I'm supposed to forget he said, and can't park for toffee. A lady said it was a white Audi and Dad said it would be." He scampered off with a magazine and was soon back. "Next time we went we saw a white Audi with a little dent and I thought it must be the same one, but Dad said it probably wasn't because Audis are really common and all their drivers are wanglers. Do you know what a wangler is?"

Presumably the first word Adam's dad could think of which started in the same way as the word he'd begun to say and thought better of uttering in front of his son. "No."

"It means people who get themselves out of trouble. I think it was the car which dented Dad's, but the man would have said it was circ… cir…"

"Circumstantial."

"Yes, and Dad just thought that because lots of people have the same car."

"I expect you're right."

Adam had delivered magazines to all the houses on that side of the road, so they carefully checked both ways to be sure no white Audis or other vehicles were coming, and crossed over.

Adam was excited to find a cigarette end outside one house on the way back. Crystal told him that if he were to pick up a clue he'd need to be very careful not to destroy evidence.

"Like fingerprints, I remember from when you came to school!"

"It's good to remember things." She gave him a tissue and he, very carefully, picked up the cigarette end.

"Is everything OK?" asked a young, very tall woman. She looked like the 'after' photos of an expensive health and beauty treatment. To avoid staring, Crystal focussed her attention on the incredibly cute toddler, presumably her son, in his pushchair.

The kid had the same afro hair as his mum, but in his case it was cut short. Hers was braided into those long intricate plaits which must take ages to get looking so perfect. Even in the cheap looking floral t-shirt and lime green shorts, she looked like a catwalk model.

"We're looking for clues," Adam said, giving their names and explaining Crystal was a police officer and one day he was going to be a detective.

"Pleased to meet you both. This little one is my son Teddy."

Crystal couldn't resist crouching down to say hello to the little boy and was rewarded by a big grin and wave.

"And I'm Beth."

That brought Crystal rapidly to her feet again. Was this the same Beth who'd worked for a short time in Paula's Posies? She matched the description given at the florist's and the chances of there being two Beths in Little Mallow who looked that stunning and had sons called Teddy was extremely unlikely.

"Do you think that really is a clue?" Beth asked.

"If the murderer lives in this house it might be," Adam said.

"I live here. I don't smoke, but I do have something to confess."

"What is it?" Adam asked eagerly.

Crystal would have stopped him asking, or Beth replying, if she'd been able to make a sound, but not even air made it out her mouth.

"I was at the fancy dress party…"

Chapter 26

Friday 5th June

"Did you see the murder?" Adam asked.

Crystal shook her head frantically hoping Beth wouldn't say anything incriminating in front of him – or her for that matter.

Beth shook her own head, though far less emphatically than Crystal had. "I didn't stay long."

"But you're letting the police know because we've asked people to do that?" Crystal said.

"That's right, yes."

"Adam, can you deliver the magazines to the last three houses and then tell my aunty we're nearly finished and I'm going to have a quick word with Beth and will be there in just a minute, please?" It seemed a really good idea to get Adam out the way, just in case Beth really did have something related to the crime to confess, and Crystal couldn't stop her. Anything the boy said would very likely come under the heading of leading the witness.

"OK," Adam said, taking the small pile of magazines from Crystal. "This one is for you."

"Thank you," Beth said, then asked Crystal to follow her into the house. "Teddy will get fretful if I don't let him out."

"I just need to take your full name and the times you arrived and left." Please don't tell me anything else.

The attempt at telepathy didn't work, as Beth pushed her son up the path saying, "It's not quite that simple. You

230

see, I used to work at Paula's Posies and left under a bit of a shadow." She let herself into the house, leaving Crystal to follow her into the living room.

Weirdly Crystal was less bothered about following a possible murderer into her home than about DI Shortfellow's reaction. Or perhaps it wasn't weird, as Crystal was certain Beth meant her no harm, and in any case she wouldn't be accepting anything to drink. On the other hand, the DI would definitely be angry if Crystal messed up. However unlikely it seemed that Beth could have killed her former boss, she'd said she had something to confess. Crystal couldn't take the risk she'd say something important, which was inadmissible as evidence because of a procedural error. She began to recite the official caution. She got as far as, "You do not have to..."

"Say anything unless I wish to do so?" Beth interrupted, and gave a brief flash of a smile, then unclipped her son, lifted him from the pushchair and sat him on the floor with a picture book.

The child circled the room slowly, holding furniture for support and occasionally stopping to turn a page. He chattered happily the whole while, as though sharing the story with the stuffed toys which littered the otherwise spotless floor.

"Well, yes. Sorry, but if there's anything you want to tell me, I have to do this first." Crystal started again and completed the entire caution. Although Beth's gaze hardly left her son, Crystal was confident she'd heard and understood.

"I realise it looks bad, me not phoning up straight away, but as you've got a kid I think you'll understand. When I heard what happened and that the police wanted to hear from anyone who was there, I was pretty sure that when you knew I'd worked for Paula you'd want me to come in and give a statement."

"That really would be best," Crystal said.

"Thing is, it's so difficult with Teddy. Getting the buggy on the bus, and he makes a real racket if he gets bored. It will be a lot easier if I can just tell you now you're here."

"OK then. Your full name is...?" Her plan was to ask for the barest details, thank Beth for her help, and get out of there.

"Bethany Louisa Phillips."

"And this is your address?"

"Yes. The house belongs to Mr and Mrs Taylor, Carol and Ken. I rent one room, but they let me share this and the kitchen too."

"And you went to the party yesterday evening?"

"When I showed the Taylor's the invitation they offered to keep an eye on Teddy if I wanted to go. They don't usually babysit. I know they'd help in an emergency, but I don't like to ask. I don't go out much socially. I'd rather be home with Teddy. I'd do anything for him, but people tell me I'll be a better mother if I have a bit of a life of my own." She took a step towards Teddy as he wobbled, then relaxed as he sat down and continued his pretend storytelling. "With it being free and so close, it seemed too good a chance to miss."

Crystal could understand that. "What time did you get there?"

"Maybe eight? I made sure Teddy was fast asleep before I got dressed. Ken lent me the ghost costume he wears for when kids come trick or treating. It's really just a huge sheet with eye holes cut in, which covered me completely. It was far too hot, and I couldn't eat or drink in it, so I took it off quite soon and was just wearing what I am now."

There were a lot of questions Crystal wanted answers to, but she'd have to wait until CID had asked them and hope DI Shortfellow would pass on the replies. "What time did you leave?"

"I got back at ten exactly. I remember because Carol joked about just making curfew. I'm sure she'll remember. I didn't hear about Paula until this morning."

"Great. Thank you. That's all very clear. Thanks for your help." She began moving towards the door.

"I'm really sorry about Paula. She was lovely. Very understanding about Teddy. Once I got a call from the nursery to say he'd had a fall and was upset and she told me to leave everything and go check on him. She'd been going to lunch, but stayed to serve until I got back."

"She does seem to have been nice."

"Muuuum," Teddy said, and tugged at Beth's shorts, making Crystal think she could escape.

"Well, thanks again, I'll leave you to..." But Beth picked up her son and carried him towards the door, then stopped. Crystal couldn't leave without pushing past.

"I have to tell you something."

Please don't!

"I said I left under a shadow. I was accused of making mistakes and stealing. I didn't do it... Not any of the things he said I did and I didn't steal anything."

"OK."

"I couldn't let the others think that of me, not when they'd been so nice, so I tried to defend myself. Maybe I shouldn't have, but I pointed out Michael sometimes served and messed about on the computer and it was him who usually sorted out the change."

"You thought he'd been stealing?"

"No, no. Maybe he thought that's what I meant 'cause he got really angry, but I was just thinking that as he rarely did those things he was as likely to make a mistake as me. Then one day when Paula came back from talking to a potential new client he suddenly said he'd caught me taking money from the till. It was the first I'd heard of it and rubbish, but of course nobody would believe somebody like me over him."

"Someone like you?"

"Single mother, very short of money and new in the job, versus the boss's husband."

"Ah, right. Difficult for you."

"I don't blame Paula, but him… Is it right he was poisoned too?'

"He was. He didn't drink much from his glass and is recovering." That wasn't a secret.

"If he'd drunk it all, would he have died?"

"Probably."

"I think he must have been the real target, not Paula. I don't know what he had against me. He's not racist, or if he is he hid it really well the first few weeks, but then he seemed to turn on me and blamed me for everything. I think he's got a nasty streak, so maybe he upset someone who wasn't going to put up with it?"

"That's certainly a possibility that we'll look into. I'll pass all this on. Don't be alarmed if CID ask for a statement. I'll let them know about Teddy, so his needs can be accommodated."

"Thank you. You've been brilliant. Sorry to keep you from your little boy."

Crystal was going to tell DI Shortfellow that Beth had both a motive and opportunity to kill Michael Roth. She wasn't also going to lie by omission. "No problem and actually Adam's not mine, just a friend."

When Crystal updated the DI she mentioned Beth's theory that it was Michael Roth, not Paula, who was the intended target. Predictably he said that was an angle they were looking into.

When Crystal and Trevor checked the computer as they came on shift that afternoon they found a routine enquiry request for them from CID. A Mr Khan who had a sub post office in his shop had sold a large quantity of stamps to a man wearing lime green gloves in early May and had the transaction on CCTV. They were to review it and take it to DI Shortfellow in the EPIC building in Portsmouth.

"I suppose that's number one priority, boss?" Trevor said.

"We don't know what time they close, so… "

"He's still open when I pop in for chocolate after a late shift." Trevor grinned. "Come on, lass. Fire up the Quattro!"

"Do what?"

"Oh sorry, I've been watching Ashes To Ashes on iPlayer."

"What's that?"

"Seriously?"

"I've never heard of it."

"It's like a streaming service for things…"

"Not that! Ashes To Ashes."

"Gene Hunt, Shaz Granger, Alex Drake, the creepy clown…"

"Like I said, never heard of it."

"Skip!"

"What's up?" asked Sergeant Freedman who happened to be passing.

"I've utterly failed in my role as mentor and tutor. The lass here is totally uninformed. Can you believe she's never heard of Ashes to Ashes?"

Imani Freedman gave Trevor a look. "Neither have I. I'm far too young, obviously. Anyway, Life On Mars was heaps better."

"Good points, well made," Trevor agreed.

"What are you two on about?"

Sergeant Freedman shook her head in a despairing manner. "You'd better find out, Student Officer Clere, or that SOLAP of yours is never going to be signed off." Then, giving Trevor another look, added, "Far, far too young."

When Crystal and Trevor introduced themselves to Mr Khan he explained that hearing the police were interested in speaking to a man who'd gone to the party wearing the striped trousers and lime green gloves reminded him of the incident.

"It was odd. He asked for seventy second class stamps, which is unusual. Most people who want a lot get books or a whole sheet, but he wanted exactly seventy. Then he paid in cash. It's over fifty pounds, so that was unusual too."

"And the gloves?" Crystal prompted.

"It was cold so I didn't think much of that, except I noticed the colour because I'd not long done some painting at home in that shade and got some on my hands. I was thinking I should have worn a pair. I'd pretty much forgotten about it until I heard about the death on the news and mentioned it to my daughter. She said you want to hear from the person who organised the party."

"We do, yes."

"When I said I'd give the man in gloves a receipt, so he could claim the money back, he just said 'no thank you' so it wasn't a business expense. They could have been for all sorts of things, but now I'm wondering if they could have been for party invitations."

"I think we'd better have a look at the footage."

"Come through. It's not very good I'm afraid. If it was I wouldn't still have it. We replaced the camera not long after it was recorded because of the poor quality and the new system records digitally, not on tape. I hadn't got round to disposing of the old set up. I can't just put something in the bin if it might be useful to someone." As he spoke, he'd switched on the playback device, which he'd previously paused at the relevant time and day.

"There's no audio, and it's black and white." Mr Khan said and clicked 'play'.

They watched a tall, slim man, wearing a dark baseball cap come in, walk up to the counter and request the stamps. He matched the description Mr Roth had given of the man he claimed had given him the poisoned glasses of wine. He also looked a lot like Mr Roth himself.

During the transaction he kept his head down and stood at right angles to the shop counter, partially leaning against it. Whether that was a deliberate attempt not to show his face to the camera was hard to say.

"You recognise him," Mr Khan said.

"I can't comment on that."

"You don't need to. I've had enough parents in here watching their darling children shoplift to know the answer. I suppose that if he's your man I'll see it on the news and be able to tell my wife I was right to hang on to this instead of making room for more stock."

"If he's our man you'll most definitely have been right and have found someone this is useful to."

"Take the whole lot, so you can play it back."

"Thank you. I'm afraid you might also be asked to give a formal statement, perhaps even appear as a witness in court."

He nodded. "I can't help the poor lady, but I'll do what I can to see her killer doesn't escape justice."

On their way to the CID HQ in Portsmouth, Crystal wondered if she thought it was Michael Roth on the tape because she'd disliked him after talking to Beth.

"Trevs, I change my mind with every fresh piece of evidence. Is that the same as keeping an open mind?"

"I reckon so. Not changing it in the face of new evidence would be the opposite, wouldn't it?"

"What do I tell the DI?"

"Everything." Then when they got into DI Shortfellow's office he said, "Boss, Crystal here has found out a few things and come to some possible conclusions. I think you'll agree she should tell you everything, no matter how trivial or apparently contradictory?"

"Absolutely. You tell me and I'll decide what action, if any, to take." As he'd been guilty of not keeping Trevor fully informed in the past, there wasn't really anything else he could have said.

As Trevor set up the device to show the CCTV footage, Crystal gave the DI every detail she could recall, including her belief the man on the recording could be Michael Roth. That she'd believed Beth but admitted if Michael Roth had her unfairly sacked that was a motive for revenge against him. "She claims to have left the party before ten and to have witnesses… actually I don't know what time Roth was given the poison, if he was."

"About ten."

"Ah."

"Does that seem unlikely?" DI Shortfellow asked.

"No, it's just that I'd thought the timings would put Beth in the clear. And I admit I was hoping they would."

"Sometimes those we'd like to be proven innocent aren't, and vice versa."

Crystal nodded. "Like the burglar who smashed his way into properties and may have had a connection with Mr Argent, as he owned a dog? He caused distress to a lot of people – I'd like him to go down for a good long stretch, but I assume you haven't found anything to link him to that murder?" She was sure she'd have been told.

"No, nothing. The man, Ashley Johnson, denies it. He also denied having stolen the jewellery he was caught carrying home in the early hours of the morning and claimed to have no knowledge of the other stolen items in his home, so it's not surprising he won't admit to having the means or a motive for murder."

"If Mr Argent had gone into Johnson's house, is it likely he'd have realised it contained stolen items?"

"I'd say so. I have no trouble believing Johnson would take violent action to ensure he kept quiet in that case, but I can't believe he'd have the intelligence or patience to trick his victim into thinking he'd won the glass which held poison. He's a thug without an ounce of charm and looks the part. If the paper printed his photo they'd have to pixilate part of it as he has a swear word tattooed on his forehead."

"Classy." Crystal's respect for the officers who'd arrested him went up a notch. Burglar and police literally walking into each other had sounded comical, but in reality it must have been quite scary.

"I can't imagine he and Mr Argent becoming friends."

Crystal agreed. "Or his neighbour, Mrs Owen, failing to mention if she'd seen someone like that visit the old man."

Chapter 27

Friday 6th June

DI Shortfellow called some of the other detectives into his office in Portsmouth CID Headquarters and introduced them. "I think you all know Trevor Harris. He's tutor to student officer Clere, who will be joining us in the autumn." This was met with friendly greetings.

Trevor played Mr Khan's footage for everyone. It was generally agreed the person shown could be Michael Roth, and that given the timings involved, number of stamps bought and the lime gloves, even if it wasn't him it might well be someone connected with the party.

"Shall I ask him about it, sir?" DS Kirk offered.

"Don't mention the footage," DI Shortfellow said. "Just that a shopkeeper recalls a man matching his description buying a lot of stamps in mid-May."

"Righto." He and the rest of his colleagues left the DI's office.

"Sir, I've just thought of another shop owner who could be helpful. Trevor and I have dealt with underage drinkers in local parks. They all get their alcohol from Gould's off licence in Gosport and if we and the kids know the owner isn't on the side of the law, others probably do and it might seem a good place to buy vape refills if you don't want to risk the shopkeeper reporting you to the police."

"Possibly, but it doesn't sound as though the owner will be co-operative."

"He might be now, boss." Trevor told DI Shortfellow of the action being taken against the shopkeeper and the possibility he was looking at a prison sentence."

"You're right, that might make him decide to be helpful." The DI made a note.

"Sir, can you remind me, what did Michael Roth say about the assistant Beth?" Crystal asked.

"That although she'd been sacked, he didn't think it was likely she killed his wife."

"Then why would he mention it?" She was asking herself as much as the DI and Trevor. Perhaps they realised as neither responded.

"Could he have been trying to plant the opposite idea, sir?"

"Possibly."

"He didn't like Beth, according to her. Maybe, because of that, he wants to incriminate her. Or if he really believed she was stealing maybe that's made him suspicious of her. Losing a part time job doesn't seem a strong motive for murder. Besides which, we don't know it was Paula who was the intended victim. Unless the killer was Roth himself, doesn't it seem just as likely he was the one being targeted or, maybe even more likely, both of them?"

"It does," the DI said.

"OK, obviously you're considering all that. He said he saw Beth at the party?"

"He thought he did, wasn't sure."

"That's total boll… bollards. Being tall and absolutely stunning she's very hard to miss, and she's black. You were there, how many black people did you see?"

"None that I recall. Most people were in disguise though."

"Beth's only disguise was a sheet over her head and whole body. When she had it on, no part of her would have been visible at all. She took it off pretty soon, and was then wearing a t-shirt and shorts. She has to be six foot tall. People either saw her or they didn't – nobody got only a glimpse."

"He might just have seen an arm and, as he'd recognised a lot of people connected with Paula's Posies, thought it could be her."

"Ah, yeah. You're right about the arm, sir. If he saw any part of her except her face his comment makes sense. But why would he recognise a lot of people? Other than Beth, none of the staff were invited, nor any of the customers I spoke to."

"What about yourself?" the DI asked.

"Case in point, sir. I went in exactly once prior to yesterday. I paid in cash and didn't give my name or address, so whatever the reason for me being on the guest list, it wasn't that I'm a customer."

"Yet you're reasonably confident in your identification of Michael Roth?"

"I'm reasonably confident it could be rather than it is, if you see what I mean?"

The DI grinned. "Worryingly, I think I do."

Crystal ignored Trevor trying to pretend he was trying not to laugh. "Mr Roth wasn't in Paula's Posies the one time I went in, but I've seen the Roth's about a few times and they both came on the day half the village helped do the gardens at the hall."

"Interesting. They'd have known that outside area existed then?"

"Definitely."

There was a tap on the open doorframe and the sergeant walked in. "Roth says it can't have been him, sir. He'd have no reason to buy a large number of stamps. I said we're trying to work out who was behind the party. He's taking it as proof the killer sent the invites and is checking to see where he was that day."

"Thanks, Captain," The DI said.

"Excuse me, Sergeant Kirk," Crystal called after the departing man.

"Yeah?"

"Did you tell him the precise date?" Crystal asked.

"Only after he asked for it."

"Right. Of course, sorry."

"No worries. Sir'll tell you, it's better to ask than die wondering."

When he'd gone Crystal said, "Sir, everyone in Little Mallow knows about the seating area behind the hall, I should think. Far fewer would know about the outside light."

"I agree," Trevor said. "Just walking by in daylight it's clear there's a path which goes down the side and there are places you can peer through the railings and plants to see part of the garden. Even though I knew about the light I couldn't see it and I wouldn't have expected an outside switch for it."

DI Shortfellow nodded. "Mr Roth stated many of the party guests have a connection to his wife, not family or close friends but people who knew her personally such as a mobile beautician, two members of her book group, the dentist they both used. There were also customers, suppliers, and some business rivals of the florist shop. That's been borne out by those we've so far interviewed. Most attendees were local, so it's not surprising some knew her, but I think it's too many to be coincidence."

"So, I was right, sir? The party was arranged to allow the murder to happen."

"That now seems most likely."

"And one, or both of the Roths were targeted deliberately, rather than it being a random killing?"

"Again yes, that's our current theory."

"Why did you ask who knew about the outside garden if they were given the drinks inside?" Trevor asked. A good question which Crystal kicked herself for not having thought of.

The DI glanced at his notes. "Mr Roth states that someone in a hallowe'en costume mentioned how nice it smelled out there which prompted Paula to want to look at the plants she'd donated to see how they were doing. He surmises they were somewhat steered out there, so it would take longer for them to get help once they'd drunk the wine."

"Possible. There were a lot of hallowe'en type costumes and they were just about the only ones who went out there until someone screamed. Do you know who that was?"

"No, but not Paula. The autopsy confirms cause of death as the nicotine. The doctor was surprised it acted so quickly – if it did indeed act as quickly as Mr Roth initially stated. He now thinks he was so upset he may have blacked out and not immediately sought help."

"Maybe it was him who screamed?" Trevor suggested. "People don't always realise they're doing it."

"Could it have been a man, Crystal?" the DI asked.

"Maybe. I didn't think of who, but why and where, and I guess most screams are high pitched. Sorry."

"That's OK. Better to be unsure than positive and wrong."

"I expect I've been wrong about some things, sir."

The DI gave another brief example of his distinctive laugh. "We do know others went into the garden as we found two glasses under a bench. We know they're not the ones the victim and Michael Roth drank from as you gave those to the ambulance crew."

Crystal took a deep breath. "I did, sir, because I hoped analysis of the contents could help Paula. But, in case it might be helpful to know how they'd been positioned, I put some others in their place. Sorry, I forgot to tell SOCO, sir."

"I'll let them know." He didn't look pleased, but neither did he seem furious, that she'd repeated his mistake of not keeping another department fully informed.

Crystal had been under some stress and had a lot on her mind. The same would have been true of the DI as he geared up for a drugs bust. Maybe she'd cost CID a little time trying to trace the non-existent couple who'd drunk from the glasses she'd placed under that bench, but the case wasn't likely to collapse because of it. As she might not be so lucky next time, it would be a really good idea not to repeat that mistake.

Chapter 28

Saturday 6th June

The bus was a slightly late leaving Little Mallow. As that was frequently the case, Arnold had allowed plenty of time. Even so, when he arrived at The Knitted Tea Cosy, Cameron was already waiting outside.

"Thank you for agreeing to see me today," Arnold said.

"My pleasure, I assure you. I was delighted you contacted me so soon."

"I wanted to explain that I gave your name to the police when I was asked who attended the party."

"And you're warning me so I have time to skip and run before they ask difficult questions?"

"No! I told them we were talking when that person screamed. They know you can't have been outside killing anyone."

"That's no help, my dear chap. Nobody was outside killing anyone, the damage was done inside by the handing over of a poisoned chalice. I could easily have done that and then approached you to establish an alibi."

"It wasn't you, I know it wasn't. Besides you don't fit the description."

"The guilty party was slim I understand," Cameron said with a smile.

"I didn't mean… Oh. You're teasing me."

"I apologise. For that, and not having the slightest qualm in giving CID your name during my own interview."

"I'm sure you realised they were bound to know that already," Arnold said.

"That was my assumption, yes. It was gratifying to hear you speak so warmly in my defence, even if I was mistaken about your eagerness to see me again."

"Sorry if I made it seem like an emergency. I'm not at my best when telephoning people." If they were to be friends it made sense to warn Cameron of that. It would also be a good idea to let Cameron know he did want to be friends. One reason Arnold had so few was that he was always too worried about rejection to make the first move. Although he supposed Cameron had done that by giving Arnold his card. "Maybe it's a good thing that after the interview with DI Shortfellow I felt the need to contact you without delay. If that hadn't been the case I'd probably have put it off until it seemed too late and never called at all."

Cameron smiled. "St Symeon's has some rather beautiful stained glass I understand."

"Yes it does. One piece is medieval. Are you interested in ecclesiastical glass?"

"It's a very recent interest. It started at the exact moment you told me your job. Had you not telephoned me before next Sunday it would have developed sufficiently that I'd have felt compelled to come to church and take a look."

"Oh." Arnold wasn't at all sure how he'd have responded to that.

"Shall we go in?" Cameron gestured to the door.

"I've just cleared that one, if you want a table," said a cheerful looking middle-aged waitress.

They agreed to have a pot of tea, so they could see if it came with a knitted cosy. Arnold was surprised Cameron ordered Earl Grey, but he did like the way he rolled his Rs as he did so. They also requested scones for Cameron and caramel shortbread for Arnold.

"Perhaps it should have been the other way round?" Arnold said into the lull in conversation after the waitress departed.

Cameron raised an enquiring eyebrow.

"Shortbread being Scottish and scones being English."

"I understand the shortbread, but what makes a Sassenach feel proprietary about scones?"

This time Arnold realised Cameron wasn't being entirely serious and tried to play along. "Cream teas are very much an English tradition, at least they are in the West Country."

Cameron ham acted astounded horror. "Scones aren't banished to a far flung corner in Scotland. Throughout the entire country we treat them with the reverence something derived from our heritage of the noble bannock deserves."

"My apologies. Perhaps you will accept a small gift as recompense for my hurtful misunderstanding." Oh dear, now he wasn't just joining in the banter, but mimicking Cameron's slightly affected manner. As a child he'd tried to behave like the other boys so he'd be liked. It hadn't been very successful then, and wasn't a good idea now.

"Perhaps."

"I have something for you. Don't open it yet." He didn't want Cameron to have to fake enthusiasm if he didn't like it.

The waitress returned with a laden tray just as Arnold slid a small jewellery box across the table to Cameron. "Oh, sorry, I… "

"That looks super, thank you," Cameron said, moving the box aside, and helping to unload the tray. "Oh, that tea cosy is just too sweet."

"Yeah, but I dunno who it's supposed to be," the waitress said, then departed with the empty tray.

Arnold admired the cosy. It was knitted, as he'd expected, and resembled a sweet old lady, knitting a tiny tea cosy. She had rosy cheeks, her beady eyes twinkled behind knitted glasses, and a chain of knitted daisies was fastened around her neck. "A lot of work has gone into that and it's very well done. Charming too."

"Isn't it?" Cameron agreed. "From the name I guessed there would be knitted tea cosies, the owners would have little choice, but hadn't expected anything of this quality."

As they poured tea and took the first delicious bite, Arnold explained he'd met the owners of the tea rooms the same evening he'd met Cameron, and learned that Mr Holbrook knitted the cosies to make their establishment memorable.

"He's succeeded. I'm eager to return to see some more."

"I understand he has some on sale."

"I wonder if he'd make them to order? They could make fun gifts. Talking of which… My curiosity is getting the better of me." He opened the box Arnold had given him. It contained a silver version of the double arrow symbol used on maps to indicate railway stations, formed into a lapel badge. Cameron didn't take it out of the box or say a word.

Arnold had made a mistake giving this sophisticated man a piece of cheap costume jewellery. He'd been thinking of Cameron when he'd finished another piece in the same material the previous evening and thought the shape might work well. It was an easily identified design and, once he'd sketched a template to follow, very easy to do. He should have left it at home.

"You made this?"

Arnold nodded.

"For me? For my station master's uniform?"

"Yes. It… I just…"

"That's incredibly kind." He took it from the box and laid it on his palm as though it were a rare and delicate treasure.

Deciding against saying he'd created it from what was practically scrap in just a few hours, Arnold took another bite of his indulgent shortbread.

"You'll have to come to see me wearing it as I oversee operations at Pollock station. Do say you will."

"I'd like that," Arnold admitted.

"Tomorrow? We could have lunch somewhere afterwards."

"I'll be at church."

"Of course. And I'm away in the week. Next Saturday at this time?"

"Saturday is fine, but if we meet elsewhere I'll need to check the buses for the time."

"You don't drive?"

"No. Never."

"I'll come and pick you up then."

"No, no." He couldn't have said why, but the idea alarmed Arnold. "There's no need. I enjoy travelling by bus."

"If you're sure. We can meet here again if it's easier?"

"It would be, yes." The card given to Arnold at the ill-fated party showed Cameron's address and it didn't appear any bus routes travelled that road. There would be a stop fairly close, but it would be easier to find that from Cameron's home than to find his new friends house from what might not be the closest stop.

"Be honest, was it the lure of the fabulous knitted cosies which made you choose to meet here, or simply the proximity of the bus stop?"

"It was a mix of both those things, and the fact I'd heard this café could possibly be a motive for the murder."

"How thrilling. Do tell."

"I heard the ladies who arrange the church flowers discussing the crime. The police officer who was present on Wednesday evening lives with one of them, so they're quite well informed."

"Naturally they would be."

"The ladies said several cafés in Gosport, including this one, have a regular order for flowers from Paula's Posies. The florist who'd helped Paula Roth start up her business has her own shop in Gosport and was apparently none too pleased Paula had snatched away her clients."

"Betrayal like that? She'd have been livid!"

"I don't know if it's actually true," Arnold pointed out. "Facts can get distorted when stories are repeated."

"Yes indeed."

"Is everything OK?" the waitress asked, although she was looking at the jewellery box Arnold had given Cameron, not at either of the two men.

"Very nice, thank you. We were just admiring these flowers," Cameron said of the stem of perfectly ordinary carnations which graced their table. "Do you know where they came from?"

"Did you hear about the woman who was killed by poison champagne at her own birthday party up in Little Mallow?"

"We did… Oh! She was a florist, so these were from her shop?"

"Paula's Posies, that's right. Poor woman. I met her once and she was ever so nice."

"So sad. What will you do for flowers now?"

"I dunno. I hadn't heard the shop was closing, but if it does I suppose we'll go back to getting them from where we did before."

"Which was…?"

"Dunno, sorry."

"That's probably not going to be of much help to DI Shortfellow, is it?" Cameron remarked when the waitress moved on to another table.

"Dunno," Arnold couldn't resist saying.

Cameron smiled and shook his head in mock exasperation. "I don't recall the champagne, do you?"

"No, and I happen to know Paula Roth's birthday was the twelfth of October. It's St Symeon's Day and extraordinarily also the birthday of Reverend Jerry Grande."

"Your vicar?"

Arnold nodded.

"Did he choose the church because of the coincidence do you think?"

"He says it's because of that coincidence he became a vicar. He learned about it at an impressionable age and it made him feel a connection with the church – both the building and in the wider sense."

Cameron insisted on paying as Arnold had the expense of the journey, and had given him the delightful gift.

As they were leaving, Muriel Grahame was coming in. "Oh, hello, verger."

"Hello, Miss Grahame. We've been blessed with another glorious day," Arnold said, and again felt he was mimicking Cameron. At least he hadn't developed a Scottish burr.

"Yes, indeed. I don't usually buy refreshments away from home, but the heat has made me unusually thirsty."

Arnold felt no compulsion to justify his own presence, but neither did he wish to appear mysterious and invite undue speculation. "Allow me to introduce Cameron Pollock. Cameron, this is Miss Muriel Grahame, a very valuable member of the church flower arranging team and the baker of exceptional coffee and walnut cakes."

Cameron and Muriel looked pleased as they exchanged 'how do you do' and 'nice to meet you'.

On the bus back to Little Mallow, Arnold decided not to test his embryonic phone skills, so instead of staying on until he reached the end of his road, he alighted at the stop nearest the vicarage. He was in luck, Jerry was at home.

"Good timing, as I was about to put the kettle on. I've been writing my sermon for tomorrow, in the hope of providing some comfort in light of recent events."

Arnold followed him into the kitchen. "I'd like to change my reading to Romans eight, twenty-eight to thirty nine, if you think that's suitable." He knew reverend Grande had decided against that week's planned reading which, in the circumstances, felt inappropriate.

"Perfect, yes," the vicar said. "That talks of God's unchangeable love in even the worst of circumstances, and chimes perfectly with what I have planned. I shall read psalm ninety-one and two. That emphasises the brevity and changeable nature of our lives. But God does not change, nor does his love which is endless."

"Were you able to comfort Michael Roth?" Arnold asked.

"Sadly no. He's not a man of faith and wouldn't see me."

"Even so, he will know you care and he has somewhere to turn should he wish it. Before I became a Christian the local minister tried to help me with something. I wasn't ready. Too hurt, too angry, but it made a small difference just to know she was there if I needed her. Eventually that led to me understanding that God too was there."

"Thank you, Arnold. That's a good thought."

Jerry cut two slices of Mary Milligan's lemon drizzle before Arnold could say he'd already had something to eat.

Oh well, it was hardly one of his five a day, but he could count it as lunch. He took a bite, enjoying the tangy syrup, before saying, "Would you mind checking if the midsummer event at the new hall can still go ahead? I think the request would be better coming from you."

"I'll be happy to make the call. On Monday, if it can wait until then?"

Arnold nodded. "If the event can still happen, do you think it would be a good idea to make more of it?"

"In what way?" the vicar asked.

"I thought perhaps the blessing and opening ceremony could take the same form as we'd planned, but that we could invite the whole village rather than just the committee and supporters. There would be room for everyone in the gardens. Then we could continue into the afternoon. Make it a community event with barbecues set up, everyone bringing food to cook outside and fun activities for the children."

"Is that feasible with the funds and time available?"

"It should cost very little and won't need much time to organise. More importantly, it would take away the association of the garden with death and darkness by filling it with life for the midsummer afternoon."

"The exact opposite of what happened before?"

"That's right, yes. We invited the local press for what we'd originally planned. I don't know if they'd have come, but I'm sure they will now. I'd like them to have something positive to report."

"And me. I don't know how much sway it will hold with the press, but for Little Mallow I think it's a wonderful idea, Arnold. Really wonderful."

The vicar had showed gratitude for Arnold's work quite frequently, but never for his ideas – perhaps because he'd volunteered very few. He didn't know how to respond except with practicalities. "For the food, I was thinking we could pin up slips of paper in the church listing things such as sausages, bread rolls, salad, soft drinks, and people could remove one corresponding to what they intend to bring. That might discourage everyone bringing the same things and encourage sharing."

"Another very good idea. Are you happy to see to all this and able to find the time? I'm aware what you do already vastly exceeds the hours you're paid for."

"There are people I'm sure will help with certain aspects, and I can manage the rest. I want to put the last event, and my part in making it happen, behind me."

"I feel that way too. What happened is not our fault. The killer must have had evil in their heart for a long time. If the mystery party hadn't happened they'd have done it some other place and time. I sincerely believe that, yet still I feel some guilt. Shall we pray?"

The moment Arnold echoed Jerry's amen, the vicar's telephone rang. "Excuse me," he said and left the kitchen. It was his practice to always try to answer calls without being overheard, in case the caller wished to speak in confidence.

Arnold busied himself washing the cups and plates they'd used.

Jerry was soon back. "Not an answer to our prayers, but an answer none the less. That was DI Shortfellow. He'd like to attend tomorrow's service, and now he's aware of it, for either himself or one of his team to come to the midsummer opening event too. He said to put him down for a pack of burgers and tub of coleslaw."

Chapter 29

Monday 8th June

When Crystal and Jason tried to arrange a third date, the first evening they both had free was the twelfth of June, the evening Ellie had invited them and Mike to share a meal at her house. That was too long to wait, so Crystal called at his flat after an early shift to give them the chance to share lunch before he went off on another job.

He'd given her an enthusiastic hug when she arrived. "It really is good to see you, but I'm running horribly late. I meant to go and get us something nice to eat once I'd packed up my stuff, but... " He indicated cameras, lenses and other photographic equipment on his table and the floor.

"I'll go get us something, no problem. What do you fancy?"

"Anything, honestly. There's salad in the fridge so you don't need to get that."

"Salad? You?"

He shrugged. "I've got this gorgeous new girlfriend. She's a cop and well fit, so I thought I should make an effort."

"Quite right too." She hadn't thought he was fobbing her off by saying he was busy, but it was good to have it confirmed. She checked the fridge. Jason had four salad items, but only if bacon counted. There were other vegetables, fruit juice and kefir. He definitely was making an effort.

"Do you have bread?" she called. "I could make us a BLT."

"That'd be great. Use whatever you need. I don't keep any of my dodgy secret stuff in the kitchen."

She made the food and carried it to the almost clear table, where he was applying what looked like a small bomb to the inside of a camera. "You know you could just pack that stuff away, you don't have to blow it up."

"Yeah I do." He aimed the device at Crystal and released a gentle puff of air into her face. "It's for cleaning the sensor. All done now." He attached a cover to the front of the camera and put it with the other stuff on the floor. A lot of it was now packed into a sturdy looking case.

"Have you arrested your murderer yet?" Jason asked as they ate.

"Not quite. We're still not sure about the motive." At least she wasn't. DI Shortfellow had shared a great deal of information with her, but even if he wasn't holding anything back, she was out walking the beat most of the time, not in EPIC where she'd hear every detail as it was uncovered.

"Do you need to be positive about that to arrest him?"

"Not if we know who did it and have evidence."

"You saw him on CCTV."

"I saw someone who looked like the victim's husband. I really did think it was, that he was guilty, and that a jury would agree, until I learned he had an alibi. He was delivering flowers in Warsash about that time."

"So he says."

"He does and the computer records show there were three deliveries in that area, plus he got a parking ticket

259

for pretty much blocking a junction with Osborne Road while he was looking for one of the addresses."

Jason ate a big bite of sandwich before saying, "It's only, what five miles away? He could have bought the stamps on the way there, or the way back."

"The timings don't fit for that and it's further than you think – almost ten miles each way. I tried it myself and it's over twenty minutes just to get there."

"Shame. I was thinking… He bought seventy stamps?"

"Yeah. The same number of people Martin Blackman was asked to cater for, which is why we think it's likely to be connected. Well that and the description."

"I came as your plus one."

"Yeah. Oh. He didn't really order enough food for everyone who was invited. Still, it was short notice and not everyone likes fancy dress. Maybe he thought half of them wouldn't come?"

"If the stamp buyer really was the party planner."

"There's the lime gloves and striped trousers, remember."

"OK, stamp guy is the murderer, but he's not Roth. You wanted it to be him, didn't you?"

"I admit I liked the idea of my ID being important in solving the case, but what's more important is bringing the right person to justice."

"Was she definitely the target, do you think? I know it was her who died, but…"

Crystal nodded. "The killer could have been after her husband or just a random nutter? Yeah, I do think they meant her to die, but it isn't definite. Some party guests have a connection to either Paula Roth or her shop.

Enough to seem like there's a reason for that, but not enough that it's impossible for it just to be coincidence."

"Would people necessarily know they had a connection?"

"Paula's Posies has only been going for about a year, so I think any suppliers or customers would be likely to remember, when they heard she was killed."

"Yeah, if they went in and spoke to her, but would they remember getting a delivery?"

"Good point. I remember the times I've been sent flowers." Then, in case he thought she didn't get many or that she wouldn't welcome more, added. "Recently that is. I got a huge bouquet at Valentine's and I only thought about who might have ordered them, not which shop they were from."

"Paula's Posies in Little Mallow."

There was only one way he'd know that. "Thank you, they were lovely."

"You're welcome."

Ignoring the annoying fact that by not letting him know she was interested in being more than friends she'd wasted at least four months of potential dates, she asked, "Why did you use that particular florist?"

"I was in Little Mallow on a job and decided to send them on the spur of the moment. That doesn't help much, does it?"

"It might... Can you remember what name you gave? For me, I mean?" As far as she could recall, when she'd checked the delivery really was for her, the lady had confirmed her address, not her name.

"Cynthia Clere. I happened to have seen that on some official looking post and guessed it's your real name, but not many people would know it."

"A clue! Sorry I missed that. You're right, not many people know. That's what was on my party invitation, which seemed strange. Like you say, it's usually only used officially, not by people likely to invite me to parties."

"The florist's records would have you listed like that and they wouldn't know you're in the police. That's why you were on the guest list."

"You didn't get an invitation though, and you were the customer."

"I paid in cash so they had no reason to ask for my address. This is proof Paula or her husband organised the party, isn't it? Either him so he had a chance to kill her, or her for her own reasons and he knew about it and used the opportunity to do away with her."

"It could be that, but it's not proof. It suggests someone with access to the computer at Paula's Posies made the guest list. I grant you it could have been one of them and if it was, it was most likely him because other than setting her up to die, or your theories about Arnold, there's been no hint of a reason for this party."

"I'm ruling Arnold out and declaring Michael Roth guilty."

"Unfortunately, we have to consider all the evidence, not just the bits which fit our theory."

"The post office guy said the CCTV wasn't working well, so the timing could have been out. If he'd not needed to look at it recently he might not have noticed."

"Perhaps. He did stop using it soon after. I'll mention it to CID, but it's a long shot. And there are other possible suspects, other things to consider."

"Such as?" Jason asked.

"Apparently a couple of people bore a grudge against Paula, and the Roths weren't the only people who'd have been able to create that guest list. All the staff, past and present, had free access to the computer. You didn't need to log on, so if anyone found themselves alone in the shop they could take a look."

"I see what you mean. There wasn't anyone actually in the shop when I went in. One of the staff was outside vaping. She practically followed me in, but other people might have had longer on their own. If I'd said not to rush I just wanted a look she might not have come in straight away."

"Vaping, did you say?"

"Yeah." He bit his lip. "I'm pretty sure. I couldn't smell it, but that's how it looked. She had something in her hand and it was really cold so I could see a huge great cloud of vapour when she breathed it out."

"The vape fluid which killed Paula was odourless. Do you remember what she looked like?"

"Very tall, slim, black, luminous jumper, quite pretty."

Beth! "I'm going to have to think about that."

"What I meant was, I hardly noticed her but if I had just happened to glance in her direction I'd have immediately seen she was absolutely and definitely nowhere near as gorgeous as you."

"I didn't mean that. You can look at all the girls you like as long as you walk right by and buy me flowers."

"Keep walking. Buy flowers. Got it."

They really needed more time together, and not just in the company of others, but that would have to wait. "I'd better go or I'll make you late."

"No, we've got," he checked his watch and looked alarmed. "Sadly you're right."

"I can do the washing up if that would help."

"It would – a lot."

As she cleaned the frying pan, plates and everything else they'd used she hoped he didn't think she was eager to get away. Her real motivation was to make sure they'd have time for a nice long goodbye kiss. As he took full advantage of that opportunity and she responded with enthusiasm, she thought all was well.

"I'll call you tomorrow," he said.

"Great – and I'll see you at Ellie's on Friday," Crystal said as she let herself out.

She was halfway home when she got a text. She'd been thinking of stopping in Lee-on-the-Solent to get an ice cream, so pulled into the Marine Parade car park. She was mentally debating the merits of ginger or lemon meringue flavours as she checked her phone. It took her a few moments to realise the message was from the mother of Dom, one of the lairy boys whose alcohol Crystal and Trevor had confiscated and who'd given the statement about which shop had sold it to them. Then she rang the station and spoke to the sergeant on duty – Dil Dylan.

"I've had a call to say a boy's in trouble, is anyone near Lee-on-the-Solent?" she asked.

"Nearish. What's happening?"

"I'm not sure, but can you get them to go to the park on Megson Drive? I'm heading there myself and trying to get more info."

"Yes, alright. Call me when you know anything."

Crystal rang back on the number which had texted her, put the phone on loudspeaker and headed to the park. "This is officer Clere," she said as soon as the call was answered.

"Oh thank God. Is someone coming? It sounds really bad. It could have been Dom."

"Officers are on the way. Tell me exactly what happened."

"I don't know, Dom phoned me in a panic. They put patches on another kid and made him drink vape fluid and now he's really ill."

"Phone 999 now. Ask for an ambulance. Tell them it's nicotine poisoning. Call me back as soon as you've done it." The mother probably had more information than Crystal, but perhaps wasn't in a fit state to give it coherently. Crystal stopped to call control herself, which would have the advantage of informing Sergeant Dylan too. Then she drove to the park, leapt out of the car and raced to the woody patch where the boys had previously stashed some of their alcohol.

At first all she saw were empty beer cans and another of those distinctive carrier bags and she thought she was in the wrong place. Then she smelled vomit. The kid was so pale and still she thought she was too late, but he was breathing heavily and had a fast pulse. Crystal checked him over, pulling off five nicotine patches as she did so. Soon she was joined by the ambulance crew and two of her colleagues on bicycles. Not far behind were Dom and his mother.

"Will he be OK?" Dom asked.

"He might if you help. Tell the ambulance crew everything." After he'd done so he returned to his mum and Crystal. "I'm in so much trouble."

"Not as much as the boy they're taking to hospital," Crystal pointed out. Then seeing how shocked he looked said, "And not so much as you would be if, like the others, you'd run away and left him to die instead of telling someone."

"Die? It was just a joke."

"I don't see the funny side, and I'm off duty, so you'd better tell it to my colleagues." Crystal returned to her car.

The door was still open and her phone in the holder. There was a patrol car in front, and an ambulance behind, meaning driving away would need more precise manoeuvring than she currently felt capable of. She stayed where she was and called DI Shortfellow. "Was the shopkeeper we think supplied the vape refills which killed Paula co-operative?"

"That's not the word I'd have used."

"I think he might be now he's implicated in another attempt to kill by nicotine poisoning." She explained the incident which had just occurred. The DI agreed with her that although the boys probably hadn't intend their victim to die, the fact he almost had, and still might, would apply useful pressure.

Chapter 30

Friday 12th June

Ellie decided against wearing the green dress. The evening was intended to be a meal shared with friends, not a formal dinner party. Besides, it was probably dry clean only and she didn't want to risk staining it as she made the finishing touches to the tagine.

Crystal was the first guest to arrive. She had a bulging carrier bag, the contents of which would be their starter.

"Does any of that need to go into the fridge or oven?"

"Not if we're eating fairly soon. It's just loads of veggies, and hummus, salsa, and garlic dips."

"That sounds nice." And as it would be eaten with their fingers would be suitably informal.

"Why aren't you in the green dress?" Crystal demanded. Then, after Ellie explained said, "Isn't the whole point to make Mike not just a friend?"

"No. Yes. It is what I want... Tonight's just not a green dress night."

"I suppose... Yeah, you're right. You don't want to wear something less gorgeous on your first actual date."

"Exactly." Or not at all. Mike so clearly wanted to be her friend that an actual date seemed less likely every time she saw him. "Come through to the kitchen."

"It smells lush in here. What are you giving us?"

"Vegetable tagine."

"I've never had that."

Ellie, sure the author's description would sound more tempting than hers, read from the cookbook. "This rich and earthy dish is sweetened with apricots and cinnamon, warmed with chillies, turmeric, and cumin, then brightened with a squeeze of lemon and generous scattering of fresh coriander."

"Like I said, lush."

The doorbell rang and both women headed that way. Jason and Mike arrived together. Mike had a bottle carrier and Jason brought a frozen chocolate bombe, carton of cream, and strawberries.

"That's cheating," Crystal complained. "I spent hours cooking for you."

"Cooking?" Ellie queried. She was sure Crystal was just joking, but she didn't want Jason to think his contribution wasn't good enough – it looked like it would be really nice.

"OK, chopping and stirring, but Aunt Agnes says that's all there is to cooking."

"If it was, I could probably manage it," Jason said.

"Actually I think she's right," Ellie said. "Unless you're rolling out pastry, chopping and stirring is pretty much it. Come on then, Mike. As the rest of us have been busy cooking, chopping or shopping for a fabulous dessert, I think you should pour us all a drink." She indicated the glasses she'd set out on the table.

"Alright, but not here. Come into the kitchen." He sounded very strange.

"OK." As she turned away she saw Jason reach for Crystal. Ellie didn't begrudge her a kiss, she just wished

Mike had the same thing in mind. Perhaps she should have worn the green dress.

Mike followed her into the kitchen, then in a loud but croaky voice said, "I'll just shut the door." He pulled it partway closed. "Can't let Crystal see what I've done." He pulled out a bottle of what was obviously sparkling wine, onto which was Sellotaped a colourful home-made label saying 'St Sym's Communion wine.'

Ellie was laughing like a hiccuping hyena even before he claimed to have swiped it from his uncle Jerry's cellar.

Crystal and Jason soon joined them and found it just as funny as Ellie had.

"Something smells amazing," Jason said.

"It really does. It's making me hungry," Crystal agreed. She began unpacking the food she'd brought.

"It's making me thirsty, come on, Mike, get pouring," Ellie said.

He opened the bottle, then one of Ellie's kitchen cabinets. He was so comfortable in her home – why couldn't he see that he belonged here, with her?

"The glasses are in the dining room," she said. "I can't think why I set the table so neatly when it looks like this party is happening in the kitchen." Then she caught sight of her friend's face. "Is something wrong, Crystal?"

"You've just reminded me about the glasses. It seemed strange they were both tucked neatly away."

"Sorry?"

"They could easily have been kicked into the bushes or even picked up when people came out to see what was going on. I reckon the killer did it on purpose – he wanted it to be obvious how Paula died, but not before it was too late to save her."

"Why would he want her cause of death to be obvious?" Jason asked.

"If it was Roth then because he'd drunk some too, so he'd seem like another victim. If it wasn't him, maybe he really was intended to die too?" Crystal suggested.

"Was it definitely a man?" Mike asked.

Ellie put up a hand. "Whoa! I know you want to talk about the murder and I'm interested too, but not until we've had something to eat and drink, OK?"

"Of course. It's just I'd forgotten about that," Crystal said.

"We'll remind you again later," Mike said. He poured them all a glass and they drank it in the kitchen as Crystal arranged her prepared vegetables and dips on platters.

"I can see evidence of chopping," Jason said, "but I reckon you bought those dips and I have it on good authority that's cheating."

"That's just where you're wrong," Crystal said as she spooned salsa out of a plastic tub which bore the name of a supermarket and the word salsa in prominent letters. "I made the garlic mayo by squeezing garlic puree into mayonnaise and… stirring!"

Mike and Jason carried in the platters of starters, leaving Ellie and Crystal to deal with the bottle and glasses. It wasn't long before the operation was repeated in reverse.

Ellie put flatbreads in the oven and 'brightened' the tagine as directed by squeezing in the lemon, giving it a stir and sprinkling on the chopped coriander. The fresh green leaves really did lift the appearance of the food.

"Jason, can you take this in, please? Crystal, there's a bowl of salad in the fridge."

Mike uncorked a bottle of red and Ellie slid the warmed flatbreads onto a serving plate. She'd worried there might not be enough, but didn't want leftovers she'd be tempted to nibble. It was fine. After serving everyone a reasonable portion there was almost half the tagine left. Crystal tore a bread in half and took the smallest piece and Ellie didn't have any herself.

Soon the first helping had been eaten and seconds accepted, and the conversation moved from words of praise for her cooking, discussion of the run of good weather and questions for Jason about photography, to murder.

"From Crystal's reaction when I said Beth used a vape, she has to be a suspect," Jason said.

"Lots of people vape," Crystal pointed out. "And even those who don't could easily buy the refills."

"OK, there's also the cash she was accused of taking from the till. The party booker used cash."

"How much was it, Ellie?"

"One thousand, one hundred and fifty pounds, most of it for the food and drink."

"That's what I thought. Paula's Posies didn't take much actual cash... remind me about that in a minute, I've got half an idea." Crystal took a sip of wine. "Beth couldn't have stolen enough tenners unless she took them all, every day she worked. The till wasn't always short and it sounds like the times it was were a mistake. She didn't strike me as dim, certainly not stupid enough to think she could steal every ten pound note without it being noticed, but some people aren't good with numbers. The errors could have been her fault, but accidental."

"The one time I went to the florist shop, Beth was outside smoking," Jason said. "Maybe she wasn't super conscientious?"

"From what the other assistants said I don't think there was a problem," Crystal said. "But maybe Roth got that impression. If he was very protective of his wife and formed a bad opinion of a member of her staff then maybe he'd jump to the conclusion that any mistakes were deliberate and malicious. It would explain why Beth was sacked."

"I don't think he was protective like that," Ellie said. To her it had seemed as though he considered Paula's Posies as a little hobby and only took an interest because he didn't think his wife capable of handling the business side of things.

"What was their relationship like, do you know?" Crystal asked. "Could he have been having an affair?"

"If he was, that would give him a motive for killing her."

Ellie shook her head at Jason's words. She didn't want to think about love turning to hate. Murder as a way out of a relationship was rare, but divorce wasn't. She'd rather stay single than go through that heartbreak.

"Would it all being tens make it easier to trace? Cash machines give twenties usually," Ellie said, hoping it would serve as the reminder 'in a minute' Crystal had requested, as well as a change of subject.

"Good point. If he drew them from the bank in one go he'd have had to order them in advance to be sure they had enough notes. If someone buying seventy stamps was remembered then a guy asking for a hundred and fifteen used tenners could be too. I don't think he took the risk."

"So where did he get them? From a shop? I don't mean by stealing, but asking them to cash a cheque, or give a lot of cashback on a card payment – although I'm not sure they're allowed to give that much."

Crystal looked at her as though she'd said something remarkable.

"What's up?"

"It's just that I'm aware of a shop where the owner isn't too worried about the law – and he sells vape refills. If we get a suspect it should be easy enough for CID to see if there's a match against his bank account."

"If, at long last, I'm going to be allowed to ask a question," Mike said, giving Ellie a wink, "Was the killer definitely a man?"

"If Michael Roth was telling the truth, then yes."

"The same applies if he was lying," Ellie realised.

"I don't follow," Jason said, which she thought a lot more polite than the expression on Mike's face.

"If he was lying and this skinny bloke in striped trousers didn't give him the glasses, then where did they come from?" Crystal asked.

"Oh. Right. Yeah, he got them himself, or she did and he put in the poison…" Jason said. "Hang on… What if she did it?"

"Suicide?" Mike asked.

"Yeah. Perhaps a pact and he chickened out, or never meant to go along with it. He might want to hide it. I don't think life insurance pays out for suicide?"

That sounded a plausible theory to Ellie.

Crystal definitely seemed to be considering it. "I hadn't thought of a pact. If he hadn't expected her to go through with it, that would explain his shock."

"Or maybe he wasn't in on it?" Mike said. "Even bigger shock then."

"Yes, because he'd have experienced symptoms with the first sip," Crystal said. "But no, because of the glasses. If this wine was poisoned," she raised her glass, "and one of us was in real trouble and the others realised they were affected too, would we put our glasses tidily away where they wouldn't get knocked over?"

Ellie shuddered as she imagined anything so awful happening again, and to people she cared about. "Michael Roth must have done that. The tidiness somehow makes it worse. So cold and calculating."

"People do odd things when they're in shock. I attended an RTI where a kid was knocked off his bike."

"What's an RTI?" Mike asked.

"Road traffic incident. We don't say accident anymore, because a lot of the crashes are caused by something other than bad luck. Whether or not that one could have been avoided I'm not sure, but it was pretty bad. When the mum turned up she ignored her son and tried to get everyone gathering up his schoolwork which was blowing about. Trevor, the guy I work with, said it was because she knew she couldn't do anything to help him directly."

Ellie wanted to be told the kid was now OK, but didn't ask – Crystal didn't look as though she were remembering a happy ending. "Are there any other suspects?" Of course murder wasn't really a cheery subject, but it was strangely fun to try to solve the one they'd got caught up in.

"Not strong ones, but nearly all the guests were connected to Paula's Posies in some way. Mr Roth mentioned a business rival who was pretty upset, claiming Paula stole customers from her. There's Beth who was, wrongly or rightly, accused of theft, and the shop's main supplier hasn't been paid in months. Oh, and there was a legal dispute over the lease of the premises."

"You're scaring me," Jason said. "I've had rivals accuse me of various dodgy dealings, needed to threaten clients who haven't paid with legal action, and had people getting shirty because their kid got in the way of my shot."

"Stuff like that must happen in all businesses," Mike said.

"Exactly. They rarely lead to murder, or even a punch on the nose, but we… well, CID, have to look into it all. Talking of which, who would have known about the outside light switch, Ellie?"

Everyone turned to look at her, making Ellie feel like a character in a play. "Everyone on the committee. They didn't all come to every meeting but the minutes were emailed to everyone. Paula was on the committee."

"So her husband would have known?" Mike asked.

"I suppose so. Then there's the people who did the work or were asked for quotes, those who came on the day to help with the gardening which includes…"

"You, me, and Crystal!"

"She could have told me," Jason said. "I don't think she did, but... "

"I didn't because I didn't know myself, but I take your point – I could easily have found out and be lying. We all could have slipped something in the wine in the hall, or enticed the Roth's outside where we'd made sure it was dark, and done it then. So, who's got a motive?"

Ellie knew Crystal was kidding and didn't seriously suspect any of them, but there didn't seem to be any prime suspects and she must have had a reason for asking about the light switch. "Crystal, I knew about the lights and helped make sure the party went ahead. That night we met, that's when it was decided. I didn't mean to meet the others there but if I had been behind it and knew both Martin and Arnold had the letters and wanted to find them, the pub or vicarage is where I'd have looked. I'd hate you to get in trouble for giving away information to a potential suspect."

"There are hundreds of potential suspects, Ellie. Talking to them won't get me in trouble – only saying the wrong thing to the person who actually did it."

"Which obviously isn't you, Ellie," Mike said with conviction.

"Coming from the man who thinks Arnold disposed of his mother, that's very reassuring." She instantly regretted that attempt to lighten the mood. She'd been touched by Mike's certainty and responded with a joke at his expense.

"That's not quite right. My theory is that she doesn't exist. I don't hold him responsible."

"Was she taken by aliens, or he delivered by them?" Jason asked.

"Good question. He seems human, so I guess they snatched her. Or maybe he's an orphan."

"Why wouldn't he just say?" Crystal asked.

"Maybe he doesn't want to talk about it? He's very reserved."

"Maybe he gets it from her, that's why we've never seen her?"

"You're right, it's a mad theory."

"Do you want to know mine?" Crystal asked.

"Go on then," Mike encouraged her.

"I can't help feeling there's a link between this murder and one which happened in Gosport back in March. There are some things in common, but DI Shortfellow thinks it's just coincidence."

"Is that the old man who was poisoned by a glass of whisky?" Jason asked.

"Mr Argent, yes. The main things they have in common are poison in an alcoholic drink and no obvious motive or suspects, except that in each case their next of kin will be better off and possibly had the opportunity to administer the poison. But there's also a feel of economy to them both."

"How do you mean?" Mike asked.

"Mr Argent had very few luxuries except those he won – he entered a lot of competitions. One was the crystal glass he drank from. The whisky was a gift from his cousin, the one who inherits. Giving him malt whisky seemed kind, but being cynical it was an investment. She knew she'd get everything if she kept him sweet, and it was the cheapest malt she could buy. Same with the party. It seems generous to provide free food and drink, but if you wanted to get a lot of people together, and persuade them to put on disguises you'd have to offer something. This was a relatively cheap way to do it."

"That's a good point," Ellie agreed. "Martin Blackman said what he was given was just enough for a couple of drinks and some food for that number of people. He provided a bit better food than he normally would for that price as he thought it would be a good advert to others who might book the hall. The money sent to book was a bit more than we were planning to charge, but saying a donation was included helped push things along."

"And as Jason pointed out, our invites suggested we bring a friend, so there were potentially twice as many people as he'd ordered food for," Crystal said.

"He wanted a crowd, I suppose," Ellie said. "And he got it. If CID discover the exact number of attendees please let me know, as we shouldn't agree to events for more than that number, unless a lot of them will be outside most of the time."

"The mystery element was clever," Mike said.

"Not as clever as Crystal and her friends in CID." It was getting late and Ellie wanted the evening to end on a happy note. "I'm sure that by the midsummer party she'll be able to tell us how it was solved."

"I'll drink to that," Jason said.

They all clinked glasses and took a sip, then Jason asked if they were ready for him to cook dessert.

"Born ready," Crystal said.

"I'll get it out the freezer then," Ellie said, having noted Jason's emphasis on the word cook.

As they cleared up from the main course and set out dessert bowls Ellie thought over what she'd heard. The only real link she could see between the two cases was Crystal. It was understandable her friend wanted to find something to crack the case, and she supposed a link would go a long way towards that, but it was most likely wishful thinking on Crystal's part.

Ellie thought the business rivalry theory most promising. There might not be much money involved, but she could remember how angry one of her mum's friends got when she thought Mum was poaching on her Avon delivery area – she'd yelled at her in the street. She'd later cooled down and apologised, but if she'd had any kind of weapon, reason might have come too late.

Jason did a great job of flipping his chocolate bombe out of the plastic mould onto a plate.

"Now, that's a useful skill," Mike said.

"But not cooking," Crystal pointed out.

"Just you watch this," Jason said. He pulled the foil lid off the carton of cream, stuck in a spoon and stirred it vigorously.

Ellie laughed so hard she almost convinced herself it would burn off the calories in the large spoonful of the stuff he put on her piece of, really gorgeous, chocolate bombe.

Chapter 31

Saturday 13th June

As Arnold got off the bus he saw the young Milligan family walking towards him. It didn't matter that he'd been seen of course. There was no reason he shouldn't be in Gosport visiting a friend. No reason they shouldn't be visiting the library in the town where they lived, which it looked likely was their intention. It was just that he'd sometimes prefer to keep his private life private.

"Mr Stewart, I know what you're doing!" Adam called, causing several people to look round.

Arnold waited for the family to catch him up and tried to smile. He didn't feel he had any choice.

"Sorry," Adam's mother, Lorna Milligan said. "He worked it out, or thought he did, just before we came out."

"How did you know?" Arnold asked the boy.

"I recognised the flower and I know your job, so I deduced it."

Arnold smiled at his misunderstanding. Anyone would think he had a guilty conscience. The boy had guessed the solution to the latest photo puzzle in the Little Mag. "Very clever… if you're right that is."

"You're mending a stained glass window, aren't you? The one that's inside the porch."

"Well done."

"Yeah, well done, son." Adam's dad clearly hadn't been certain the suggested solution was the correct one.

"I knew you must be mending it because it used to be a bit broke and isn't now. Did you make a new piece of glass?"

"No, it needs to be special, very old, glass. We've been waiting to find some the right colour, which is why it's been broken for such a long time. When it came, I cut it to the right shape and soldered it in."

"What's shouldered?"

"Soldering is like gluing but with metal which is heated so it melts. "

"Is it dangerous?" Joshua, Adam's older brother, wanted to know.

"I do have to be very careful. I wear special gloves and goggles for protection when I clean the metal and solder it in place."

"How do you know how to do it?" Adam asked.

"I learned at school, in metalwork classes." The theory at least. Back then it had seemed fiddly to Arnold. He preferred tasks with quicker, more obvious, results. That led to Arnold taking a college course in building maintenance.

"St Symeon's is lucky to have you," Lorna Milligan said.

"Thank you."

"We're going to the library," Adam announced.

"I guessed as much."

"Are you a detective too?"

"We're all carrying books you numbskull," Adam's brother informed him.

"You're the numbskull. And a dimwit."

"Knucklehead."

"Doofus."

As the boys good naturedly called each other stupid in ever more imaginative ways, Lorna said, "We heard you were one of those helping the Roths. That must have been difficult."

"A very distressing situation."

"Have you heard anything more about it?"

"I understand Mr Roth has made a full recovery and the police are investigating a number of leads." He mentioned a few of those, including the theory of business rivalry taken to extremes, and the possibility of revenge by a disgruntled former employee. He was only repeating what everyone else knew, but it was nice to be considered as a possible source of information.

"We won't keep you," Lorna said as her husband went to separate the boys whose mock argument sounded close to becoming the real thing. "I expect you're busy."

"I'm going to see a friend. Someone I met that night in the new hall."

"That's nice. I'm glad some good came of it all."

Lorna Milligan's words felt like a blessing. When, a few minutes later, Cameron opened his arms offering a hug, Arnold felt little hesitation about stepping forward into the brief embrace.

"Have you heard any more about the murder?" Cameron asked as they walked to where he'd parked his car.

"Do you recall the lady we met as we left The Knitted Tea Cosy?"

"Muriel Grahame, was it?"

He nodded. "She has a younger brother whom everyone refers to as Old Bert. He's an enthusiastic allotment holder. Obsessed some might say. His own plot is immaculate and he often helps others with theirs, if they'll let him. One in particular had become quite overgrown. The tenant hadn't wanted Bert's interference. Yesterday they realised they couldn't cope and allowed him to start clearing the end which had been neglected for some time."

"He didn't find another body?"

"Nothing quite so dramatic. Paula Roth died from drinking vaping liquid. What Old Bert found was a canvas bag containing several refill bottles."

"The murder weapon, in effect."

"The police believe so. Bert didn't know what they were and guessed at insecticide. He doesn't approve of that and it was him talking about murdering God's creatures which made someone else connect them with Paula's death and contact the police. There's no reason for people to hold on to the bottles and they can go out with the normal household rubbish, so it was suspicious they were dumped like that."

"And would never have been noticed if the killer had followed that commonplace course of action. Were there fingerprints?"

"I don't know for certain, but assume so. The police are asking people to provide theirs so they can be eliminated from the investigation."

"Have they requested yours?"

"No. Perhaps I should volunteer?" That hadn't occurred to him before. Now it had, it seemed the obvious thing to do.

"I'll do likewise. The answer will tell us something, even if the charming DI won't." He stopped the car. "This is me." The house was a large bungalow, with dormer windows in the roof.

Once inside Cameron offered Arnold a drink, and the opportunity to change into something 'more railwaylike'. "There really should be a better word for it. Ships are nautical, planes aeronautical."

Arnold tried to think of something suitable. Railonautical? Trackological?

"Stationmaster, driver or guard?"

"Um… " Oh dear, Cameron thought Arnold had agreed to wearing a uniform. He wouldn't feel comfortable getting undressed in front of Cameron, but neither would he like to make a fuss about not doing so.

"Really it comes down to whether you prefer flags, whistles or all the power."

"I don't think too much power would be good for me." Arnold neither wanted to risk causing any damage nor to deprive Cameron of the aspects he most enjoyed.

"You make the tea then and I'll go and look something out for you. That's if you'd like tea. Help yourself to anything else you'd prefer. There's wine in the fridge… "

"I would like tea, thank you."

There was Early Grey tea in Cameron's cupboard, in a small pack behind a larger box of the regular kind. Arnold used the one closest to hand. Cameron seemed less affected today, which Arnold preferred. He liked the plain tea better too.

Arnold had only just poured boiling water into the warmed pot when Cameron reappeared dressed the same way as when Arnold first saw him. He carried more clothes, which he draped over a chair. "Pop those on and bring the tea up, would you?" he said, then went out again.

Dressed as a guard, and carrying two cups, Arnold ascended the stairs. As he'd half guessed, the attic had been converted into space for the trains. The set up was more impressive and extensive than he'd imagined. The track was ingeniously laid out, with lots of twists and turns and various intersections. Alongside the tracks were areas of landscape in different stages of completion and all kinds of little models. There were realistic looking trees and houses, some apparently still being built by workmen small enough to drive the tiny cars on the ribbon like roads. "This is incredible."

"Once you go beyond laying out tracks and start to build a world for the trains to go through, it's hard to know when to stop."

Arnold could easily believe that. Whenever he made anything he was proud of he immediately wanted to attempt something better or more challenging. He glanced at Cameron's chest and was pleased to see the railway logo inspired lapel badge he'd created was fixed in place.

Evidently Cameron saw him looking. "Looks rather good, doesn't it?"

Arnold was happy with his workmanship, but the scale was wrong. "It's too small. I'll order a slightly thicker gauge wire and try again."

"If that's not an awful lot of work I'd be delighted to accept. I've been wearing this one as a tie pin at work, where it's been much admired. It's the perfect size for that."

Arnold hoped he wasn't blushing. The idea of Cameron publicly displaying his gift made him feel warm and childishly happy.

"You could sell them if you wished," Cameron said. "Several people asked where I acquired it and if other designs could be made – initials, star signs, that kind of thing."

"I do sell a few pieces," Arnold admitted.

"Do you have an online shop?"

Cameron looked up Arnold's website, bookmarked it and promised to pass on the details to those who might be interested. "It doesn't give your name," he said. "Do your parishioners think that because you work for the church you should do nothing else?"

"Something like that." He had no idea how the residents of Little Mallow would react to the idea of the verger supplementing his income through his craftwork, he'd simply not thought to share something which felt so personal.

Cameron encouraged Arnold to try operating the trains. "In my head there's a great deal of engineering and complicated procedures involved. In reality you push the appropriately numbered green lever forward to move the train. The further you push, the faster it goes. If disaster threatens, then press the red button. That cuts all the power."

The levers were easy as they were labelled 1, 2 and 3, but there was more than one button on the control panel and they were all dark. It was probably the larger one in the centre, as the four smaller ones were the same size as each other and arranged in a neat row. He couldn't risk it.

"Do you mean this one? I'm colour blind, so… "

"Oh, are you?" Cameron said, with no more surprise or concern than if Arnold had mentioned being left handed. "Yes, the big one in the middle. The others… Well try them and you'll see."

Three of the buttons controlled the signal lights, station illumination and street lights for the roads Cameron had put into the landscape he'd created. The fourth, which raised the barrier on the level crossing, was Arnold's favourite.

Arnold operated the trains without needing to push the 'in case of disaster' red button, but was happy to relinquish the controls after a few minutes. He preferred deciding which route each train was to take, setting up the points accordingly and activating the level crossing. What he liked best of all was hearing Cameron talk enthusiastically about the trains and the environment he was creating for them.

Cameron had made some of the buildings himself, using cardboard, papier-mâché, sweet wrappers, and all manner of bits and pieces. "It's very time consuming, especially sourcing the materials, yet thrilling when you find something perfect. Those drainage tubes were drinking straws from a martini. They made me lightheaded, firstly because they were far too thin to use comfortably and then when I realised they'd be perfect for the construction site."

"It's very good. I particularly like the fact that you've included model buildings in the process of being built by model people." He indicated a collection of animals. "Are you going to have a farm?"

"That was the intention when I bought them. I've made plans for a barn. If I can source the right size corrugated cardboard and paint it rust brown it will be a convincing tin roof."

"That will be perfect." Cameron's scenery was attractive, but realistic. He'd built a housing estate and supermarket where some might have masses of chocolate box cottages and thatched barns.

"I'll whittle matches for post and rail fences. The gates will be a challenge. I sent off for some, but look…" He rummaged through a box and produced a few gates of the right size, but nothing like the correct quality. They were clumsy, two dimensional pieces of garish orange plastic.

"What about metal ones? Could they work?"

"That would be ideal, but I've not found any in the right scale yet and… Can you possibly mean…?"

"Let me have photos of what you'd like and tell me the dimensions, and I'll give it a try."

"That would be wonderful. Thank you. Now, where shall we go for lunch?"

Over fish pie for him and grilled plaice for Cameron, Arnold told Cameron about the community event to be held in the new hall. "Because of the rush to get everything ready for the first booking there wasn't an official opening. We want to have one now, to begin to put the tragedy in the past and create happy memories there." He repeated what he'd said to Jerry about replacing the dark memories with sunshine. He took a deep breath. "Will you come as my guest?"

"You'd like the two of us to create happy memories together?"

That's not quite how Arnold would have phrased it, but that was the gist. "Yes."

"In that case, I'd be delighted. When will it be?"

"Next Saturday, midsummer."

"Bother. I'm attending a family wedding that day. I'd considered asking the happy couple if it weren't too late to inflict a rearrangement of the seating plan on them, to include you, but decided that wouldn't be fair. Still, it sounds as though you'd have had to decline the invitation if it had been offered."

"I would."

Cameron reached over and put his hand on Arnold's. "I'm sure we'll have other sunny afternoons together."

Chapter 32

Thursday 18th June

Crystal became ever more sure the murders of Colin Argent and Paula Roth were linked. There was little evidence to back that up – everything she'd noticed could be coincidental. All her thoughts were so jumbled in her head she was almost in danger of losing track of which were facts and which just wild supposition.

She called Trevor. "Are you busy? I need someone to talk to."

"Never too busy for you if you need me, lass," he said gently.

"It's OK if you're busy. I mean I'm OK, I just wanted to go over the murders, try to get it straight in my mind."

"You really do mean talk to, not with, then?"

"I suppose. Not that I won't value your insights."

"I was about to do the ironing. I'll put you on loudspeaker and carry on with that."

"Thanks, Trevs." Crystal mentioned the things she felt the cases had in common. Even to her it didn't sound a particularly long or compelling list.

"CID are actively working both cases and they'll be solved in time," he pointed out.

"Sooner would be better, and not just for the police. Aunty Agnes has been hearing rumours. Some people share my opinion that two recent and fairly local murders must be linked. There's talk of a serial killer, which could soon lead to fear, even panic."

"It could, and you're right that would be best avoided."

"Beth won't be able to get a new job if she's suspected of killing her last boss. Rightly so if she's guilty. There's no getting away from the fact that, if she didn't steal from them, Beth has reason to resent how the Roths treated her. She'd had access to the client list. She could have made deliberate computer errors to throw suspicion from her thefts and so, if she was seen printing off that list, she could claim she'd done so by mistake."

"If Beth did steal from the Roths, would she have tried to kill them for learning the truth?" Trevor asked.

"That doesn't work for me. It wasn't as though they'd pressed charges. And the covering of her tracks, if that's what she'd done, began before she had any reason to want revenge. The only way that would make sense was if she'd already planned to kill them and took the job for that reason."

"Is that likely?" Trevor prompted.

"I can't see Beth as a cold-blooded schemer and surely if there was something in their pasts to warrant murder the Roths would have known and not employed her? Mr Roth would certainly have mentioned it if he'd considered Beth's motive stronger than the theft of a few tenners. And there was the party. No other staff had been invited, so why was Beth? "

"Easy to arrange if she organised it," Trevor pointed out.

"Beth could have known enough to make the bookings, and send out the party invitations, but she didn't appear to have the money to fund it."

"Appearances can be deceptive."

Crystal sighed. She'd liked and trusted Beth, thought her a loving mother with a forgiving nature. It could all have been an act. If the woman could work with people she intended to kill and persuade her colleagues she was a lovely friend who'd made a few little mistakes, then she could rent a single room in a house in order to establish the idea she was hard up. Crystal didn't believe that was the case, but it was a possibility.

"I'd do anything for Teddy," she'd said. Her colleagues, Liz and Dawn, said the same. What if the Roths had done something which could harm Teddy, or discovered something which might lead to Beth losing custody of him? Could Michael Roth be his father? If so, he couldn't know – he'd have told CID. With Paula dead there would be no reason to hide it.

"You still there, lass?"

"Yeah, just forgot to do the out loud part of the thinking out loud. Admittedly I don't know Beth well, but I don't think she's guilty – of anything." Or maybe just didn't want to?

"Your instincts are pretty good, and I heard what the other florists said about Beth. I agree she doesn't seem a likely killer."

"And it wasn't her on the CCTV, was it?"

"That's true. Is Michael Roth still a suspect?"

"Yeah. When we saw that CCTV footage I was certain we'd found the killer. I was wrong, but the fact he didn't buy stamps from that post office on that day doesn't prove he didn't either arrange the party, or take advantage of it to kill his wife."

"Any reason he'd want her dead?"

"Paula's life was insured, but that wasn't a new thing and there's nothing to suggest an urgent need for money. Michael Roth's business is doing well, and he seemed able to do as he liked, even when it came to Paula's Posies. We don't know of any problems in their marriage."

"I doubt he'd have said anything even if there was."

"Probably not. Maybe there wasn't anything." Paula's staff, Dawn and Liz, had mentioned the couple being polite to each other. That didn't suggest the kind of fiery and passionate relationship which, if it soured, could turn to anger and hatred. "They were on good enough terms to go to the party together."

There was a clanking sound, probably from Trevor putting the iron down. "And your other suspects?"

"Mostly rumour, wild speculation and jumping to conclusions, pretty much like me thinking Lucy Carter is involved with both crimes."

"You still believe that?"

"Yeah. I'm not absolutely certain, but I feel like there's a connection. There are things they have in common, like both sorts of poisons being given in wine and the doses being much higher than needed to kill. The killer, or killers, wanted to be really sure of getting their result."

"That's extravagant, but earlier you said these were low budget murders," Trevor pointed out.

"I've been thinking about that. The whisky was the cheapest malt Lucy could buy, but it was malt. He'd almost certainly have drunk the blended stuff, but he'd be more likely to associate malt with the competition he thought he was runner up in, and so use the glass as soon as he got it. Maybe she even told him it was on offer to encourage that rather than saving it for a special occasion?"

"If she was the killer."

"Yeah. If not, she was just being nice and maybe seeing the offer was what prompted that. The party though… I think the fairly low expenditure there was deliberate. To get a good crowd, especially with the short notice, he needed it to be local. Plenty of people would walk down to take a look, even if they wouldn't have bothered driving or getting a taxi, so the new hall was by far the best option."

"Especially as the organisers wouldn't be used to taking bookings, so would be excited by the first one and not realise how odd it was."

"Exactly. And the more money was spent, the more suspicious it would be that it was paid for in cash. And maybe catering for fewer people than invited was deliberate too? When the wine looked like it was about to run out there was rush to get a top up. I saw that happen, but can't say if Roth was there, let alone whether someone wearing those green gloves handed him a couple of glasses."

"So it could have happened just as he said?"

Crystal had been thinking more along the lines of Roth having made sure nobody could be certain he'd lied, but she had to admit it was possible he was an innocent victim."

"Could Lucy Carter have planned the party?"

"In theory, yes. Getting the customer list from Paula's Posies would have been difficult, but it's possible she managed it. But why would she? She has no reason to try to kill the Roths and wasn't even at the party. If she is guilty, she wasn't working alone."

"OK, then. Anyone you can definitely eliminate?"

"As her accomplice, not really, but there are other theories which seem very unlikely. A rumour has gone round that Cassie, the mobile beautician Paula used, claimed the deceased spread rumours Cassie snooped whenever she got the chance. As Paula asked her to come to the house to do her nails on the day of the party that seems unlikely to be true and would be a very slight motive if it were." Crystal laughed. "I did look her up online. She's got lovely blue eyes."

"She's in the clear then! You mentioned a business rival the other day. Anything in that?"

"Not really. When Paula first started she was mentored by another florist and there was apparently a falling out when some of her customers started using Paula's Posies. I'm not sure it's true and the cost of hosting the party would far have outweighed the small amount of profit she made... unless she didn't host it and simply took advantage of the situation?"

"So you're back to needing to know who organised the party and why?"

"That has to be the key to the whole thing, doesn't it?"

"Reckon so. Bear with me a minute, lass." There was the sound of footsteps and more clanking.

No doubt CID were considering every aspect Crystal had thought of, and more. Other than routine enquiries passed her way, which she'd eagerly take on, how else could she help? What should she look for? Anyone could buy vape refills, but cyanide was harder to obtain, as a

Home Office license and photo ID were needed. There was an alarming number of legitimate uses for the stuff. They ranged from pest control and gardening, through metal cleaning and electroplating to printing and photography.

"That's just for film processing and I'm all digital, so I'm in the clear," Jason had told her.

"That's what you say!"

"Come into my darkroom and see what develops if you don't believe me!"

"Ha! Gotcha! If you don't use film you don't need a dark room!" That was despite having been in his flat often enough to be sure there wasn't one.

"OK, I confess. Now get those handcuffs out."

Crystal laughed at the memory, even as she ruled out following that line of enquiry. CID would do a far better job of tracing the cyanide used to kill Mr Argent and linking that to his killer, and tying the vape refill bottles to Paula Roth's murderer, than Crystal could hope to achieve alone. They'd be better at tracking the purchaser of the whisky glass and the party organiser too.

What about people? If it was the same killer, or two different ones working together, establishing a link between them would be a real breakthrough. How do you prove a link between two people when you don't know which two to connect, or whether it's just two or a whole gang?

In the case of Paula Roth's murder there were too many potential suspects for Crystal to make an attempt. With Mr Argent it was easier. The only suspect, so far, was Lucy Carter. The main thing against her was inheriting Mr

Argent's house. As his only relation that was to be expected, so was a long way from being evidence. She had given Mr Argent the whisky. The whisky which contained no trace of the cyanide which killed him. That was in the glass, which might have been delivered by a tall, slim man.

Mr Roth was tall and slim, as was the person he claimed gave him the poisoned wine. DI Shortfellow was tall and slim. Crystal almost wished she'd thought of mentioning that when he'd given her a fright by pretending to think she'd been the person in uniform who'd visited Mr Argent the day he died.

Beth was tall and slim. Close up she was definitely female, but seen at a distance might be mistaken for a male delivery driver if that's what the witness expected to see. Obesity might be on the rise, but not being fat wasn't quite unusual enough to count as evidence. It did mean people's idea of slim covered a wide range – she made a mental note to share that pun with Jason.

Lucy Carter wasn't overweight, but at about five foot four and curvy, unlikely to be taken for a tall man. She did benefit from one death though, and potentially had a slight link to the other. Crystal's best plan was to keep an eye on Lucy Carter, whenever she had the opportunity.

There was the sound of footsteps and then Trevor said, "I'm back with you. Where have you got to?"

She didn't ask where he'd been. There had been a sound like running water and she didn't want to know if he'd been doing anything other than filling the kettle.

"I was thinking about what CID will have covered and what I might be able to add to that."

"And?"

"I'm going to chase my wild hunch that Lucy Carter is a link between the cases."

"Good luck, Lass."

Her chance came two days before the midsummer party.

Crystal was on a rest day, Jason on a shoot, Ellie was teaching, it wasn't worth driving up to see her parents as they were coming to stay with Aunty Agnes for the weekend, so she was free to amuse herself by snooping on Lucy Carter. The slight drizzle was a snag as it would be hard to look natural just loitering. Delivering Little Mallow's Little Mag had worked well before, but she didn't have any. Adam's presence had led to Crystal's conversation with Beth and he'd love to join a stakeout and be useful at noticing things, but he'd be at school. The best idea she could think of was to buy a bag of sweets and stop to unwrap one when she wanted to linger. Not brilliant camouflage, but she did like that home-made treacle toffee Adam's grandmother sold in the post office.

Initially Crystal thought her luck was mixed. There were some toffees left, but Mary Milligan didn't rush to serve her as she was on the phone.

"Yes, of course I'll have Adam… No, I can't… I suppose I'll have to close the shop while I drive down."

Crystal mimed driving and pointed at herself.

"Hang on a tick, love, " Mary Milligan said.

"I can pick Adam up if that helps," Crystal said.

"That's very kind, but the teachers won't let you."

Crystal reminded Mary Milligan that she was a police officer. "I can show them my ID. Adam knows me, and so do the teachers."

"It would be a help. There's been a gas leak at his school, so they're all evacuated. Heaven knows what I'll do with him when he gets here."

"I have a few errands to do, which Adam could help me with if it's OK with his mum."

After passing on the offer and ending the call, Mary said, "Lorna, my daughter-in-law, says thank you and to apologise in advance for the many, many questions he'll ask."

Crystal gave Mary Milligan her phone number and in return was given the address of the place the school was evacuated to and two packs of toffees. "Don't count on them keeping him quiet though, I've tried that!"

Adam was disappointed not to be driven away by a uniformed officer in the patrol car, but when she explained they were going undercover to try to find the car which dented his dad's, Crystal was forgiven.

"The white Audi?"

"That's it. Which supermarket was it in when the damage occurred?"

"Morrison's." He'd asked Crystal about her mum, dad, siblings and every family pet they'd ever had, and shared the same information about himself, and moved on to making her justify never having visited an active volcano, all by the time she pulled into the car park.

There were two white Audis. Crystal and her side kick walked casually by. Or as casually as you can be whilst one person is interrogating the other about her taste in socks. She'd misheard his question at first and was very relieved to be able to answer with, "Black while on duty, and striped the rest of the time."

One car was undamaged. The other had a scratch down the side.

"I can see red paint," Adam reported.

"Well spotted. What colour is your dad's car?"

"A really weird one."

Presuming red wasn't weird, Crystal suggested they try elsewhere.

"OK. I don't think that car was involved in a crime, do you?" Adam said.

Two could play inquisitor. "Why do you think that?"

"Because the red paint could be evidence, so they'd have cleaned it off."

"How would they do that?"

"With special stuff."

The kind of special stuff you need a Home Office licence to buy and which smells of almonds? Crystal thought better of mentioning cyanide and instead asked, "Metal cleaner? Do you know anyone who uses that?"

"Mr Stewart the verger does."

Arnold? He wasn't particularly tall, but neither was he short, and he had lost weight recently.

Chapter 33

Thursday 18ᵗʰ June

Don't get excited, Crystal told herself. Arnold probably just used Brasso on the church candlesticks.

"Adam, how do you know that?"

"He told me about it when I discovered he sho… soldered the church window."

Not Brasso then, something more specialised.

"Mr Stewart doesn't drive, so I don't think that's his car, do you?" Adam said.

"No. I think he must be entirely innocent." Despite the possibility Arnold was able to obtain cyanide, a fact which she'd pass on to CID, he seemed an unlikely murderer. She didn't want to risk more harmful rumours spreading about those involved with, but not responsible for, the murder.

Crystal was amazed when they spotted another white Audi in Lucy Carter's road. Adam had been right about them being common. The cars were so close together they couldn't see the registration plates, or spot whether there were any dents as they drove by.

"What we'll do is park and walk back. When you see the car, ask me for a sweet. We'll both take one, then you move a little way forward to unwrap yours. That will give me a chance to look at the front and you can check the back."

"OK. What are our code names?"

"What do you think?"

"I can be Gene Hunt and you're Alex Drake."

"OK." Those names sounded familiar. Weren't they the ones Trevor had mentioned as characters on a TV show? "Where did you get those from?"

"Mum and Dad call each other that sometimes when me and Josh are getting ready to stay with Granny and Grandad."

Crystal should probably stop asking the kid questions.

"Alex, can I have a sweet, please?" Adam said.

"You sure can, Gene."

Adam hadn't even taken his sweet out the bag before Crystal had checked the car's registration. It wasn't Michael Roth's car. So as not to spoil Adam's fun, she let him continue. Clever kid improved on her idea by dropping his wrapper and pretending to follow it, so he could get a quick glance at the far side.

"I didn't see any dents," he reported, "but I couldn't see properly without going into the road."

"Let's walk all the way down the road and come back on the other side."

"OK, Alex."

Doing that revealed no sign of damage to the car, which Crystal was relieved about. If Adam thought they'd found the car which she'd told him was the reason they were there, he'd be expecting some action from her. She'd better try and think of something just in case. She also needed an excuse to go to Warsash and look at the spot where Michael Roth got his ticket. Ah!

"Gene, I've just remembered something."

"You can call me Adam now we're not on an operation."

"Right. Of course." There were rules to this madness?

"What did you remember?"

"A white Audi got a parking ticket in Warsash not long ago. Do you think we've got time to check it out before I drop you off at your granny's?"

She wasn't surprised he did think so. "We'll give her a call to let her know." Crystal dialled and then handed Adam the phone. Their adventures so far sounded dramatic the way he explained them but, other than added excitement, were accurate. He'd make a great witness.

There was yet another white Audi in Warsash. It wasn't the right model.

"We don't know what model hit dad's car, just that it was a white Audi."

"Good point." He'd make a good detective too – and she'd be a rubbish criminal mastermind if she couldn't even remember the cover story she'd made up and, just moments ago, listened to being described in detail. "I don't think we're going to find the car which hit your dad's. Sorry about that."

"That's OK. Thank you for helping me try. I suppose I should go to Granny's now and help her with her stocktaking. That's counting *all* the things. We don't take them anywhere. It takes Granny aaaaaaages."

Crystal was fairly sure she only did it when Adam was there to help. He really was a sweet kid, but trying to keep him occupied whilst running the post office and shop couldn't be easy.

"We could do a little bit of training for when you're in the police if you like?"

"Yay!"

"Sometimes it's good to put yourself in another person's position. If you were a burglar which house would you pick?"

"The one with the best stuff in?"

Not what she'd been expecting, which was something about easy access and lack of alarms, but it made sense. "How would you know which that was?"

"I'd go in and look." He didn't say 'obviously' but it was in his tone of voice.

"How would you manage that without making them suspicious?"

"I could pretend to be selling carpets and measure up to see how much it would cost and then I could look in all the rooms. And they might say when they would be out so I couldn't come then to bring the carpets and I'd know when to go back to steal stuff. And when I was there I could check for alarms and how to get in."

"OK." If Adam was ever accused of anything Crystal was going to make sure she wasn't the one to interview him as he'd probably run rings around her.

"Suppose you were a traffic warden…" she wasn't sure where she was going with that.

"I wouldn't come here."

"Why not?"

"There's no yellow lines and no 'no parking' signs, so people couldn't be parked in the wrong place."

"Good point." A very good point – why had there, very conveniently for Michael Roth, been a traffic warden in that area able to give him proof he wasn't somewhere else?

After showing Adam how to walk the beat, and eating a few more sweets, Crystal drove him back to his granny in Little Mallow – via the street where Mr Roth lived.

"Another white Audi," Adam said hopefully.

"Come on, Gene, let's check it out."

"Sure thing, Alex!"

With the aid of more treacle toffees and their dropped wrappers they discovered Michael Roth's car was free from dents. It wasn't however free from interest. Crystal discovered that it's hard to stay calm when you think you've just solved a double murder.

"Did you notice anything inside the car?" Crystal asked, as they walked back to hers.

"A sat nav *and* a map."

"Why would he have both?" She wanted to keep Adam talking, and thinking, while she got a grip on her excitement.

"He doesn't like to ask people the way, even when it's really obvious he's lost and will be late and there are plenty of people about he could ask and will never have to see again."

"Yeah, that's probably it." And Adam's dad definitely had an aversion to asking for directions.

"And he had a bottle of water, which is sensible, and no rubbish, and a baseball cap."

"Can you describe it?"

"Easy! Dark green with a red dragon like the one on the flag of Wales."

Roth was no more Welsh than Mr Argent, who'd had the same hat hanging in his hallway, had been. That had still been wrapped in cellophane, she remembered. Either Lucy Carter had given it to Roth after clearing her cousin's possessions from the house, or Roth had gone there and helped himself. Crystal remembered that during the meal at Ellie's they'd discussed the possibility Roth was having an affair and how that would give him a motive for killing his wife. Ellie, because of having lived in Little Mallow for years, was the one of them most likely to have any idea about that and she'd not denied it – just looked uncomfortable. Maybe she'd had her suspicions Roth was unfaithful, maybe not. Oh! The guy buying the stamps wore a baseball cap. Crystal was certain she'd found her link.

"Is it a clue?" Adam asked. Possibly not for the first time.

"It might be, yes."

"I wish I could remember where he got them from."

Them? "Mr Roth has more than one hat like that?" If Welsh hats were on sale locally then both the victim of one murder and husband of another having one wasn't as significant as it had first appeared.

"No, Mr Stewart did."

"Arnold Stewart the verger?" He could be having a relationship with Lucy. They were about the same age and single, but would have no reason to hide it – unless it was the motive for a crime. Ellie and Mike had both said he'd be good at keeping secrets, and he used 'special stuff' to clean metal prior to soldering it.

"He gave them to people. I thought he said it was something to do with a prize, but Old Ber... I mean Mr Grahame, said he wouldn't tell anyone, so I don't think that's right."

"Don't worry, we can ask him."

"He might be at the church. We could go now."

"Sorry, Adam I didn't mean me and you, but the police. This could be a big clue though, so please don't talk about it to anyone."

"Not even Granny?"

Especially not Mary Milligan who presided over the post office, general store and gossip hub. However it wasn't a good idea to teach children to keep secrets. "No, but you'll only have to keep it quiet for a little while, and can tell your Mum and Dad, but please say it's important not to tell anyone else just yet and that they can call me if they have any questions. Now let's get you back to your gran."

By the time she'd dropped Adam off at the post office, Crystal was thoroughly confused. She stopped to have a think, before going back to Aunty's and being asked yet more questions. Crystal tried calling Trevor, but he didn't pick up. DI Shortfellow or one of his colleagues would, but she wanted to get things as straight as possible in her own mind before calling them.

How many hats were there? It seemed very likely Mr Argent had won his and that, if he'd won two or more, he'd have given the surplus ones away. Had Roth's hat come from Arnold or Lucy? If it was her, then she may have done other favours for him, such as faking a parking ticket so he'd have an alibi if anyone remembered him buying stamps for invitations to the party at which he killed his wife.

Michael Roth's alibi being provided by someone with the same job as Lucy Carter had seemed to Crystal to be a potential link between them, but may have meant nothing. If Lucy Carter really had issued that ticket, it surely had to be more than random chance, especially as it wasn't a likely area for any traffic warden to be on duty.

If the two of them were working together he could have been the one to buy the whisky glass and deliver it to Mr Argent after the cyanide was added. Supposing they were having an affair, which was very likely if they were trusting each other to this extent, then he might well prefer to be a widower than a divorcee who had to split all his assets with his wife.

But how had Arnold got hold of his hats? What Adam reported Old Bert Grahame saying suggested Arnold would rather people didn't know the answer to that question. Surely that wouldn't be the case if he'd won them as a prize himself. The chances of him having done that in the same competition as Colin Argent were very small. And what would be Arnold's motive for killing either Mr Argent, or Paula Roth, or both of them?

Arnold having organised the party was plausible, he had definitely pushed for the hall to be completed so it could go ahead. He might have access to cyanide. He could have been mistaken by Mrs Owens for the late night delivery driver. Like her sister thinking a traffic warden was a police officer she probably saw what she expected to see. It would have been possible for him to have given the poisoned glasses to Michael Roth – but in that case they were both in on it. Arnold's flamboyant outfit of burgundy satin and turquoise silk wouldn't have been mistaken for blue trousers with red stripes and lime green gloves.

There was only one thing Crystal was absolutely sure of – the dragon hats were a link between the two murders. She called DI Shortfellow and told him everything she'd discovered and what she thought it could mean.

He laughed. "Well, thanks for clarifying things! We'll have another chat with the verger and I'll check who issued that parking ticket. By the way, the owner of that off-licence you suggested could be the source of the vape refills denies ever selling more than one of the things at a time. Given the prices he charges, that might be true."

"Or he realises the implication of the purchase and has decided to keep quiet?"

"That's entirely possible. There's been another interesting development, which means we're going to ask him again."

"Development, sir?"

"We've got a match for the fingerprint found on one of the vape refill bottles."

"Lucy Carter, Michael Roth, or Arnold Stewart?"

"Bethany Phillips. She's… "

"Beth who used to work at Paula's Posies and, to use her own phrase, sir, left under a shadow."

Chapter 34

Thursday 18th June

Arnold's phone rang as he was fixing the loose end of a pew. The display gave no name or number, so the call was probably spam and it wouldn't matter what he did or didn't say.

"Hello."

"Hello, Mr Arnold Stewart?"

"Yes."

"This is Detective Constable Hetherington from Portsmouth CID."

In that case it mattered very much what Arnold said. He kept quiet.

"We have a few more questions for you."

Arnold tried to employ Jerry's advice to speak slowly and in complete sentences. Recognising the woman's voice as the patient officer who'd organised tea for him when he was interviewed by DI Shortfellow helped a little. "What would you like to know?"

"It would be better to speak to you in person," she said.

It would. A lot better – if he could get to the CID building. "I am at work. I don't drive."

"You're at St Symeon's Church in Little Mallow?"

"Yes."

"We'll be there in about twenty minutes."

"OK." He was relieved not to have to leave the sanctuary of the church and reassured by the officer's time estimate. It would take longer than that to drive round from their offices in Portsmouth, so they must already be in the area. That suggested they just wanted to check something with him, rather than they felt his earlier statement had been incorrect or incomplete.

Arnold went in search of Jerry, to inform him of the expected visitors, but got no reply at the vicarage. After that he continued working on the pew. It couldn't be left as it was, or someone might injure themselves.

DI Shortfellow came, as well as DC Hetherington. She recited the official caution and asked if he understood. He did, but couldn't remember if that had happened at his previous interview. It probably had, as he'd been expecting the proceedings to be formal.

DC Hetherington showed him a photograph of an elderly man. "Do you recognise this person, Mr Stewart?"

"No. He's definitely not one of our congregation and I think I'd recognise him if he lived in Little Mallow."

"That's Colin Argent. Does the name mean anything to you?"

"Silver."

"Can you elaborate, sir?" she asked.

"Argent means silver. It's an old fashioned word." Arnold added that last bit as he didn't want to imply he thought she should have known.

"Did you obtain any silver from him?"

"No, I don't think so. I do buy silver, but from companies, not individuals." As the police apparently knew about his jewellery making, there was no point trying to hide it. How had they discovered that – and why? Arnold was beginning to feel uncomfortable.

"Do you own a green hat, decorated with a red dragon?" the officer asked.

How could they possibly know about that? "I might have done once. I'm not sure."

The church door opened before Arnold could say anything more. It was Jerry, and he approached Arnold and the police. "Good afternoon. Can I help with anything?"

Arnold introduced them all, getting flustered when he realised he'd pointed out that the man in the dog collar, offering assistance in a church, was the vicar. "They've come to ask me some questions about… " He trailed off. He'd almost said 'about Paula Roth's murder' as that's what he'd expected from the initial phone call, but the questions suggested something else.

"We were just asking Mr Stewart if he owns a green hat with a red dragon on it," DI Shortfellow said.

"That's Old Bert's," Jerry said. "Bert Grahame is a retired gardener who sometimes helps with the church grounds. I remember the hat because I wondered if he had a Welsh connection. That's my heritage you see."

"I gave it to him," Arnold said.

"It's useful you've remembered that," the DI said. It sounded as though he thought Arnold only admitted it because Jerry was likely to reveal that fact.

"I couldn't immediately place it from your description. I'm colour blind." That sounded like an excuse – he was making this worse.

"We have a warrant to search Mr Stewart's place of work," DI Shortfellow said.

Jerry looked as surprised as Arnold felt.

"Of course, if it might be of any help in your investigations, we're happy to assist," Jerry said. "It might make things easier if you tell us what you're looking for."

The police officers both looked at Arnold. "Silver?" he suggested. Then he explained to Jerry that they'd asked him if he recognised someone who had lost some silver.

Jerry was shown the photo, confirmed the man wasn't one of his parishioners and added that he wasn't known to him personally. "Now what, precisely, is it we can help you look for? You're welcome to look at the little silver we have. There are a couple of interesting pieces, but I can assure you they've been here a very long time."

Arnold knew the questions and search concerned him directly. The church was only relevant as his place of work. That might explain them not answering Jerry's question. "I'm happy for anything you'd say or ask me to be said in the presence of Reverend Grande." He hoped that would indicate he had nothing to hide.

DI Shortfellow gave a nod and DC Hetherington said, "We're looking for cyanide, or any indication that you've ever had any in your possession. We'll also need to search your home, sir."

"Cyanide! Why would Arnold have cyanide? And didn't poor Paula die from nicotine poisoning?"

"That's correct, sir," DI Shortfellow answered the last of Jerry's questions.

"I have a licence which permits me to buy cyanide," Arnold said. "But I've never done so. I understand you can't take my word for that." He took his keys from his pocket. "Do you need me to be present in my flat for the search? I'd rather not." Of course they'd have to go through all his personal things, but he didn't want to see it happening, or the expressions on their faces.

"That won't be necessary."

DC Hetherington took his keys, and left the church.

Arnold admired Jerry's composure, and silence, after the initial shock at the mention of cyanide. The vicar must have questions he wished to ask. No doubt the police did too, but the DI said nothing further until DC Hetherington returned with several colleagues, who carried bags of equipment.

Chapter 35

Friday 19th June

Friday was a fun day for Crystal. Her parents, whom she'd not seen properly for months, came to stay with Aunty Agnes for a long weekend. They were joined by her cousin Yvonne who was also staying over.

"I'll sleep on the sofa and she can have my bed," Crystal had offered. Yvonne was a couple of decades older than Crystal, so more likely to suffer from the lack of a proper mattress.

"Or I bet that Jason would let you stay with him if you asked nicely. If I was your age and he was my fella, I would."

Crystal hadn't needed to ask – he'd offered as soon as he realised the house would be full.

Crystal, her mum, Aunty Agnes, and cousin Yvonne, each baked a cake for the midsummer event in the new community hall, chatting and laughing as they worked. Thanks to the insulating properties of the thick walls of Aunty's cottage, having the oven on for hours on such a glorious day was just about bearable.

Crystal's dad made a big thing of not getting involved in the 'girlie stuff' and stayed outside – to pick flowers for the little posies Yvonne would make. Every time a cackle of laughter came from the kitchen he'd yell, "I heard that, you know!" through the window which set them off again.

Despite not being at work, Crystal spent a lot of time on the phone with various colleagues. Her family were very understanding about her repeatedly excusing herself to make or take calls, and not being able to tell them what was happening. It was Crystal who was most frustrated with only getting snippets of information and having to keep those to herself. Trevor was the one person she could discuss it with, so he got a call whenever she'd spoken to anyone else. Luckily, when he heard there was cake surplus to requirements, he agreed to come over.

It wasn't until Crystal introduced Trevor to her cousin Yvonne she realised having him on the premises might make him a worse listener, not a better one. Yvonne's eyes were a beautiful bright blue, and Trevor wasn't a man to miss details.

At one point Crystal beckoned him out of the deckchair next to Yvonne's and said, "Let's save time. Yes she's single. Yes she's about your age. No she doesn't live locally. Yes, she generally visits quite often. Yes, it'd be really weird if the two of you got together. Now, back to the latest developments from CID… "

"I was just talking to your cousin, lass."

"And gazing into her blue eyes. And now we're done with that conversation. The DI said…"

When news came through of an arrest Crystal wasn't able to conceal her reaction.

"What is it, love?" Aunty Agnes asked.

"Give us a hint at least," Mum pleaded.

"You'll put us out of our misery, won't you, Trevor?" Yvonne smiled sweetly.

He laughed and put his hands up in surrender. "They've made an arrest."

"You say that as though there might be another," Yvonne prompted.

"That's the hope," Crystal said. "And that's why we absolutely can't tell you anything else."

Various attempts at bribery were made. Crystal and Trevor resisted everything from as many unripe plums as they wanted from Aunty's tree, to all the cash the others had on them – which as they were in the garden in lightweight summer clothes was absolutely none. Trevor almost succumbed to the offer of embarrassing photos of Crystal as a child.

Saturday 20th June

On Saturday there were just enough fluffy white clouds to highlight the beautiful blue of the sky. Exactly the right amount of breeze off the sea to keep people comfortable without stirring up dust.

It wasn't just the weather which behaved. Jason came to Aunty Agnes's early so he could meet Crystal's family properly before they went to the midsummer party. She loved that although they'd had very few dates he'd wanted to do that. And she loved her family for not making a big deal of it – or offering to find those hideous school photos. Instead they asked about his work, gave him tea and roped him into helping with the party preparations by slicing salad ingredients.

"Slicing's the same as chopping, right?" Jason asked, making him and Crystal laugh.

As a group, they walked over to the new hall. Aunty, despite never needing to hold Crystal's arm when they went anywhere together, decided she needed Jason's support. Crystal walked on her other side, so she could do her best to steer the conversation should that seem wise. Thankfully just her presence was enough to stop Aunty asking or revealing anything super embarrassing.

There was barely room to add their cakes to the range of food set up inside the new hall, and more was being brought in. That included the most fabulous carrot cake, made by Ellie.

"No Mike?" Crystal asked.

"He's helping get the barbecues lit."

"I'll go and give him a hand," Jason said.

Dad decided to join them.

Almost everyone Crystal knew in Little Mallow was there, although one tall, slim figure kept themselves apart – and there was one person she knew would be in the custody rooms at EPIC. The villagers were joined by a fair few non-residents. Most of those, other than Adam and his family, Crystal didn't know. A few she thought she recognised from the first, ill-fated party. She guessed some were reporters and laughed when told they'd initially been turned away, and Mary Milligan had sold out of everything which could be drunk or barbecued before they were admitted. Mary and her husband had arranged a couple of hours cover for the Post Office, and joined the throng in and around the new hall. Trevor was there, but nobody at all from CID.

Reverend Jerry Grande made a short speech of welcome, gave a blessing and said prayers for all those who already had a connection with the hall or would have in future. He didn't say Paula's name, but when he spoke of moving forward into the light, she was remembered. As the amens following a short prayer died away, DI Shortfellow arrived, accompanied by Sergeant Kirk and

DC Hetherington. She motioned for Crystal to join them, as the DI took the vicar's place, making it clear he intended to address the crowd.

After introducing himself and his team, in which he included Crystal, he said, "I'll keep this brief. We thought it would help everyone enjoy the afternoon to know that we've arrested two people in relation to the deaths of Paula Roth and a man from Gosport. One of those arrested has confessed to all the crimes and we're confident the other will soon become much more helpful... in, well, helping with our enquiries."

That got a polite chuckle swiftly followed by a barrage of questions.

The DI put up his hand. "I'm sorry, but as this is still an ongoing investigation there's not a great deal more I can tell you right now. However, I would like to trespass on your celebration a moment longer to say the arrests were possible thanks to hard work from my team in CID, Officer Clere who I'm delighted will be joining us officially very soon, and a young man whom I'm sure will be an asset to the force if we're ever lucky enough to have him. Where are you, Adam Milligan?"

Space was made for Adam to step forward and shake hands with the three detectives. It was the first time Crystal had ever seen him silent, but there was no doubt he was pleased. There was a round of applause and then the questions started again.

The vicar and DI exchanged a few words and then Reverend Grande, barely audible over demands to know who else had been killed, who'd done it and how, declared the new hall open and that the first batch of sausages were ready. That last remark was so effective Crystal wondered if she'd ever disperse an angry mob by saying, "Oh look, burger van."

"Sir, which of them confessed?"

"Roth. He didn't say a word until we asked where he got the hat with the Welsh dragon on. Lucy gave him three of the things without saying they came from her cousin. As Roth didn't want to explain to his wife where he got them, he passed them on to the verger, suggesting they be used as raffle prizes or similar. The verger felt bad about giving one to Bert Grahame to protect his head from falling debris when clearing the church gutters, although probably not as bad as he did when we started searching his home and the church for cyanide!"

"Poor Arnold."

"Fortunately, once Roth started talking he didn't stop and had confessed before SOCO had ripped up Arnold's floorboards or climbed into the bell tower. Roth gave us everything from the start of his affair with Lucy Carter to buying the crystal glass which they coated with cyanide and he delivered, to arranging the party, obtaining nicotine and the attempts to frame one of his wife's staff."

"Beth?"

"Yes. The vape refill bottle with her fingerprints on it was hers, taken from her bag. Her using an odourless vape made him decide on nicotine instead of the rest of the cyanide Lucy had kept when she sold off the antique and junk repair shop she inherited. All Beth's 'mistakes' were created by Roth, including fake deliveries to Warsash when he bought the stamps. The green gloves and baseball cap were supposed to make us think it was Beth concealing her identity."

"Instead of letting us link the two crimes and therefore solve them?"

"Precisely. "

"Did Roth say why they killed Mr Argent?"

"Simple greed. They wanted what Carter would inherit and had made an attempt over a year previously, by lacing an almond slice with cyanide. He'd either not eaten it, or survived doing so. They'd planned to make another attempt after they'd killed Roth's wife, but worried there would be little left. Argent had started giving more money to charity and had requested a quote from one of those equity release companies."

"They usually offer free gifts, he might have seen it as a prize."

"Possibly. The quote was a couple of months old and he'd done nothing about it but, according to Roth, Lucy became convinced he'd give away all his money before she could inherit. They'd already thought up the plan to kill Roth's wife when she started asking awkward questions about where he'd been after he visited Lucy, so they decided there was no time to waste."

"Them failing at the first attempt on Argent probably explains why they used so much cyanide and nicotine when they were successful."

"Indeed. We did realise that in both cases a very high dose was given, far more than needed to kill, but didn't see it as a link. You did, I think?"

Crystal nodded. "At first I just thought it was because the poison was put into alcohol which made them feel similar, but with Mr Argent there was still quite a lot left in his glass and with Paula death was far quicker than would be expected from nicotine poisoning, so it did seem the killer had wanted to be very sure they used enough."

"That feeling you had, that the crimes felt the same, you let me know if you ever experience that kind of thing again."

"I don't know how reliable that is. They were the first murders I've had anything to do with. For all I know they'll all feel the same."

"Perhaps. Your hunch about where the vape refills were bought was right in any case."

"The shop owner admitted it?"

"No. Unlike the sales made to those under age lads he had no reason to deny selling vape refills to an adult, but was so evasive and unhelpful he must have known there was something wrong with the purchase. Then Roth confirmed the man cashed a cheque, paying in used tenners. He's been charged as an accessory to murder."

"Excellent!" His shop had already lost its alcohol licence. Crystal wouldn't be at all sorry if the man lost his freedom too.

"Your friends are looking for you." The DI gestured to where Jason, Mike and Ellie were waiting. "You have fun and don't tell them more than you have to, and I'll do the same with the press."

Crystal did try to avoid giving more information.

"You can trust us not to blab," Mike said. "Ellie's a responsible schoolteacher, I'm a vicar's nephew and Jason... Jason's got a terrible memory, isn't that right, mate?"

"That's right, uhhh, what's your name again?"

"I can't give you precise details, but perhaps there are a few things I can share in general terms," Crystal relented. "Michael Roth and Lucy Carter both benefitted financially from apparently unconnected murders. I knew if a link could be proved between the two crimes, finding who was responsible was likely to be much easier. Roth didn't appear to have a motive, but if he'd expected his marriage to end then he would have, as his wife would have been entitled to a share of their joint assets."

"And if he was having an affair then he might be expecting that," Ellie said.

"Exactly. I guessed at an affair with Lucy Carter, and remembering she was a traffic warden, I realised she could have faked Roth's alibi when he was buying the stamps, and she made sure she had one when Roth delivered the cyanide to her cousin and again when he killed his wife."

"How could she fake a parking ticket?" Mike asked. "They have to take a photo and that can be checked online."

"True, but they're only looked at if the person the ticket's issued to tries to get out of paying. She just found another car of the same make, parked legally, wrote the ticket using Roth's registration plate, put it on the windscreen to photograph it and then took it off again to give to Roth, knowing he wouldn't challenge it."

"That's why you asked about the outside lights?" Ellie said. "He made sure it was dark when he took Paula out there so she didn't notice him pouring the nicotine into their wine?"

"That was probably more to make sure nobody came out and tried to save her while there was a chance of that.

In his first statement he said people were talking about the plants she donated and they went out to look at them. It was probably him who suggested it and he waited until her back was turned."

Crystal was pleased to see Arnold approaching, at least she was until she saw how anxious he looked. But then he often did. She gave him what she hoped was a reassuring smile and enquiring look, to make it easier for him to say whatever was in his mind.

"The first lot of food has gone," Arnold said. "If you tell me what you'd like, I'll put some on for you."

"Thanks, Arnold. You know how to look after your friends."

Arnold beamed at Mike's words. Had the poor man been worried they'd resent his intrusion? To prove she didn't, Crystal walked back to the barbecue area with Arnold and saw to it that they all stayed chatting to him as their food was cooked and eaten.

"Why does Arnold look so awkward whenever anyone says what a good idea this party was?" she asked Ellie when the two of them went in search of cake for everyone.

"Because he thought of it. I'm starting to think he doesn't realise how much people like and appreciate him. I think that's why he sometimes seems a bit reserved and odd."

"Is there anything we can do?" Crystal asked.

They made a start without realising it. Arnold didn't just looked pleased they'd brought him a slice of cake as well as one each for Mike and Jason, he looked surprised – as though it hadn't occurred to him that 'everyone' included him.

DI Shortfellow strolled over and introduced himself which Crystal thought a bit odd considering he'd already done that to the entire crowd, until she realised it was a hint for her to introduce her friends. Why? Was he just being friendly, or was there something he wanted to know? If there was, he was going to have to ask.

"This is Jason, Ellie, Mike… "

"Mike Ellison?"

"Yes," Mike said, looking a little taken aback.

"And you've met Arnold already," Crystal continued, sure now that DI Shortfellow had joined them for a reason. She seriously hoped it wasn't just to demonstrate he was capable of checking up on any men she spent time with.

"I have, yes. Arnold, when you put forward your idea of a coded letter I confess to being sceptical. However Roth has confirmed you were right and I was wrong… "

"Code?" Crystal demanded. "What code?"

"I'll leave Arnold to explain how he worked out that the odd wording on the letter he received about the booking of the hall was both an attempt to disguise the sender's identity and to implicate someone else in the crime – and how he did his best to stop us becoming sidetracked by that diversionary tactic."

"The inspector gives me too much credit," Arnold said.

Crystal and the others didn't let him get away with hiding behind a wall of modesty, so he explained his theory the letter writer had selected the wording carefully. "I wondered if it could be someone who wrote for the Little Mag and they thought I might recognise their style so changed it."

"Michael Roth did have a few pieces in," Ellie said. It didn't sound as though she'd enjoyed them much.

"He did and if he'd written in his usual style I might well have thought it familiar."

"What about implicating someone else?" Mike asked.

"Umm, I picked out the unusual words and made an anagram of the initial letters. One possible interpretation was that it was a suicide note from Paula."

"But it wasn't that?" If it had been, Crystal thought the DI would have said so, not talked of implications and diversions.

"It seems not."

"Come on, Arnold, out with it," Mike encouraged.

"The other interpretation of those letters involved moving the 'me' from the start to the end, so that instead of indicating Paula as the writer it appeared to be a signature. I knew Mike couldn't be guilty, so I told the inspector there was nobody in Little Mallow with the initials M.E."

"Thanks, Arnold, but how did you know I was innocent?"

"Because you're a good person."

When Crystal's family joined the group, Ellie and Crystal positioned themselves so Arnold couldn't just melt away. It was Crystal who did that when she saw Beth and her son Teddy, who'd had his face painted like a daisy, watching Dawn and Liz.

Crystal walked over, positioning herself between Beth and her former colleagues, so they formed one loose group.

"So, you solved it. Well done," Dawn said, stepping closer to Crystal and therefore Beth.

"It wasn't just down to me, but I did help. I wanted to thank you for your help too."

"Did we say something useful?"

"Several things, but particularly how nice Beth is. When I met her myself I agreed she couldn't have done what Mr Roth said she had, and I wondered why he'd lied." That wasn't exactly how it happened, but Beth had lost her job because of a murderer's attempt to incriminate her. Crystal didn't want her to lose friends too.

She saw the two florists exchange looks, then Dawn nodded and Liz said, "So, we didn't know if… that man… would want to keep Paula's Posies and we asked the landlord what would happen if he didn't."

"So, the rent's paid for almost a year and he said we could try to carry on ourselves if Roth wasn't going to," Dawn continued. "Looks like we might be able to now. They'll be stuff to sort out and I don't know if we'll be able to make a go of it… " They both looked at Beth.

"Are you offering me a job?"

"Yeah."

"Of course."

"I'd love that. Thank you."

"That's great news! I'll come in and buy flowers as soon as you're open again." Crystal returned to her friends and family, who'd been joined by the vicar and Trevor.

Reverend Jerry Grande finished what must have been a good anecdote with, "… I've never seen anyone shin up a ladder as fast as Arnold did that day!"

All those who'd heard the rest laughed, including Arnold himself when Mike referred to him as, "My hero."

Crystal's parents, cousin and friends started asking more questions about the murder and she was fighting a losing battle fending off the questions until Aunty Agnes interrupted. She thanked Arnold for all his efforts and added, "This has been a lovely afternoon, but it's hard work enjoying yourself and I'm going home for a little snooze now. Crystal, I know you and this charming young man must leave soon, so will you walk back with me to fetch his car?"

"Of course we will," Crystal said.

"Trevor, can I offer you a lift back to Gosport?" Jason asked.

"Thanks but I've got the car. Actually we should probably make a move quite soon... Yvonne is interested in seeing how the castle renovations are going, so I said I'd show her."

"You'd better go now before it gets dark," Agnes said and cackled.

"What am I missing?" Jason asked as they set off.

"Yvonne used to work at the castle in the school holidays and she's one of its trustees," Agnes explained. "She needs to be shown the way and what's going on just as much as we all need to worry about getting home before dark at four o'clock on midsummer's day."

"You're wicked," Jason said.

"And you're cheeky... I don't mind that, but I don't like lateness. Ten o'clock sharp tomorrow morning."

"OK, where and why?"

"My kitchen. To chop vegetables. Seems to be your special skill, and there's a lot of people to cook lunch for. You'll soon learn that, in this family, we all pitch in."

328

"Fair enough. I'll chop and Crystal can stir."

Once they'd seen Aunty safely home Crystal said, "Guess we'd better get to yours before it's dark?"

"Good plan. But about the flat… Now my favourite neighbour has moved out I don't have any reason to stay there. I'm thinking of buying somewhere in Portsmouth. Would you like to come to the viewings with me?"

"Yeah, sure. You know how nosey I am and I'll be able to let you know if it's a good area or somewhere I'm likely to have to visit while on duty."

"That'd be handy, but not what I meant. I know you're happy in Little Mallow for now, but you might want to live nearer work eventually?"

"Oh. Yes. Yes, I probably will."

As Jason drove along the seafront towards his flat he beeped his horn and they both waved at Ellie and Mike who were walking hand in hand towards the beach.

Crystal's phone rang just before they reached Gosport. It was DI Shortfellow.

"You're not on duty and not yet part of CID, so there's absolutely no obligation for you to come round to Pompey and pop into the EPIC building and sit quietly behind a two way mirror."

Of course there wasn't, which meant he thought she might like to do that. "Lucy Carter is ready to confess?" she guessed.

"Her solicitor is on the way. Don't break the speed limit, officer Clere."

Thank you for reading this book. I hope you enjoyed it. If you did, I'd really appreciate a short review on Amazon, Goodreads – or anywhere else.

I can be found at www.patsycollins.uk You may like to sign up for my newsletter and get an exclusive mini ebook set in Little Mallow, plus news of the latest releases, special offers, competitions and behind the scenes insights. A link can be found on the website, or you can use subscribepage.io/ItLSNa

The next book in the series is –

Loyal Friends and Deceitful Neighbours in Little Mallow

The picturesque seaside village of Little Mallow is suffering a spate of robberies. Arnold Stewart, verger of St Symeon's interrupts a burglary in progress and saves the church's antique silver. His friend, schoolteacher Ellie Jenkins, is another victim. Who can be responsible? And are they also guilty of other, far worse, crimes?

Naturally, police officers Crystal Clere and Trevor Harris are investigating, and young Adam is asking many, many questions. Arnold's kind-hearted employer Reverend Jerry Grande is praying for answers, and for those involved. Cameron isn't so much interested in solving the crime as keeping Arnold safe and showing him the beauty the world has to offer. All those people are old friends of Arnold's.

His new friend Aurora is more interested in solving the mystery of Castle View. There's definitely something odd going on at the house next to Arnold's flat. Against his better judgement Arnold finds himself involved. He's even more suspicious of the neighbours to his other side. They're hiding something – he really hopes he's wrong about it being a body!

Can Arnold and his friends untangle the lies being told in Little Mallow?

More Books by Patsy Collins

Novels –

Firestarter
Escape To The Country
A Year And A Day
Paint Me A Picture
Leave Nothing But Footprints
Acting Like A Killer
Loyal Friends and Deceitful Neighbours in
Little Mallow

Short story collections –

Over The Garden Fence
Up The Garden Path
Through The Garden Gate
In The Garden Air
Beyond The Garden Wall

No Family Secrets
Can't Choose Your Family
Keep It In The Family
Family Feeling
Happy Families

All That Love Stuff
With Love And Kisses
Lots Of Love
Love Is The Answer

Slightly Spooky Stories I
Slightly Spooky Stories II
Slightly Spooky Stories III
Slightly Spooky Stories IV
Slightly Spooky Stories V

Just A Job
Perfect Timing
A Way With Words
Dressed To Impress
Coffee & Cake
Not A Drop To Drink
Criminal Intent
Crime In Mind
Making A Move
Days To Remember
A Clean Bill Of Health

Non-fiction –

From Story Idea To Reader
(co-written with Rosemary J. Kind)

A Year Of Ideas:
365 sets of writing prompts and exercises

Printed in Great Britain
by Amazon

49292614R00185